You know what I am . . . you have always known . . .

And this was also true.

Here, in my dad's bedroom in the middle of the night, I finally accepted that. The man I had given myself to, the man I had secretly fantasized a future with, the man I wanted to grow old with . . . wasn't really a man at all. And somewhere, deep in a forgotten corner of my mind, a memory struggled to break free. It urged me to accept the truth about Gabriel. And as I did so, another truth was revealed. It didn't change a thing, God help me! I'd loved him before consciously knowing he was a vampire . . . and I still did.

Also by Carla Susan Smith

A Vampire's Promise

A
VAMPIRE'S
SOUL

Carla Susan Smith

KENSINGTON BOOKS
KENSINGTON PUBLISHING CORP.
www.kensingtonbooks.com

KENSINGTON BOOKS are published by

Kensington Publishing Corp.
119 West 40th Street
New York, NY 10018

All Kensington titles, imprints, and distributed lines are available at special quantity discounts for bulk purchases for sales promotion, premiums, fund-raising, educational, or institutional use.

Special book excerpts or customized printings can also be created to fit specific needs. For details, write or phone the office of the Kensington Special Sales Manager: Kensington Publishing Corp., 119 West 40th Street, New York, NY 10018. Attn. Special Sales Department. Phone: 1-800-221-2647.

Kensington and the K logo Reg. U.S. Pat. & TM Off.

First Electronic Edition: July 2014
eISBN-13: 978-1-60183-291-7
eISBN-10: 1-60183-291-5

First Print Edition: July 2014
ISBN-13: 978-1-60183-292-4
ISBN-10: 1-60183-292-3

Printed in the United States of America

Acknowledgements

As always, I am grateful to the following people who continue to help me achieve my dream:

To my husband, Jack, for always being there.

To our son, Joe, thanks for just being you.

To Nachette and Paul, Valerie and David, Beth and Rick, the best in-laws ever!

Tremendous thanks again to Lynne Harter for continuing to be my first editor.

And to Alicia Condon at Kensington, thanks for telling me I can do this!

CHAPTER 1

There are some people who will tell you that if you fall in a dream it's a bad thing. I'm not talking about a fall because you've twisted your knee or turned your ankle. I mean taking a dive off a high-rise building or stepping into an open elevator shaft on the twenty-fifth floor. The kind of descent that pretty much guarantees that if you do reach the bottom, you're not going to walk away. Hell, you're not even going to get up. And when you step over that ledge, you're filled with absolute terror, because there's no way you can change the outcome. And these people, whoever they are, will tell you that if you actually do reach the bottom in your dream, then in the waking world you're dead.

Really? How the fuck would anyone know?

I've had a few nightmares in which I've fallen, and it's a truly horrible sensation. I always wake up just as I'm going into free fall with my stomach behind my rib cage and my heart in my throat. I feel helpless and panicky both at the same time, and my limbs tremble as I try to catch my breath. But I've never reached bottom.

At least not yet.

I can't say for sure that I was dreaming about falling, but I woke in the grip of the same kind of anxiety, soaked in perspiration, tendrils of hair clinging to my neck and cheek, and my heart was pounding hard enough it had to be bruising my rib cage. But at least I wasn't dead. I also wasn't alone.

Sitting bolt upright in my bed, I took in a wild gasp of air, and stared at the wicker chair in the corner. Whatever I thought I'd seen was now gone, leaving behind an empty seat. The only immediate threat to my safety would be getting my foot tangled in the bed covers spilling onto the floor.

I shook my head, which, given the sudden pounding, was a bad idea. Lying back down, I put an arm over my eyes. This had to be the worst hangover ever. Easily a hundred times more awful than the one following the puke-fest my best friend Laycee put me through when I turned twenty-one. That particular episode had been bad enough to serve as a dire warning on the pitfalls of drinking tequila, but apparently I'd not heeded my own advice. So much for good intentions. I'd gotten so drunk I couldn't even remember drinking!

My tongue felt thick and fuzzy, and the nasty taste in my mouth said there was a good possibility I might have licked the living room carpet at some point. I swallowed—a tentative action that had my throat screaming and seemed to confirm the carpet-licking theory. Whatever I'd done, it was way worse than anything that had happened the night I celebrated my legal status.

Raising my arm, I opened my eyes a fraction and focused on the square of pale light dancing across the ceiling. It stretched almost to the far wall, which meant the sun was heading toward the horizon and I'd been asleep for most of the day. Of course, that might not have been so long depending on when I'd actually made it to bed.

In an effort to minimize the sloshing of my brain against the inside of my skull, I carefully turned my head and checked the clock on the bedside table. The bright red display read 5:05, and the small dot in the upper corner said it was definitely p.m. Yep, I'd slept all day, which only partially explained why I felt like shit. The rest of the blame was going squarely on the shoulders of Jose Cuervo and whomever he'd brought with him.

Dear God, please don't let me have done anything embarrassing, but if I did, don't let it be posted on Facebook.

The haze fogging my brain started to lift, and in its wake I was bombarded with a series of weird, fragmented images. Any hope of being allowed to recall the events of the last twenty-four hours in a manageable dose was blown right out the water. Taking a page from the sink-or-swim school of accountability, I got shoved in the deep end as everything came rushing back. Ignoring the pain in my head, I bolted for the bathroom.

Somewhere between crossing the threshold of my bedroom and falling to my knees before the porcelain goddess, my cerebral cortex exploded into a B-horror-movie nightmare. Kind of like *Twilight* on steroids, but without the generous budget or teenage cast. As I bent over the toilet, it took a little while for my brain to remember I'd already expelled the contents of my stomach several hours before. If I continued to dry heave, I was going to rupture something.

Slowly I got to my feet and gripped the edge of the bathroom sink with both hands. The face looking back at me in the mirror almost had me falling down again.

Jesus H. Christ—was that me?

I'd aged ten years overnight. Forget about getting wasted on tequila; I looked like I needed a hospital bed, and a machine that gave a reassuring beep so I would know I was still alive. My face was drained of all color. Even my sun-kissed freckles looked washed out. Dark circles ringed my eyes, and there was something white and crusty caked at the corner of my mouth. The woman in the mirror stared back at me with accusing eyes.

How could you not have known? She demanded in a shrill voice.

I wasn't ill, and I most definitely was not hung over. It was much worse than that. Panic now threaded through me. Like a wisp of smoke that turns into a flame that becomes a fire, it threatened to run out of control. I took a step back, hitting my heel on the base of the bathtub. A shower seemed like a good idea. Pulling back the curtain, I stepped into the tub. I needed both hands to turn the faucet on, but once the water washed over me, it sluiced away my panic. Numbness took its place, and leaning my forehead against the fiberglass wall, I gave my aching body over to the shower's pulsating spray. It wasn't until I tasted salt on my lips that I realized I was crying. I didn't fight it. Instead I shut down what remained of my rational thought process and let the tears flow. God knows I was overdue for a sob-fest.

I have no idea how long I stood there. I wasn't consciously aware that the water temperature had changed from warm to freezing until the sound of my chattering teeth forced common sense to prevail. In all the years of its existence, I was pretty sure this was the first time the hot water tank had ever been emptied. Wearily I turned the faucet off and stepped out of the tub.

I didn't remember taking off my underwear, but obviously I had as my bra and panties lay in a soggy pile in the bottom of the tub. It was just as well, really, because my fingers were now so cold I doubt I could have managed the intricacies involved in unhooking a bra. I wrapped a towel around me, tucking the end between my breasts. Dealing with my hair was going to take more effort than I was currently capable of, so I simply ignored it. If I couldn't comb the tangles out later, then I'd cut them out. Satisfied with my problem-solving skills, I shambled back to my bedroom.

I was in shock. I knew this because my body's physical response was eerily reminiscent of my reaction on hearing my dad had died, and the state trooper who'd been with me at the time told me I was in shock. I had all the symptoms that were typical of a traumatized condition. Chills, erratic breathing, clammy skin. Who was I to argue with a state trooper?

My core temperature, already lowered by the cold shower, fell a little further, and I began to shake as if I was having a seizure. Curling up in a ball, I hugged my knees to my chest and waited for the spasms to pass.

My boyfriend is a vampire.

Oh . . . fuck . . .

CHAPTER 2

The realization that the man I was in love with was something other than human churned up enough bile to sting the back of my throat. Everything that had occurred during the past twenty-four hours played back on one long mind-loop with far too much realism for a practical joke. Besides, Gabriel would never be so cruel as to play such a sick, twisted prank, and I don't remember anyone laughing, least of all the woman with moonlight hair whose alabaster skin had been stained with her own blood. Lying on black satin sheets, she'd stared at me with terror in her eyes. It was an image I was going to carry to the grave.

You know who I am . . . you know what I am . . . what I have always been . . .

The voice that had taken up residence inside my head began to whisper softly, insistently, and this time I had no difficulty recognizing it. How could I have not known it was Gabriel's voice all along? The cadence was so familiar, the phrasing of words uniquely his own, and he told me everything I wanted to hear, everything I needed to hear. It had always been his voice speaking inside my head. Only now I didn't want to believe what it was saying.

My lover was a vampire.

Only vampires didn't exist . . . did they?

We weren't still living in the Dark Ages, when every waking moment was governed by superstition, for God's sake! This was the modern world. A world filled with the Internet, cars that could parallel park themselves, and cell phones with more apps than a normal, sane person would ever need. A vampire had no business in a world of shiny chrome and glass. They belonged in an era of horse-drawn carriages, foggy streets, and butt-ugly Victorian décor. And yet I had seen the proof with my own eyes. Shuddering, I forced myself to take a deep breath so I could examine this barely believable event with something that could pass for logic.

In the relative normalcy of my home, surrounded by the trappings of my ordinary life, I had no problem telling myself vampires were not real. They were a work of fiction, springing from the mind of a brilliant writer with a gift for the macabre. And I almost had myself convinced too, except . . . well, what was that saying about a grain of truth being embedded inside every nightmare? Every fairy tale? Every legend? Stories about creatures who survive by drinking the blood of the living had been a part of folklore long before Dracula became a household name. Suddenly all those shows on the History Channel about Vlad the Impaler drinking the blood of his victims took on a completely different light.

But if such stories are true, then vampires are our natural enemies; they hunt down humans in order to sustain their own existence. A vampire is the real wolf in sheep's clothing—looking like one of us, moving among us, becoming us, the ultimate predator, with seduction as the only weapon needed for us to hand over our humanity.

Fangs? Yeah, they were real. Gabriel's were long and white, and they looked wickedly sharp. He hadn't tried to hide them once he knew I'd seen them, even going so far as to allow me a second look, as if to confirm it wasn't my vivid imagination. You can't fake something like that. But fangs are just a tool, used to perform the coup de grâce. Caught in a vampire's thrall, most humans would probably give themselves up long before they ever saw fangs.

And what egotistical sense of arrogance declares that human beings can have no predators save for each other? Assuming you're at the top of the food chain doesn't necessarily make it so . . . or mean you can't be dragged down a rung or two.

The tremors racking my body began to lessen as my temperature climbed back up to somewhere near normal. I let go of my knees, feeling the ache in my muscles as I stretched out my legs, and rolled onto my back. If I was going to survive this, then I had to accept, without any doubt whatsoever, that the world was not the same place it had been yesterday. It was not as I had always supposed it to be.

Vampires do exist.

My boyfriend is a vampire.

I took a couple of deep breaths, letting the implication of those words flow through me. In my struggle to accept this new reality, I received a pretty hefty smack upside the head by a highly relevant, extremely personal, and totally unalterable fact. It was one thing to have been going to the movies and out to dinner with a vampire, but I'd also been having sex with one. An awful lot of sex.

Whoa—talk about seduction! I don't think my ignorance of Gabriel's true nature was going to score me any brownie points, but then again, who was I going to tell?

Oh. My. God.

If vampires are the undead, did that make me some sort of closet necrophiliac? I don't remember this being covered in *Twilight,* but perhaps I'd given up reading the book by then. My mind began to fill with every erotic moment I had shared with Gabriel. Things I'd done to him. Things he'd done to me. Things we'd done to each other, and—oh shit!—in this bed, too! As if on cue, every detail of our last intimate encounter filled my head.

I had been on the verge of falling asleep when he'd slipped between the sheets and curled himself around me. The warmth of his breath fanned my skin as his hands and lips coaxed me into wakefulness. A delicious shiver ran through me when the tip of his tongue teased the outer edge of my ear before continuing its journey down to the spot where my neck and shoulder met. His mouth latched on, sucking with enough force to make my flesh sting erotically. Wrapping one arm around my waist, he cupped a breast with the other, using his thumb and forefinger to bring my nipple to a sensual fullness that ached for the touch of his mouth.

The feel of his erection, hard and magnificent against my ass, made me moan. A heat of my own exploded between my legs and I became wet. The hand that had been around my waist now slid between my thighs, and needing no encouragement, I opened for him. Gabriel slipped one finger, and then a second, inside my body, making me gasp at the delicious friction he created. I pushed back against the heel of his hand, and he quickly brought me to the brink of my climax, taking me over the edge when his thumb rubbed my clitoris. While I was still riding the swell of an orgasmic wave, he rolled me over and gave my nipple the attention it was craving. His mouth was exquisite. Lapping with his tongue, he drew the swollen bud between his lips and then scraped the sensitive tip erotically with his teeth. In response, I arched my back and grabbed a fistful of his long hair, making sure he didn't stray from his task.

And then he was inside me.

I wrapped my legs around his hips, enjoying the fullness of having his throbbing cock fill me. I stroked my hands across his wide shoulders, down his arms, and across his heavily muscled chest. Returning the favor, I rolled his eager nipple between my own thumb and forefinger. Gabriel closed his eyes and groaned softly, and the tremble in his body told me just how close he was to coming. I clenched my pelvic muscles, drawing him farther inside me. It was the only provocation he needed. He pulled back and then thrust forward, coating himself with my body's liquid silk until he brought us both to climax in an explosive rush that left me spent . . . and wanting more.

A sudden hysterical bubble of laughter burst out of me. No wonder he'd been so blasé about not getting me pregnant. I wanted to crawl into a hole and die. Fuck him! Except I already had, and that's why I was in this god-awful mess right now. My brain was fried. Any logic I was trying to use to deal with my situation was quickly becoming unraveled. I had no idea what the hell I was thinking. So I did what any girl in my predicament would do. I screamed—loud and long, and just a hair's breadth shy of hysterical. And then I did it again for no other reason than that I could.

Why had this happened to me?

A few months ago my life had been perfect. Okay, maybe that was a slight exaggeration. Being a virgin at twenty-five wasn't my idea of perfection, and while I might not have been desperate, I had been starting to get a little concerned. It wasn't as if I hadn't been trying to change my status, and there had been a couple of times when I'd truly thought it was going to happen. But something inevitably went wrong. It always did.

Until Gabriel.

I'd just known, somewhere in my heart—and pelvis—that he was *The One*. Except this time when it all went wrong, it hurt worse than any other time before. His dumping me, on my front porch of all places, when I was on the verge of giving myself to him, had been devastating in a way I'd never thought possible. And it was more than just my pride that was damaged. The pain I felt was very real.

Wallowing in misery punctuated by bouts of self-pity was not an experience I ever wanted to repeat. I don't care how necessary it was in helping me move on from Gabriel's unexplained behavior. And then, when I was certain I'd gotten him out of my system, guess who came calling on Halloween, of all nights? Can you say "trick or treat"?

I'm still not really sure what prompted the sequence of events that followed his arrival on my doorstep that night, but I do know that it was more than just satisfying a basic need. At least it was for me. And there's a part of me that knows, deep down, that I wouldn't have changed that night for anything in the world. But now I know why I always woke up alone.

Hindsight, as they say, is twenty-twenty. Looking back with my improved vision, I could easily slap myself for my ostrich imitation. Burying my head in the sand had simply put off the inevitable. Gabriel had tried to tell me about himself; as I recalled, he had actually said that knowing the truth would change how I felt about him. Only I'd dismissed the notion. I couldn't blame myself really, not when I'd assumed the truth involved obstacles I could get my head around—normal *human* obstacles like drugs or prison. Shit like that. Never in a million years would I have believed the truth meant embracing the world of the supernatural.

I'm in love with a vampire, for Christ's sake! How sick is that?

My head became a whirling mass of mixed emotions, with fear of the unknown leading the parade and threatening to paralyze me. There are times when being afraid is a good thing, when it can save your life even, but this wasn't one of those times. Those are the times when changing the situation you're in is a real possibility, and that didn't apply to me. There was nothing I could do to change what Gabriel was. That being said, there was only one outcome I could see in my future. An outcome that hinged entirely on one question.

How long was Gabriel going to let me live now that I knew the truth about him?

CHAPTER 3

It's an odd feeling knowing you're going to die. Actually we all know we're going to die, we just don't have the date marked on the calendar. Death is inevitable. I'm sure someone very clever said that. Now that I knew the truth about Gabriel, there was no doubt in my mind that I was going to die. I might not know the date, but I figured getting next year's calendar would probably be a waste of time. It all came down to vampire self-preservation. You didn't need to be a rocket scientist to realize that vampires have been preserving themselves for a very long time. There was a reason their existence wasn't common knowledge. I was living on borrowed time.

I told myself that if it was up to Gabriel, and only Gabriel, then I might be given a chance. His feelings for me were strong enough that he might protect me. But it wasn't just about him. There were other vampires whose existence I was now aware of. Other vampires who also knew about me.

Was there any way I could survive this? Perhaps Gabriel's belief that I was somehow promised to him would be my ace in the hole. What was it he'd said? *You are a Vampire's Promise . . . given by word . . . accepted by deed . . . bound by ritual to keep safe that which has been surrendered.* I had absolutely no idea what that meant, but it was obviously significant to Gabriel, and it might buy me some time.

Yeah, but for how long? What had been surrendered, and by whom? Whatever it was, I knew I didn't have it. And it wouldn't take Gabriel long to realize the same thing. And what would happen then? Back to square one . . . I was going to die.

None of this made any sense to me, and maybe it wasn't supposed to. Maybe it made sense only to those with extra-long canines. It didn't matter what scenario I conjured up in my head, or how I moved the scenery and players around, it all came back to the same thing. I was going to die.

Would Gabriel do it himself? Drink me dry, as he had with the woman on the bed? Except . . . I don't think he actually did that. Thinking back, even though I told myself I didn't want to, it occurred to me that I hadn't actually seen Gabriel drink her blood. He'd punctured a hole in her neck, but then he'd let her bleed out. Now, why would he do that? Weren't vampires thrown into a frenzy at the sight and smell of blood? If that were true, Gabriel had to be the king of self-control.

I told myself that he hadn't had time to drink her blood because my puking on the carpet had interrupted him, only that wasn't true either. There'd been plenty of time before I started tossing my cookies, but Gabriel hadn't even made an attempt. Maybe there was something in her blood he hadn't liked. What if she'd been infected with AIDS or something? Or was the truth really a lot simpler than that? Was it possible Gabriel had killed the woman just because he could? It might have been a show of power, but for whose benefit? Certainly not mine, and I didn't recall seeing anyone else at the party.

I began to blink rapidly as tears spilled down my cheeks. I had no idea why I was crying or who I was crying for. Was it the woman I'd watched die, or myself because I'd done nothing to help her? It made no difference that my head told me saving her had been beyond my power. She'd been dead before I ever got inside that room, but my heart said I should have at least tried. Now I was filled with self-loathing for my weakness—not so much at being unable to prevent murder, but for allowing myself to be seduced so easily by Gabriel.

And realizing the woman on the bed could easily have been me.

But Gabriel had never bitten me. Never even tried to. When it came to using teeth on skin, I was the one who'd been the aggressor. Even now I could recall the taste of his blood as it filled my mouth. A spicy sweetness laced with just enough pepper to tantalize my taste buds as it washed down my throat. Granted, it hadn't been anywhere near a mouthful, but the experience had been off-the-wall amazing. So there it was, I had drunk a vampire's blood.

Shit! Shit! Shit!

What the hell did that say about me? I had no idea, but Gabriel had been right about one thing. Knowing the truth about him did change everything between us. How could it not? Even the most rock-solid relationship in the world was bound to slip into a different perspective when your boyfriend needed to supplement his diet with a couple of pints of O-negative.

Taken at body temperature. Directly from the vein.

And speaking of diets, how was it Gabriel could eat regular food? And drink like he did? Was he an anomaly in the vampire world? Was the only vampire I'd spent any time with unable to exist on blood alone?

My hands began to tremble. Truth be told, I don't think they'd ever stopped in the first place. This was all too much for me to deal with. I needed a drink. Ideally something that was at least eighty proof, only I'd yet to replace the bottle of bourbon Laycee and I had destroyed this past summer. Coffee would be a poor substitute, but I would make do. The stronger the better.

Catching sight of myself in the mirrored closet door, I threw on sweatpants and a T-shirt. Then, gritting my teeth, I dragged a brush through the bird's nest that was passing itself off as my hair. Ten minutes later I had a long braid hanging over one shoulder. Taking a hard look at myself, I was grateful not to be scared shitless this time by the face that looked back at me. I definitely looked better. Not a hundred percent, and nowhere near my old self, but then I doubted I would ever be my *old self* again. The world was not the place I had always believed it to be.

I had just reached the bottom of the staircase, my foot on the last riser, when I froze at the sound of a knock at the front door. I hesitated, my hand still wrapped around the newel post. I wasn't expecting anyone, and surprise visitors hadn't been working out so well for me lately. The only person I could think of who might drop by at this time on a Saturday was Laycee.

Ordinarily I would have welcomed her company, but right then her timing couldn't have been worse. No way was I going to be able to look her in the eye. She would know something was wrong, and figuring it involved my Mr. Right, she wouldn't let go until she'd forced me to spill my guts. What was I supposed to tell her?

Hey, Laycee, how's it going? Remember when I busted your chops for sleeping with a married man? Well, I can beat that one hands down. The guy I've been sleeping with—he's a vampire! The real deal with fangs and everything. A real hoot, right?

I snagged my bottom lip with my teeth. Somehow, I didn't see that going over too well.

The knock came again, a little sharper this time, as if Laycee could sense me hesitating and was mildly pissed at being kept outside in the cold. Lord knows, it was no use pretending I wasn't there. Maybe, if I was lucky, I'd be wrong. Instead of my BFF it would be some idiot wanting to sell me a magazine subscription . . . or siding for the house . . . or religion. If I was very lucky it would be that guy from Publishers Clearing House telling me I'd won a million dollars. Wouldn't that be nice? The chance to forget all my problems while vacationing in some tropical paradise.

The distance to the front door seemed longer than usual, but that was because my brain was suddenly inundated with erotic flashbacks. My mind spewed forth a moving collage of me naked, panting, and coming. More than once. I think the only place Gabriel and I *hadn't* had sex in was my dad's bedroom, and no way in hell was fornication of any kind taking place beneath that ceiling.

Crossly, I told myself that now really wasn't the best time to be thinking about vampire sex, no matter how hot or spectacular it might have been—or how much I was going to miss it. Taking a deep breath, I went toward the front door. With my best smile frozen in place, I flipped the dead bolt, opened the door, and found Aleksei, Gabriel's second-in-command, standing on my ho-ho-ho Christmas doormat.

Awww . . . fuck! Another vampire.

I took a step back and mentally slapped myself. Of course! Laycee was in the mountains with Jake and would be gone all weekend. How wonderful, how perfectly normal. My best friend, whose life was filled with the type of difficulties I'd have given my right arm to have, was enjoying a lust-filled weekend with the biggest complication she had—namely, her still technically married boyfriend, who also happened to be the town sheriff.

Staring down at the black military-style boots on the other side of my threshold, I suddenly realized I'd never needed a dose of Laycee's double-wide, trailer-park common sense more than I did at this precise moment. It would be the perfect antidote to the gothic nightmare that apparently had no intention of ending or restricting itself to my sleeping hours. Unless, of course, I was still actually asleep.

I raised my eyes and stared at the huge figure framed in the open doorway. The army greatcoat and camouflage-style pants didn't surprise me, but the T-shirt made me look twice. Emblazoned over the familiar eagle, globe, and anchor logo were the words *USMC Protecting Your Nuts Since 1755*. On anyone else such a declaration would have made me smile, but on Aleksei I had to wonder if it was a statement of fact.

God, he was big!

I'm sure that somewhere in my subconscious I'd already registered this fact, but the last time I'd been this close to him, my brain had had other things to worry about, witnessing my boyfriend commit murder being top of the list. Looking up at the face that was now staring down at me, I realized I was peeing-my-pants terrified. I thought about screaming, but who would hear me? I had no close neighbors, and if he'd come here to hurt me, I sure as hell wasn't going to be able to fight him off. Even if I managed to reach the kitchen ahead of him, I was all out of garlic.

My entire world, everything that I had never questioned, had just been flushed down a paranormal toilet. Any lingering doubts I might have about vampires being confined to the limits of a writer's imagination were gone. Last night had shown me that, and the confirmation was standing in front of me.

Folding his arms, Aleksei shifted his weight so he now leaned against the doorjamb. He peeled back his lips and, with an almost lazy insouciance, dropped his fangs. I made a noise that might have been a yelp and felt my whole body stiffen. His fangs didn't look as big as Gabriel's had been last night, but they were big enough.

"Is good you know what I am," he said, as his mouth widened into a grin. "Now, invite me inside, Rowan."

And I almost did. My mouth opened, and I felt my tongue forming the words when something snatched hold of me, and gave me a good, figurative shake.

This is the only ace in your hand—use it, goddammit!

"Are you kidding?" I shot back. "Just how stupid do you think I am?"

The big guy frowned and then began stroking his chin, almost as if he was giving both parts of my response serious consideration. If he was trying to be funny, it wasn't working, and nothing pisses me off more than having my intelligence insulted. Dream or reality, he'd just told me he couldn't come inside my house—at least not the first time—without being invited to do so. Gabriel had also needed me to invite him in, and withholding my permission was the only weapon I possessed. Hopefully it would be enough.

"I don't think you stupid at all. Asking for invitation is only politeness." His voice was a deep rumble that I found strangely comforting. "Gabriel would not like me to be rude."

Screw Gabriel. What about me?

Narrowing my eyes, I looked at him. It wasn't that I thought he was lying, but I definitely got the sense he was holding something back. Sighing, he pushed himself off the doorframe and straightened up to his full height. He was an impressive and very scary sight.

"Do you really think we haven't found way to get across threshold?"

My stomach curdled. Maybe Gabriel hadn't wanted to be rude that first time either. "You d-don't have to b-be invited in?" I stammered.

He gave a nonchalant shrug before giving me a sly grin. "Is better, but not necessary." Tilting his head back, he ran both hands down either side of the open doorway, as if feeling for a weakness in the framework. "It will hurt like bitch, and I'll have headache for week, but can be done. And you will need new door."

I don't know if it was the way he spoke, his accent and the way he stressed certain words, but it sounded like I was being threatened, the suggestion being that more than my front door was going to need re-placing when he was through.

Bullies threaten, and I don't like bullies. Even if they come pack-aged like a brick outhouse. If Aleksei wanted to scare me into invit-ing him inside, he had gone about it the wrong way. Any initial fear I'd felt at seeing him on the other side of my door had now vanished. I'd been scared enough these past twenty-four hours. Nothing he said or did was going to top it. All his veiled threat did was piss me off, causing my temper to spike recklessly.

"Then knock yourself out!" I snapped before slamming the door in his face.

Immediately I jumped back to a spot halfway down the hall, wait-ing for the only barrier that separated us to be ripped off its hinges. If Aleksei made good on his threat, it would prove what an idiot I was.

But nothing happened.

I hadn't realized I'd been holding my breath until I was forced to exhale, which the vampire on the other side of my front door heard.

"Rowan, you must invite me in. Is for your safety."

The frustration in his voice was evident, and I'd be lying if I didn't say it felt good to hear it. Hah! Score one for the puny human. But even so, I was still scared half to death. My heart was beating so hard, I expected it to burst out from between my ribs and flop around on the carpet, kind of like a fish out of water.

"You can't come in without an invitation," I muttered, more to myself than the closed door.

"No, I cannot."

He sounded royally peeved. Guess I wasn't playing nice. Hearing him loudly expelling his own rush of air, I could almost picture his expression as he tried to get a handle on his temper. "I am sorry I told you untruth."

Oh well, that changed everything. I mean if he was *sorry* . . .

"Go away, Aleksei, I'm not going to invite you in, no matter what you tell me."

"But Rowan, you might have danger—"

"You think?" My knees turned to jello. "Do you think I'm so stu-pid I don't realize Gabriel needs me to disappear now that I know what he is? What you all are?"

The sound of his fist banging on the door's wood paneling made me jump. The door was sturdy, but it was also quite old. I had no idea how much of a battering it could take. Not from a vampire.

"Gabriel is not problem," the big guy growled.

Yeah? After last night I wasn't so sure. "What do you mean?" I yelled back, but the only answer to my question was silence.

Hurrying to the living room, I went to the bay window, which gave me an unrestricted view of the front porch. It was empty. Somehow I doubted Aleksei was hiding in the hydrangea bush at the bottom of the steps. I had a pretty good idea where he was headed, and a hollow feeling swirled in the pit of my stomach. How long did I have before Gabriel showed up?

CHAPTER 4

The unopened bottle of Jack Daniels sitting on the kitchen counter next to the coffeemaker brought me to a screeching halt. I didn't know whether to laugh or cry at the realization that my vampire boyfriend knew me a lot better than I was willing to admit. But perhaps it wasn't that much of a stretch to suppose I might need something stronger than coffee. Or maybe he just figured a face-to-face would go a lot better if one of us was drunk. At least now I knew who'd stripped me down to my underwear and put me to bed the night before.

I got a glass from the cupboard, cracked the seal on the bottle, and poured myself a generous measure. I downed it in one go, spluttering a little as my throat caught on fire. Refilling my glass, I repeated the action. The idea of being totally shit-faced when Gabriel arrived seemed like an excellent plan. Carrying the bottle in one hand and my glass in the other, I pulled out a chair from the kitchen table and sat down. Might as well be comfortable while I waited.

Forty-five minutes later I made an unsettling discovery about the way my body processes alcohol. Terror negated the intoxication I was hoping for, even at eighty proof. The level of liquid in the bottle had dropped by at least a third, and I didn't have so much as a decent buzz. Fuck! There was a distinct possibility I was going to have to deal with Gabriel stone cold sober after all.

Folding my arms on the table, I leaned forward and put my head down. I just couldn't catch a break. Instead of strapping some steel to my spine and making me brave and bold, all the bourbon seemed to be doing was activating my tear ducts. That my tearful breakdown was witnessed by kitchen appliances was just wrong.

"Rowan . . . Rowan . . . wake up."

My shoulder was being shaken, and although I understood the words, I really didn't want to open my eyes. I was feeling good, tranquil and stress-free, the way I imagine I'd feel after having a great massage at some swanky spa. All I needed now was cucumber slices on my eyes and a pedicure. That this particular fantasy was tinged a glorious shade of sippin' whiskey bronze only added to the ambience.

"Rowan, dahlink . . . open your eyes for me."

Dahlink?

The firm pressure of fingers on my shoulder brought me back to reality. The dull ache in the small of my back said I'd been hunched over the kitchen table for longer than I'd thought. I opened my eyes and blinked owlishly at the face smiling down at me.

"*Anashayshzia?*" From the way I slurred her name, it occurred to me I'd finally hit the technically wasted mark. *Well, it's about damn time!*

With her arm about my shoulder, the lovely blonde helped me come a little more upright. I caught the scent of her perfume. Yves St. Laurent's *Opium,* a classic that smelled wonderful on her. Somehow I wasn't surprised by her choice. Everything about Gabriel's friend was lovely, elegant, and classic. I wasn't surprised that she and Gabriel were close.

"You need coffee," Anasztaizia declared, giving me a sympathetic shake of her head. "Lots of good Russian coffee, I am thinking."

Lovely, elegant, but not very bright. Coffee was the last thing I wanted. I wanted more bourbon. No, I *needed* more bourbon. I tried telling her this, but all that came out of my mouth was an incoherent perversion of the English language. Anasztaizia was not, apparently, well versed in drunken bourbon-ese, and she frowned at me. I was dismayed when she picked up my glass and the bottle of Jack Daniels and placed both on the counter, out of reach.

"Is bad to drink alone, dahlink." Slipping off her coat, she draped it over the back of an empty kitchen chair and pulled from the depths of her oversized purse a brightly colored canister. "Filters?"

I mumbled, and waved a hand peevishly at the cupboards lining the wall. If she was going to cut me off, then she could find the damn filters all by herself. Apparently Anasztaizia was a whiz at sign language because she found the right cupboard on the first try. I put my elbow on the table and plopped my chin in my hand, watching as she made herself at home in my kitchen. A lot of women are proprietary about their kitchen, but not me. Want to bake me a cake? Go right ahead!

I wiped my mouth on the heel of the hand that was holding my head up. My tongue felt thick, my head thicker. By rights I ought to have been passed out under the table, and I had no idea why I wasn't. I stared at the clock on the wall, but my focus was off, so it took me a couple of tries to read the hands correctly. I would have sworn on a stack of bibles that I'd put my head down for only a couple of seconds—okay, five minutes at most—but according to the clock I'd misplaced two hours. *Two hours?* Sheesh!

Anasztaizia busied herself making coffee. I had no idea what she was doing in my kitchen—well, I knew *what* she was doing; it was the why that was a complete mystery. And it was one I didn't have time to solve right now. If Aleksei had been gone for two hours, then Gabriel was going to be here any minute. Actually I was kind of surprised that he wasn't here already, but in any case I had to get rid of Anasztaizia before he showed up. I didn't care how friendly she was with him at her family's restaurant; being caught up in my drama was not something she needed.

I stood up—a monumentally bad idea as the kitchen took a wild lurch forward, forcing me to sit down again in a hurry. With both elbows on the table this time, I cradled my head in my hands and moaned. It was a few moments before I felt brave enough to try moving again. Turning my head slowly seemed to be okay.

"Anashtayshza . . . you gotta go," I implored. "Gab . . . Gab . . ." Good Lord, I couldn't even say his name!

"Gabriel is not coming," she said, rescuing me from verbal ineptitude. "At least not tonight." Crossing her arms, she leaned back against the counter and gave me a look that said she knew a lot more about my current predicament than I was aware of. "He does not know that you have refused to invite Aleksei inside."

He doesn't? How come? And how do you know I wouldn't invite Aleksei in?

I would have bet even money Aleksei had headed straight for his boss when he'd left my doorstep earlier, but now, if I understood Anasztaizia correctly, it would seem not. I stared at the Magyar beauty; her blond hair shimmering beneath the overhead fluorescent gave her an angelic halo. I didn't understand what was happening, and being semi-drunk was a definite impediment. I wanted to apologize for my inebriated state, but a sudden bolt of pain stabbed me behind my eyes, leaving a horrible throb in its wake and forcing me to look away.

"You are very lucky that Aleksei came to me instead."

Luck was just a matter of degree. Drunk or not, it seemed to me that one problem had been exchanged for another.

"Why would he do that?" I asked, wondering if more than the bourbon was confusing me.

After setting the coffeemaker to brew, Anasztaizia pulled out a chair and sat down opposite me. "Because he thought you might prefer to talk to me first."

"I don't understand," I mumbled, as the pain in my head began to settle into a slow, steady, barely tolerable throb.

"Of course you don't." She patted my hand gently. "Trust me, this is not the ideal way to find out someone you care about is a vampire."

There's an ideal way?

Despite the fact that my very eyelashes hurt and I was probably risking blindness, I opened my eyes wide at her words. I should have been shocked, but I wasn't. Who was I kidding? Of course Anasztaizia knew exactly what Gabriel was. The way she dropped the V word without batting an eyelid was proof enough. I had known, of course, that her friendship with Gabriel had been established long before he and I had become an item, but what surprised me now was the expression on her face. I wasn't so drunk I couldn't see she was angry. I just hoped it wasn't because I was too shit-faced to fully appreciate her coming to my rescue. If that's what this was. God knows, I hadn't sent the big guy to get her—why would I?—and if she knew Gabriel was a vampire, I was willing to bet she knew Aleksei was one as well. If she wanted to bust someone's balls about being forced to hold my hand, then she could take it up with him. I felt certain he had a set big enough to kick.

Of course there was always the possibility I was on the wrong track. Perhaps the beautiful Hungarian shared Katja's disdain for my relationship with Gabriel. Maybe she also had ideas about being with him, and if that were the case, I'd rather it be her than the psychotic Goth Queen who'd schemed to take Gabriel from me. But if Anasztaizia was here to lecture me about my love life, she was in for a disappointment. A verbal sparring match becomes pretty much redundant when one of you has difficulty stringing more than three words together.

As I prepared to let Anasztaizia know, shit-faced or not, I was no pushover, her expression shifted. Something in her face said she wasn't here to pass judgment on either me or my relationship with Gabriel. As I bathed in the unexpected warmth of her acceptance, a far more mundane question came to mind.

"Howdja get in?" I asked, recalling the two tries it took for me to drop the dead bolt once I realized Aleksei was gone.

Smiling, she gave a dismissive wave of her hand, nearly blinding me with the diamond on her ring finger. The thing was the size of a doorknob. Despite my condition, the girly part of me, the part that loves makeup and high heels, wanted to *ooh* and *aah* and ask how many carats it was.

"One of the things you need to remember," Anasztaizia said, her voice bringing me back to the here and now, "is that many vampires can manipulate locks. Opening a door is not a problem. Crossing the threshold is the problem. They cannot enter any premises if they have not been invited to do so by the proper authority."

"What does that mean . . . *proper authority?*" I was amazed at my ability to coherently string together this many words.

"It must be the person who actually resides on the property," she continued. "It cannot be a guest or visitor. I cannot invite Aleksei into your house, and neither can your best friend." She pointed at the floor with her forefinger. "This is *your* home, Rowan, only you can invite a vampire—any vampire—inside."

I wasn't so drunk I didn't see the flaw in what she was saying. "But that's not true of every building, is it?"

"No, I'm talking about personal dwellings only. Any building open to all people is common ground, and no invitation is needed."

A sudden image of murder and mayhem, vampire-style, in the downtown library filled my head, and I shuddered. "And they only have to be invited one time, right?" I asked, moving on from imagined carnage in children's fiction. I didn't really need an answer because Gabriel had only asked me to invite him in the very first time. I'd been so impressed by his insistence, I'd thought it was some quaint Norwegian custom. Hah! Since then, he'd pretty much been able to come and go as he pleased. "So I guess you're not a vampire then?"

"No, I am not," Anasztaizia replied wistfully. She might not be a vampire, but her expression told me she wanted to be one. "Aleksei unlocked the front door for me, and now I apologize for entering your home uninvited." She leaned forward, her expression becoming earnest. "And Aleksei is very sorry that he lied to you."

Yeah, right, of course he is.

"Um . . . where is he?"

Anasztaizia motioned her head toward the front door, a graceful gesture that made me think there wasn't anything she did that was clumsy. "He is waiting outside." She hesitated, a small wrinkle appearing between her eyes. "You really should invite him in, Rowan. He is only here because Gabriel wishes it."

I stared at her, aghast. Was that supposed to make everything all right? Had she any idea what I'd been through? *What I'd seen?* Twenty-four hours ago I'd had no reason to question the reality of the world I inhabited, wouldn't have realized I *could* question it. Its configuration was dictated by a natural order that had kept me safe for the past twenty-five years, and it was all I'd ever known. Now all bets were off.

My ordinary life, the one where I fell in love with Mr. Right, got married, and had his babies, had been destroyed in the blink of an eye. My blissful ignorance had been shattered. The curtain hadn't just twitched, it had been yanked open, and I'd had no choice but to view what lay behind. It would have been better if there had been a wizard with an ego as big as all get-out, but instead I'd found another world. One that apparently coexisted with mine, but a world no human was ever meant to know about.

And it made no difference how it had happened. I hadn't asked to look behind the curtain, it had been forced on me, and now that I knew . . .

You're in sooooo much trouble!

The sputtering sound of the coffeemaker coming to the end of its brewing cycle was a welcome interruption, as was the wonderful aroma that now filled the kitchen. No coffee I made had ever smelled this good, not even the Starbucks blend I occasionally treated myself to. Taking two mugs from the cupboard, Anasztaizia filled them with the dark brew, setting them down on the table before going to the fridge for the half-and-half.

"Is Aleksei going to kill me?" I blurted out. "Is that why he's here?"

The milky stream hiccuped in mid-pour. I can honestly say the sound of my voice cracking startled me as much as it did my Hungarian visitor. She just hid it better. I felt scared and resigned all at the same time, knowing there could be only one response to my question. Anasztaizia didn't really need to answer because I already knew what she was going to say.

"Rowan, if Gabriel wanted you dead, you can be assured of two things," she said calmly, as she pushed one of the steaming mugs across the table toward me. "First, he would never instruct another to take your life."

Curling my fingers around the handle of the coffee mug, I watched the creamy surface do a slow rotation while I waited for her to continue. She didn't, and when I raised my eyes, I knew it was because she wanted to be certain she had my full, and undivided, attention. "And the second?" I asked, barely able to get the words out.

"You would already be dead."

Picking up the second mug, she turned and walked out of the kitchen and down the hall. I heard the front door open, followed by some murmuring, and then the door closed again. I tensed, still not completely believing in a vampire's inability to cross a threshold uninvited, but Anasztaizia returned alone, minus the mug of coffee. Seating herself across from me, she clasped her hands together and put them on the table.

"Aleksei has been sent by Gabriel, is true," she began, "but not to hurt you, Rowan. He is here to protect you."

It sounded suspiciously like a fox being asked to guard a henhouse.

"Why?" I asked.

"Because no one knows where Katja is."

Ah, not a fox but a vixen. I pictured the gorgeous dark-haired vampire in my mind, seeing her push her dislocated shoulder back into place while her eyes burned with pure hatred. I'd tried telling myself it was just hot temper, something she would get over, but I knew that was a lie. The beautiful Goth Queen wanted to hurt me in the worst possible way. And she was more than capable of doing so. "Do you really think she'll come after me?" Part of me was absolutely terrified by the possibility, while another part was intrigued in an odd, academic way.

"Is difficult to say," Anasztaizia replied with a shrug. "Katja has always had a bad temper. She is unpredictable."

"So you've met her?"

"Only once, but it was enough."

"Yeah, wish it had been only once for me."

Reaching across the table, Anasztaizia patted the back of my hand. "I'm so sorry, and I wish, with all my heart, this was not happening to you."

But it didn't change the fact that she was glad I knew the truth. It was something we now had in common. We were two humans who had crossed paths with vampires.

"Is she really that dangerous?" I asked, my hand tightening around the mug of coffee before me.

"Katja doesn't like being told she cannot have something, especially something she has set her heart on having. I think she has desired Gabriel for a long time."

"Well, she can have him," I declared hotly. "As far as I'm concerned, we're through!"

Sighing, the lovely blonde rearranged her hands so the left was now resting on top of the right. The enormous diamond caught the light, winking at me as if it had a secret it wanted to share.

"You are not being truthful, Rowan, and even if you were, it changes nothing." She effectively halted any protest from me with a raised brow. "Gabriel wants you, and only you. Katja is humiliated by his rejection, especially as it happened in front of you. Pride will not let her forgive such an insult, or you for being what Gabriel desires."

"You didn't hear me," I said with a shake of my head that I instantly regretted. *"I don't want him."*

I didn't realize I was clenching my teeth until I felt an ache running along my jawline. It took a supreme effort, and the understanding that I was in danger of cracking a tooth, to relax the muscles in my face. Anasztaizia's look of frustrated disbelief wasn't exactly helpful. Neither was the hollow feeling in the pit of my stomach.

"Rowan, dahlink, I heard you perfectly, but it is *you* who doesn't listen." She tapped a well-manicured forefinger on the table for emphasis. "Gabriel is a vampire, and vampires do not give up those they claim for their own. They are the most possessive creatures to ever walk the earth. Whether you want to be or not, you are now a part of Gabriel's life, and he is not going to let you go. No matter what."

I opened my mouth to protest, but snapped it shut without saying a word. I was too bewildered by the warmth her words had stirred up inside me. Gabriel wanted me, and only me. Why did I find that so reassuring?

CHAPTER 5

It still sounded like a bad high school melodrama on TV—the head cheerleader getting all pissy because the captain of the football team was taking his geeky lab partner to the prom instead of her. I picked up my mug and almost got a lapful of hot coffee because my hands were shaking so much. I was grateful for Anasztaizia's steadying hold on my arm, even if I was nearly blinded by the door-knocker diamond.

I needed to take a step back. Sipping my coffee, I decided a change of subject was needed. Kind of like a time-out. Anasztaizia and I were both women, surely there was something else we could talk about? Something that didn't involve the opposite sex. Or vampires. I took another swig of coffee, and the tremble in my hand began to lessen. "This is really good," I said, tapping a nail against the mug. "Is it from your restaurant?"

"No, it's a special blend I keep at home. It's Russian."

"Russian?" I felt my forehead wrinkle. "I thought you were Hungarian."

"I am, but my boyfriend is Russian. I keep the coffee for him."

Her gaze flickered toward the front door, and I almost fell off the chair as understanding crashed over me like a bucket of cold water.

No wonder Aleksei had gone to her instead of Gabriel. Sometimes I am so stupid!

"But—you're human!" I blurted out as if this might be news to her.

"Well . . . so are you." Her eyebrows pulled together just enough to make her look worried.

"Yeah but, but . . . Aleksei . . . he's a—"

"Vampire, I know." Dropping her voice to a whisper, she leaned toward me. "I hate to be the one to tell you this, Rowan, but so is your boyfriend." The worried look vanished as a smile twitched at the corner of her mouth. She was teasing me, only I wasn't sure how to respond. "Rowan, I know this is difficult for you. This is why Aleksei came to me. He thought I could help, but first you must tell me what is problem."

Excuse me? I wondered in how many other homes, around other kitchen tables, a similar conversation was being conducted. I was willing to bet it was a big, fat zero. We were talking about *vampires,* for God's sake, and Anasztaizia couldn't see what I was having a problem with? I sucked in a breath and forced myself to remain calm. She was only here to help, I reminded myself, and she was from another country, a different culture, so maybe she really didn't understand where I was coming from.

"Sorry, but I'm having difficulty getting my head around the fact that they kill people," I said tersely. "And don't try telling me they don't—I know, I saw it."

"Yes," she agreed matter-of-factly, "what you say is true. Sometimes they do kill people, but I promise you they kill only very bad people."

Oh wow, well that was a relief, except who decided what was bad enough to get your throat ripped out?

"And they drink blood," I continued, "human people blood!"

I was starting to babble, and I saw Anasztaizia's expression turn slightly alarmed.

"They are vampires, so they do have to drink blood," she agreed warily, "this you know. Of course human blood is better, but they can survive on animal blood if no other is available." The doorknob diamond flashed as it moved across the table and came to a rest on the back of my hand. "Think of it like . . . um . . . a diabetic needing insulin," she finished brightly.

"Diabetics don't kill people to get what they need," I snapped coldly.

"Well . . . neither do vampires."

One of us was very confused, or in a state of serious denial. Apparently Anasztaizia's relationship with the big guy outside my front door didn't include seeing him eat. At least not the essential part of his diet. She couldn't have, or else she would never have just said what she did. I knew what I'd seen. God knows I was never going to forget Gabriel puncturing that woman's neck with his fangs. I was about to contest her statement when it suddenly hit me that, in all honesty, I couldn't. While I had watched Gabriel inflict the wound, I hadn't actually seen him drink her blood.

The stain on his mouth and chest had occurred from the initial severing of the artery and the resulting subsequent struggle. In all truth, I'd not seen Gabriel put his mouth on her again. Anasztaizia curled her fingers around my hand, making it look for a moment as if I was the one wearing the enormous diamond.

"Rowan, vampires never feed from those they kill," she said in a soothing singsong, "and they don't kill those from whom they feed." The grip on my hand tightened imperceptibly as she slowly pushed aside the collar of her blouse with the other hand. My eyes were drawn to the creamy column of her neck, and I saw two small puncture marks centered inside the faint shadow of a bruise. "Aleksei fed from me earlier tonight. The mark will be gone by morning."

Yanking my hand free, I jumped up and knocked over my chair. It was enough to make me forget the pain thumping in my head. "You let him do that to you?" I asked in a horrified gasp. "For God's sake . . . *why?*"

A brief flash of irritability crossed her face as she smoothed her collar back into place. "Why would I want him to use someone else?"

Any number of reasons sprang to mind as revulsion and fascination flowed through me, each fighting for the upper hand. My head was now swimming with a lot more than the effects of too much bourbon. A hole had been punched in the fabric of my understanding, one that was big enough to drive an eighteen-wheeler through. It was a hole I doubted could ever be patched.

Staring at the table, I saw the diamond winking at me from Anasztaizia's hand. The significance of the finger she was wearing it on hadn't occurred to me until now. Aleksei was a lot more than just a boyfriend. He was her fiancé. Jeez—was she actually going to *marry* him?

Rising from her seat, Anasztaizia started toward me, but I held up my hands, warding her off. "Please," I begged, feeling the hard edge of the sink up against my butt, "stay where you are. I don't know if I can take any more."

It really wasn't her fault. She was only trying to help me get a handle on the reality that had been forced on me. But the image of Aleksei, and those fangs, puncturing the creamy skin of Anasztaizia's neck was too much for me to take in. My brain was threatening to shut down completely.

Not wanting her to see how close I really was to losing it, I did an abrupt one-eighty and covered my face with my hands. As I pulled in a few shuddering breaths, I felt her hand making soothing circles on my back.

"I'm so sorry, Rowan," she said softly. "I didn't mean to frighten you. Neither of us did. I forgot how difficult it must be to accept what I am telling you, what you have seen. It must be like a very bad movie. In my culture, stories of vampires are told in the nursery and so are very commonplace. It takes great trust to accept that what I am saying to you is true, but"—she gave my upper arms a light squeeze—"I swear to you, it is the truth."

Something in her voice penetrated the chaos in my head, and I turned back around to face her. "How did you and . . ." I doubted she had met Aleksei through E-Harmony.

"As a young girl I ran away from home and ended up in Budapest with no money, no friends, and nowhere to stay. This is one of many mistakes I have made with my life." She gave me a rueful smile and shook her head. "I was befriended by a girl named Marta, who said she could help me."

"Anasztaizia, it's all right, you don't have to go on." I didn't want to make her relive something she'd rather forget.

"No, it's okay. It was long time ago."

Not that long, I thought to myself. If she wasn't my age, she only had me beat by a year or two.

"The first thing Marta did," Anasztaizia continued, "was to give me to her boyfriend, who raped me. He raped all the new girls. It was how he broke them in."

I gasped. Even though I had assumed whatever she told me was probably going to be bad, I hadn't expected that. "H-how old were you?"

"Fourteen." She sat back down at the table, her hands in her lap. As she continued speaking, I noticed she played with the diamond ring on her finger, as if reminding herself she now lived a different life. "I had been prostitute for six months when I was saved."

"Saved?" Somehow I didn't think she was talking about the biblical sense.

"The man I was with decided I hadn't been good enough, and he wanted his money back. I refused, so he hit me." She gave me a different type of smile this time. "He only got to hit me once."

"Aleksei?"

"Yes . . . Aleksei."

"Did you know he was a vampire?"

Opening her mouth, she tapped a tooth. "Oh yes . . . I knew."

"And you weren't afraid?" I asked incredulously.

Her fingers stilled, and she gave me a look that I couldn't read. "Marta's boyfriend had already made sure I stopped being afraid. Of anything."

I didn't know what to say. I couldn't imagine being forced into a life of prostitution at any age, much less fourteen. "So what happened next?"

"Aleksei took me home."

"Home?" She'd been with him since she was fourteen?

Apparently my expression told her what I was thinking.

"He took me back to my family, and made me promise to finish school."

"But you saw him again, right?"

"Not in the way you are thinking." Propping her elbow on the table, she cupped her chin in her hand. "When he came to see me, he was more like annoying big brother. He was not boyfriend. I was in love with him from first time I saw him, but Aleksei wanted me to know boys my own age . . . and my own kind. It took me some time to persuade him he was only male for me." She gave me a wonderful, sunny smile. "He wouldn't even kiss me without my father's permission!"

"Really?" I was filled with an odd admiration at Aleksei's restraint. As lovely as Anasztaizia was now, I could only imagine how tempting she must have been when she was on the cusp of womanhood.

"Aleksei is very old-fashioned," she said with a soft laugh, "even for a vampire."

"Your parents," I said hesitantly, "they didn't know, did they?"

"My mother, I think, did, although she did not say, and my father has suspected for some time. He wants me to be happy, and he knows Aleksei makes me happy." That much was blatantly obvious.

I came and sat back down opposite her. "Does it hurt?" I blurted out.

"What?" The change of topic startled her.

I pointed at her neck. "Does it hurt when he . . ." I let my voice trail off, not certain I knew how to refer to such an intimate act.

Reaching across the table top, Anasztaizia took hold of my hands, gripping them lightly, her thumbs rubbing gently across my knuckles. "Are you sure this is what you want to know?" she asked gently.

No, I wasn't sure at all, but something inside me had been woken up, and it was saying I needed to know. Not trusting myself to speak, I nodded.

"Very well," she sighed and took a moment to gather her thoughts. "It only hurts first time," she said quietly, "but I think that is because the mental struggle is hard to deal with. The physical part is much easier, but there is no way you can prepare for how you will feel."

"What do you mean by mental struggle?"

"Before first time, Aleksei wanted me to know as much as I could about what was going to happen. Sometimes is better to know nothing. To just do and feel the experience, to, how you say . . . go with the flow?" Something she remembered made her lips curve upward in a private smile. "First time you will fight, but in the end that which is stronger will win."

I couldn't imagine any situation where I would ever be stronger than Gabriel. And then I wondered why it would matter, because I also couldn't imagine him drinking my blood. Anasztaizia, guessing the path my mind was wandering on, set me straight.

"This is not about physical strength, Rowan. The fight will be inside your head." She tapped her temple with her forefinger. "Blood is the life force of the body, it is not meant to be given to another. Not like this."

"But people donate blood all the time," I said, thinking about the latest Red Cross drive I'd seen advertised in the Sunday newspaper.

She laughed out loud. A wonderful sound that made everything she was saying easier to hear. "This is not quite the same thing."

She was right. The difference between having a sterile needle put in my arm and Gabriel sinking his fangs into my neck were like night and day. The first felt like an almost philanthropic act, the other a violation.

"Never underestimate your own instinct for survival," Anasztaizia continued. "You are being asked to go against your strongest urge, and to give freely what is most precious to you. Ignoring your own needs because your desire for another, and his needs, are stronger." I swallowed and gently pulled my hands free of her grasp. It was a lot to take in. "How often do you . . . ?"

"Each vampire is different." She made another graceful lift with her shoulders. "The older the vampire, the stronger he is, and the more control he has over the hunger." She looked at me, her eyes frank with curiosity. "Gabriel has not yet tried to—"

"Oh my God—no!" My hand instinctively went to my throat. "Never!"

"Ah well . . . he is very strong."

There was something in her tone, a sort of fatalistic inevitability that said this *was* going to happen to me, and the sooner I accepted it, the better. Either that or the amount of bourbon in my system was finally taking over and eighty-proof Tennessee whiskey was dulling my comprehensive reasoning.

A voice inside my head whispered that maybe things weren't so bad after all. I might be involved with a vampire, but I was still alive and hadn't given up as much as a single drop of blood. If Gabriel had wanted to feed from me, he could have done so at least a half dozen times by now. Perhaps Anasztaizia was right. It was just a matter of viewing it in the proper context. Blood was every bit as necessary to a vampire as insulin to a diabetic. It was the method of extraction that I was going to have to come to terms with.

"Do you think," I paused, feeling my cheeks burn, "Gabriel will want to feed from me?"

Her gaze was unflinching. In all the times we'd met, I'd never noticed before that her eyes were the most gorgeous shade of turquoise.

"I don't think," she said, choosing her words carefully, "Gabriel wants to feed from anyone else."

Oh . . . shit.

I closed my eyes and felt the room spin as my brain threw random images at me. Unfortunately, they all seemed to be from the same B horror movie. I was almost overcome by a collage of heaving bosoms, heavy eyeliner, and ridiculous lacey nightgowns. But in the middle of this grotesque nightmare, Anasztaizia threw me an unexpected lifeline.

"Rowan, surely you must know Gabriel will not force you. He will wait for you to give yourself to him."

And what if that never happens? What then? How long can he last without blood?

Until he's forced to use someone else.

A sudden panicky feeling began deep in my stomach. I looked around my kitchen, trying desperately to find something that would anchor me back to the mundane reality that had been my life a short while before. It felt like a dozen lifetimes had passed since then. Anasztaizia stared at me, her eyes filled with concern, and sensing, I'm sure, the turmoil in me.

Everything was the same, and everything was different.

Yesterday morning I had no idea that the human race coexisted with supernatural creatures, and now the proof was irrefutable. Inanimate objects could not take me back to the life I'd once had because that life, and all that it comprised, no longer existed for me.

I think life likes to test us every now and then, just to see if our coping skills are in need of a few improvements. I got pushed into the deep end to see if I would sink or swim, and I had absolutely no intention of going under. Sharing a world with vampires was going to take a different set of coping skills, and the sooner I took advantage of the instruction being offered, the better. I gave Anasztaizia a wobbly smile.

"I think I'd better invite your boyfriend in."

CHAPTER 6

Before opening the front door, I braced myself for the very real probability that my guest on the other side would not be in the best of moods. I didn't know if Aleksei was the type to hold a grudge, but I couldn't count on him not still being pissed at my refusal to let him in. I thought about asking Anasztaizia for tips on dealing with a ticked-off vampire, but I wasn't sure how objective she would be. Squaring my shoulders, I told myself to ignore the fact that Aleksei was a vampire. I should treat him like any other guy with a chip on his shoulder—in his case, a really, really big shoulder.

The first thing he did was snarl at me. The second was drop his fangs. So much for trying to ignore the vampire part. He apparently had no intention of letting me forget exactly what he was. I took a step back and began rethinking the wisdom of inviting him inside.

"Aleksei . . ."

The voice coming from behind me shifted his focus, and I was stunned at his transformation. Hostile attitude and fangs both disappeared at the slightly disapproving tone in Anasztaizia's musical lilt, allowing me to see their relationship wasn't at all one-sided. Completely smitten, Aleksei would do absolutely anything for this woman.

"It's all right, Rowan," Anasztaizia murmured from behind me as she placed her hand on my shoulder. "He's just a little unsettled."

Unsettled?

A dozen different adjectives to explain the big guy's state of mind bounced around inside my head. Every one of them was normally used to describe an act of violence. *Unsettled* wasn't one of them.

"Please," the exotic blonde continued in a low voice, "you have to invite him in."

Swallowing, I looked at the vampire standing on my cheery ho-ho-ho Christmas doormat and, taking a deep breath, asked, "Aleksei, won't you please come in?"

He stepped over the threshold and brushed past me, almost flattening me against the wall. In a way I could understand his reaction. If vampires were as possessive as Anasztaizia had said, then being kept waiting on my porch must have been absolute torture for him. He was looking for reassurance that his girlfriend had not been harmed by walking into the proverbial lion's den, alone and without his protection. The fact that she had done so of her own free will was completely irrelevant. My actions had made it a necessity. It was something I didn't think he was going to forgive, or forget, anytime soon.

After closing the front door, I turned to see Anasztaizia being swallowed up inside the army greatcoat as Aleksei wrapped his arms around her. Low murmuring was interspersed with chaste kisses administered to her forehead, temples, and nose. And then a decidedly unchaste one was placed on her mouth. I could almost feel the raw heat as I quickly lowered my gaze. Was that what Gabriel and I looked like?

"You sent me away," Aleksei growled, glaring back at me over the top of Anasztaizia's head.

"Well, you lied to me!" I shot back, using whatever bourbon was still in my system to be reckless. "So I guess we're even."

Extricating herself from his embrace, Anasztaizia caught hold of Aleksei's chin and spoke to him in a sharp tone. I didn't understand the words, but I caught the general gist. She was telling him to knock it off. His chest moved as he took a deep breath, and I felt a palpable drop in the tension. Taking his hand, Anasztaizia led him back to the kitchen.

Aleksei pulled out a chair, took off his coat, and draped it over the back. He then set about moving it next to his girlfriend's so the two chairs were now side by side. I hid my grin by covering my mouth with a hand before resuming my own seat. Anasztaizia busied herself making a fresh pot of the delicious coffee.

"You are first person never to have believed me," Aleksei grumbled, folding his arms across his chest. "And I am sorry to lie to you," he added with a sigh.

I knew the apology was being given at Anasztaizia's behest, and I got the feeling it wasn't something that happened very often. I decided I could be magnanimous.

"Apology accepted," I told him.

He grunted and stared at me. I told myself he was regarding me with newfound respect, but who was I kidding? He was probably calculating how much pressure it would take to snap my neck, and judging from the size of his hands, it wouldn't be much. But he *had* underestimated me earlier. Something I was sure he wouldn't do again.

"Gabriel has told me to answer questions."

"What sort of questions?" I ventured warily.

"About vampires," he said with a scowl. "There are things you are wanting to know, yes?"

Although Anasztaizia had assured me that if my demise was something Gabriel wanted, I'd already be pushing up daisies, I hadn't totally believed her. I did now. It was plain to see Aleksei was not thrilled by the prospect of being my go-to guy for all things vampire. And I didn't see Gabriel wasting his second-in-command's time making him play twenty questions if he was only going to kill me afterward.

"So, what do you want to know?" he asked.

"About vampires?" I stared at him for a long minute before giving him a sly smile. "How about . . . *everything*."

Of course I didn't need to know that much. I already knew at least three things about vampires that couldn't be disputed: drinking blood was necessary to their survival, daylight was a big no-no (which explained why Gabriel never stayed the night with me), and they had to be invited to cross a threshold. But it was good to see the big guy momentarily flummoxed by my answer.

"Actually there are only three things I want answers to," I said, holding up the appropriate number of fingers.

"Only three? You are surprising me, Rowan." Aleksei being sarcastic, who knew?

"Yeah well, they're kind of biggies, so don't get excited."

"Tell me." He smiled, first at me, then at Anasztaizia, who put mugs of hot, steaming coffee in front of us.

"What does it mean . . . I'm Gabriel's Promise?"

Anasztaizia's sharp intake of breath took me by surprise. Apparently they hadn't been expecting that. Score one for me. Their hesitation and the way they surreptitiously glanced at each other made me even more curious. And also scared.

"You do not know?" Aleksei asked quietly, spooning sugar into his mug.

I sighed. "Would I be asking if I did?"

"This I cannot tell you. Ask me different question."

Not the informative start I was hoping for, but I wasn't about to give up just yet. "You can't tell me *anything*?" I prodded stubbornly.

He glanced at Anasztaizia, who made the tiniest movement of her head. "All I can tell you is you are bound to Gabriel by ritual. One that cannot be broken."

"What exactly do you mean by *bound*?" I wasn't sure if he was referring to kinky leather restraints or something with matrimonial implications. Neither prospect gave me the warm fuzzies.

"I don't know," Aleksei said, looking angry. "Talking about a Promise is forbidden."

"You're kidding, right?" We hadn't even begun to play twenty questions and he was already shooting me down. "You can't tell me about it even though it involves me?"

Ignoring me, Aleksei raised his mug to his mouth.

"Why not?" I asked, sounding like a bratty kid who can't get her own way.

"Because it is not permitted," Anasztaizia said firmly, taking her seat next to Aleksei and patting his beefy bicep. "No vampire is allowed to talk of a Promise. Doing so, even among themselves, means punishment."

These were vampires we were talking about, and from the little I'd seen, they were a pretty resilient bunch. Katja had actually pushed her dislocated shoulder back into place while crab-hopping down a hallway with a swollen knee. What kind of a punishment could they possibly be given? Lock them in a room and make them listen to Justin Bieber CDs until their ears bled?

"So who *can* tell me what being a Promise means?"

"Gabriel," they both said together. Right. Should have seen that one coming.

"So, what is second question?" Aleksei had obviously decided we were done with the whole pesky Promise issue, and he was ready to move on. My feelings didn't seem to count for much, but as I was already treading on thin ice with him, I let it drop.

"How does someone become a vampire?" I asked. "Do you just have to bite them?"

He rolled his eyes, and Anasztaizia reached for his hand.

"Rowan! You smart girl saying stupid words!" he chastised. "Think about what you say. If this is how vampires are made, then the world would already be full of vampires."

Embarrassment made my face burn. He was right, of course, but in my defense, the prospect of vampires running rampant across the planet wasn't something I generally thought about. If all it took to create a vampire was simply being bitten by one, then both species would have died out centuries ago. No wonder Aleksei was annoyed with me—I was annoyed with me! Hadn't Anasztaizia shown me where her boyfriend had had a little nibble earlier? And she was very definitely not a vampire. Good Lord, what was wrong with me?

"And you should know not every human can be made vampire," Aleksei said. "Only those possessing the proper marker can be turned."

"What's a marker?"

It was Anasztaizia who answered me. "Think of it as a recessive gene."

Did I really look like the type of girl who reads *DNA Digest* or *Genetics Weekly*? What did I know about genes, recessive or otherwise? I counted myself lucky to remember enough basic biology to recall how many pairs of chromosomes were in the human body.

"It makes it possible to survive the transition," she clarified, "and helps with adapting to a vampire existence."

I brought my gaze back to Aleksei. "And do I have this marker?"

"No," he said very decisively.

"How do you know?"

"You are a Promise."

"And that means I can't be turned into a vampire?"

"Exactly!" He looked positively smug.

"So I'm bound to a vampire," I said slowly, "but I can't be turned into one."

Two heads nodded at the same time, and though I felt sure this was a good thing, I was uncertain which one of us the distinction affected more—Gabriel or myself. The idea that a vampire would be bound to a non-vampire, and vice versa, struck me as potentially problematic. However, the look on Aleksei's face suggested I'd have more luck asking my toaster oven for further clarification. This dealt with my being a Promise, and I decided not to annoy him by asking questions he wouldn't answer. Gabriel was going to have a lot of explaining to do. "So how do you change someone?" I asked instead.

"Vampires cannot change a human," he said. "It is something only a Fallen can do."

"A Fallen? What's that?"

"They are the Original Vampires," Anasztaizia said, keeping her voice so low I almost didn't catch what she was saying, "and they are the only ones who can let you look death in the face, but not take his hand." I appreciated the romantic spin, but it didn't really tell me anything. My feelings must have been evident because she gave a small sigh before continuing. "To turn a human into a vampire, the process must begin at the exact moment of the final heartbeat—too soon and the body will not respond. The skill is in knowing which beat will be the last, and only the Fallen possess this knowledge."

For the next few moments the only sound I could hear was the low hum of the motor in my fridge. It sounded like it was only a couple of revolutions from conking out.

"And Gabriel is one of these Fallen vampires, isn't he?"

"Yes," Aleksei said, crossing his arms over his chest.

"And he turned you into a vampire, didn't he?"

"Yes." He jutted out his chin as if daring me to dispute it. Why would I? It hadn't been that difficult to figure out.

I looked at Anasztaizia. "Is he going to make you one too?"

She shook her head. "No . . . I cannot be turned." The regret in her voice said she would like nothing more, and seeing her hand disappear inside Aleksei's huge paw, the reason why also wasn't difficult to figure out.

"Did he make Katja a vampire?" I asked.

"No," Aleksei said with a shake of his head. "She was turned by Ryiel."

The rush of relief I felt was quite unexpected and very intense. If Gabriel had turned the exotic beauty into a vampire, then, to my mind, her feelings for him would border on the creepy and incestuous. "So . . . who's Vladimir?" I asked.

"You know Vladimir?" Anasztaizia looked at me with surprise.

"He was in the house," I told her. "He asked Katja who I was."

"And she told him?" Anasztaizia seemed stunned by the idea.

I nodded. "Yeah, but I got the impression he wasn't very happy at me being there." I paused and looked at both of them. "He told her that if things went south he wouldn't be able to protect her."

"He said that?" The blonde pursed her lips, looking faintly troubled.

"Well, not in those exact words," I said, "but I'm pretty sure that's what he was implying."

"I didn't know Vladimir was there," Aleksei said, his mouth becoming a grim line.

"Maybe I've got the wrong guy? Tall, aristocratic-looking. Like a movie star from the fifties with a great widow's peak."

An odd snorting sound made both Anasztaizia and me stare at Aleksei. Covering his mouth with a hand, he seemed to be giving his full attention to the floor, fascinated by the patterned linoleum. Unfortunately, having shoulders as big as his was sometimes a liability. I could tell he was trying not to laugh by the shaking motion they made. I looked at Anasztaizia, who spread her hands and shrugged in bewilderment, as puzzled by the big guy's reaction as I was.

"What's so funny?" I asked when he finally raised his head and looked at both of us.

His mouth continued to twist in a humorous smirk. "You think Vladimir is aristocrat."

I didn't think it was that funny, but what did I know about vampire humor? "From your reaction, I guess it's fairly safe to assume he's not, then?"

Clarification was delivered with a deep rumbling chuckle. "Son of goat herder from Carpathian Mountains."

I still didn't think it was *that* funny.

"Why would you think it was Vladimir who turned Katja?" Anasztaizia asked curiously.

"When I asked Katja if he was her father, she said *in a way,* so I just sort of assumed . . ." I let my voice trail off, acutely aware of the other definition of the word *assume.*

"Well, he is, *in a way,*" Aleksei said, generously coming to my rescue. "Vladimir is the one who asked for Katja to be turned. He was guardian."

"She needed a guardian?"

He nodded. "Yes, it was his responsibility to see her through the transition, then help her to live as vampire."

"And is the guardian always a male?" I asked curiously.

"Not always. A female can be guardian."

Who would have thought equal rights were alive and well, and had very sharp teeth? "You said Vladimir asked for Katja to be made a vampire." I could see Aleksei's eyes gleaming with interest as he wondered what I would inquire about next. "Is a request to turn a human ever denied?"

"Sometimes." He sounded hesitant. "If there is good reason."

"Such as?"

"Instability."

I thought I'd misheard him, or misunderstood. Katja didn't strike me as being exactly level-headed. In all fairness, I had no idea what her personality had been like as a human, but I was willing to bet the basic fundamentals hadn't really changed. Still, I felt like Aleksei was leaving something out.

"Can a person change their mind? Do they have any say in this?"

"Of course." The big guy looked faintly annoyed with me. "They can always refuse, but I have never heard it happening."

No, I just bet he hadn't. Saying *no* to a vampire didn't seem like much of a choice at all. I sat for a few minutes, toying with my rapidly cooling mug of coffee, as my mind ran through everything I'd just been told. I wanted to be certain I had the order of events straight.

"So only a human with the proper recessive gene, and who wants to be turned, can be made into a vampire." Aleksei nodded and seemed quite pleased that I'd caught on fairly quickly. "But they can be turned only by an Original Vampire, one of the Fallen, right? And Gabriel and this other vampire—Ryiel—they're both Fallen . . . so how many are there?"

"How many what?" Anasztaizia asked, her eyes shining brightly.

"How many Fallen?"

"Nine."

"What happened to the rest of them?"

"The rest of who?" Now it was Aleksei's turn to ask.

"The Fallen. Nine doesn't seem like an awful lot. Weren't there more of them?"

He shook his head and looked puzzled. I was guessing no one had ever considered this before. "No. There have only ever been nine," he stated emphatically.

My life was rolling down a path where everything was a lot more complicated than what I'd known before. I had no idea where exactly a Fallen existed within the vampire hierarchy, but it seemed to me that it was pretty high up. I hadn't failed to catch the reverence in Aleksei's voice when he said the word "Fallen."

I fixed my gaze on the Santa and Mrs. Claus salt and pepper shakers, standing guard on either side of a wedge of holly-printed paper napkins. Time passed. It could have been a minute or fifteen or fifty before Anasztaizia's gentle voice broke the silence.

"Rowan, is there anything else we can tell you?"

Breaking my trance, I smiled at her before bringing my gaze back to Aleksei's scarred face. "Yeah," I said slowly, "how do you kill a vampire?"

CHAPTER 7

If revealing vampire secrets made Aleksei uncomfortable, then the idea of sharing information on this particular topic turned him downright prickly. I couldn't really blame him, I suppose, but it did make me wonder just how broad a directive Gabriel had given him. From the look on his face, if I hadn't crossed a line yet, then my toes were dangerously close to the edge.

The vampire's face turned cold, his eyes steely, and I felt a shiver go down my back, the kind my father always said meant someone was walking over your grave. As a smart-mouthed teenager I'd been quite scornful of all my father's favorite sayings, and this one was no exception. How would anyone know where I was going to be buried? What if I decided on being cremated instead, with my ashes scattered at sea? Did that mean instead of people walking over my grave, a school of dolphins was now swimming through the area? Such a possibility still ranks very high on my *Way Cool* chart.

I'm pretty sure the temperature in the kitchen dropped a few degrees as Aleksei asked, "You want to know how to kill a vampire?"

Not trusting my voice, I nodded. The sudden warmth of his smile took me completely by surprise. All I could assume was that he had forgotten I was human and, to his mind, a physically inferior species. Perhaps my sudden inability to speak had reminded him. At any rate he obviously decided there was no harm in telling me. What was I going to do with the information? It wasn't like I was ever going to be able to actually put into practice anything he told me. Every vampire I'd met so far could flatten me with one hand tied behind his or her back. Including Vladimir, the not-so-aristocratic matinee idol.

As it turns out, killing a vampire isn't that easy.

"So, the whole stake-through-the-heart thing isn't true?"

Aleksei's scornful laugh was enough of a reply in itself. "Vampires cannot be killed like that. Is stupid fairy tale."

"Why not?" Curiosity got the better of me. "I mean, you do have a heart, right?"

It was a pointless question because I already knew the answer. I'd been lulled to sleep by the steady, rhythmic beat of Gabriel's heart on more than one occasion, and I wasn't about to forget those other times when it went all jackhammer in his chest, usually as he was coming. I suspect most women get an incredible rush knowing they can evoke this type of physical response in a man. Knowing I could do this to a vampire was suddenly a hundred times more delicious.

"Yes, I have a heart," Aleksei said, "but becoming vampire makes other changes."

"That recessive gene again," I said with a smile.

He grinned back and tapped his sternum with the tips of his fingers. "Is true. It protects heart with muscle that is very strong."

"Strong enough to stop a knife?"

"You want to try?" he challenged me.

It was Anasztaizia's lack of reaction that told me it was a fruitless challenge on my part, even though I was tempted for maybe half a second or so. "Just asking," I said with a nervous, shaky laugh.

"The only sure way to kill a vampire is to cut off head and burn body." He emphasized the point with a dramatic slashing gesture across his throat.

Of course it was. Why didn't I know that?

"Is that the only way?" I asked, because if there was a psycho-vampire bitch out to get me I wanted to be sure I had all the bases covered. Just in case.

Aleksei shrugged. "Well, there is also staking out in sun."

"Does the sun have to be shining or will plain daylight do?"

He stared at me with suspicion. "Why do you want to know this?"

"Because sometimes having the proper information can make all the difference," I told him. "So, which is it?"

"Daylight is for weakening, sunlight for burning." He leaned forward, his expression almost gleeful. "But I should tell you no human can kill a vampire. Only one vampire can kill another vampire."

The superiority of his tone was just a little too smug for my liking. It explained why he'd suddenly overcome his initial reluctance to answer me. I was no threat to any vampire whatsoever. And that really pissed me off. Granted, I could see how decapitation might prove a little tricky for someone not blessed with homicidal, maniacal tendencies—as well as a very big axe—but I was infuriated at how easily he dismissed the resourcefulness of the human race.

"You don't think a human could stake a vampire out in the sunlight?" I asked, pursing my lips.

Aleksei adopted the kind of exaggerated patience rarely seen outside of a first-grade classroom. "First you must catch vampire and overpower him, something you have not the skill or strength to do. Even the weakest vampire will always be stronger than the strongest human."

It took me a minute before I realized he wasn't being a condescending asshole, he was just stating facts, and respecting me enough to be bluntly honest. I notched down my irritation, trying not to let it cloud my thinking.

"But what about crosses, holy water, and garlic?" I asked. "Couldn't those be used to subdue a vampire?" The look on Aleksei's face said his estimation of my IQ had just crashed through the floor. "Oh, sorry," I mumbled, "I'm guessing they don't have any effect, do they?"

"No silver chains or bullets either," he added helpfully.

"I thought silver was only for werewolves."

He scratched his chin, thinking. "So I have also been told, but I never met anyone who killed a werewolf, so I don't know if such a thing is true."

The kitchen tilted slightly. Not enough to disturb anything. The cabinet doors didn't swing open, and my mug didn't try to slide into my lap, but it was enough of a nudge to tell me my reality had just slipped a little further.

"Are you saying . . . werewolves are real?"

"Of course." The corner of Aleksei's mouth twitched as he tried to suppress a grin. "And I'll tell you something else humans have wrong—they don't change because of moon."

Was this something I absolutely had to know? Of course it was. "So, why do they change?"

"Bad temper."

The grin he'd been trying to contain refused to be held back. *Do vampires ever need to floss?* I pondered as the impressive display of his teeth dazzled me. I doubted they went to the dentist, but hey, you never know.

"All werewolves have bad temper," Aleksei continued, his voice bringing me back to the here and now. "Actually, now I think about it, all shape-shifters have bad tempers."

"You would too if changing broke every bone in your body," Anasztaizia interjected.

I stared at her. "All . . . shape-shifters . . ." I muttered, gripping the edge of the table with both hands.

"Sure." Aleksei nodded and seemed very pleased with himself. "Werewolves are just one kind."

Of course they are. Silly me.

I told myself he was only giving me information he thought would be beneficial to my overall well-being. Unfortunately, I wasn't sure how to categorize this particular brand of helpfulness. The only way I could control a sudden attack of the shakes was to sit on my hands. The last thing I needed was for Aleksei to see just how badly I was rattled. It was hard enough accepting the existence of vampires. Other supernatural creatures were going to have to wait their turn.

I had the dismal realization I would be no match for Katja in a physical fight. In truth, I'd known that after seeing her take on Gabriel, but I'd been optimistic that Aleksei might reveal a possible vampire weakness. Anything that would give me an edge if I ever needed it. Now I realized that if Katja was truly determined to get to me, there was nothing I could do to stop her. Except stay in my house. Suddenly the idea of Aleksei being able to cross my threshold was rather comforting.

"I guess it's safe to assume that you're not immortal, then?"

"Nothing is immortal, Rowan," Anasztaizia said in a soft voice. "Everything will die. Even vampires."

"Then I don't get it. I thought the whole attraction of being a vampire was the chance to live forever."

"Is that what you would want to do?" Aleksei asked, giving me an unfathomable look. "Live forever?"

"I don't know," I backpedaled hastily. "It's not something I've spent much time thinking about."

"Well, it's not something a vampire can give you."

Somewhere close to midnight I managed to persuade Aleksei he needed to take Anasztaizia home. I promised him, cross my heart and hope to die, that I would be perfectly all right by myself. As long as the rule about vampires crossing thresholds was true, then I was safe. Katja had never been invited inside my house, and couldn't cross any threshold, front or back, uninvited.

"Don't underestimate her, Rowan," Aleksei warned as he helped Anasztaizia put her coat on. "If she comes here, she will try to get you to let her in. Like most females, she is very cunning."

"I get it, really I do, but unless she can hypnotize me into saying *come into my house,* there's no way she's getting through the door." I paused as I realized what I'd just said. "Uh, she can't do that . . . can she?"

"No," Aleksei said with a shake of his head, "and female vampires must have physical contact to cross a threshold. Words alone are not enough." He frowned, thinking about something. "She might pretend to be injured," he told me.

"Why would she do that?"

"To get your sympathy. If you thought she had a twisted"—he pronounced it *tvisted,* which made me smile—"ankle, you might think her weak and let her in inside. All she would need is to hold your hand, yes?" He winked and gave me a sly smile. "Why do you think bride is carried over threshold?"

My mouth dropped open. That thought had never actually occurred to me, and I didn't know if Aleksei was teasing me, but I wondered how many grooms would gladly chuck that tradition right out the window if there was any truth in the vampire's words. Shaking my head, I assured the big guy I wasn't going to open the door for anyone. At all.

"Not even for me?" he teased.

"Why would I need to? You've been given an invitation, and I know you can open locks."

It was obviously the right answer because Aleksei looked very pleased with himself. And me. Now I had two vampires who could come and go in my house whenever they pleased. Of course, I wasn't sure if Gabriel was going to make use of the privilege again. Or if I even wanted him to.

Of course you do, my inner bitch whispered silkily in my head. *Not only can he tell you all the things Aleksei won't, but I know you're nowhere near done with that body of his . . . not yet . . . admit it.*

I wanted to snap out something cutting to shut her up, but my sarcasm well was currently dry.

"Come, we must let Rowan rest." Anasztaizia bent to kiss my cheek. "This has been a difficult day for her."

That was putting it mildly.

Taking Aleksei's hand, she steered him toward the front door, something I found oddly reminiscent of a bear being led around a circus ring by the trainer's beautiful assistant. It didn't take much imagination to picture Anasztaizia in a sparkly costume with feathers in her hair.

"Lock door," Aleksei instructed once he and Anasztaizia were on the other side, feet planted on my ho-ho-ho mat.

Even though I knew he had my best interests at heart, I wasn't completely helpless. I was smart enough to lock a door, although I wasn't really sure how much good it would do. What was to prevent Katja, with her own set of lock-picking skills, from opening it and throwing in a couple of tear gas grenades? Or regular grenades, come to think of it.

"Remember, not every vampire can open a locked door," Anasztaizia reminded me.

"It is a skill Katja never acquired," Aleksei added.

"Are you both reading my mind now?" I asked.

Aleksei gave me a sly look. "You play poker?"

"Not really," I said shaking my head, "I'm not very good at reading cards."

"Problem is with face," he chuckled, "not cards."

I refused to believe I was guilty of broadcasting my emotions so openly. If my face betrayed my feelings, especially now, then the stress of the past twenty-four hours was surely responsible. But hearing that Katja did not possess lock-picking skills made me feel better. And judging from the smile Aleksei gave me, my face hadn't been shy about broadcasting this.

CHAPTER 8

I had promised Anasztaizia I would get some rest, but it was a promise I knew I was going to break the moment I said the words. Sleep was out of the question. I might be tired physically, but mentally I was Red Bull six-pack wired.

The first order of business was to try to get a handle on the information dump I'd been given, put it in some sort of perspective. Hah! Easier said than done. The more I sifted through all I'd been told, the more I realized just how totally unprepared I was to deal with this newfound knowledge. My inadequacy would be laughable if it wasn't also completely terrifying. I found myself jumping at every sound I couldn't immediately identify. Each creak and groan the house made as it settled, noises I'd heard all my life, now sounded sinister.

I set about tidying up the kitchen. After washing and rinsing our mugs and the coffee carafe and filter basket, I set them to dry in the draining rack. Next I rearranged the chairs around the table so everything was back in its proper place. Then I spent the next half hour or so moving aimlessly from one room to another, picking up this, putting away that. Being able to sense Gabriel's presence in every room wasn't helping my well-being. If anything, it only added to my anxiety. His presence surrounded me. Somehow he'd managed to saturate every space in my house with his essence. I could say, with all honesty, that I had no idea how I was going to react when we next came face to face, but I knew such an encounter was a foregone conclusion. It was simply a matter of when it happened, not if.

I desperately needed to talk to someone. Anasztaizia was a wonderful woman, but let's be honest, when your boyfriend is six-and-a-half-feet of hulking Russian vampire, your opinion is bound to be a tiny bit biased. I'd never needed Laycee so much, but reaching out to her was impossible. What would I say? There was no way to spin this and make it sound believable, and Laycee could always tell when I was hiding something. She wouldn't rest until I spilled absolutely *everything* to her in full detail. No, it was better to leave my best friend out of this. Probably safer as well, and I meant that in a very real way.

So it made perfect sense to seek refuge in my dad's room. It was the one place that Gabriel had never been.

The faint trace of Old Spice aftershave took me by surprise as I opened the door. It was so slight I doubt anyone else would notice it—anyone human, that is—and it brought a hauntingly familiar ache to my heart. But as I opened myself up to the expected sharp pang of grief, I couldn't help noticing it was not so overwhelming as usual. Was that time working its own brand of healing, or something being with Gabriel was responsible for? Was I moving on? I shook my head. Gabriel's influence on anything remotely connected with my dad was not something I wanted to think about just now.

How long was it since I had last been in this room? Early spring maybe? I seemed to recall throwing open the window so the room could get a good airing, so . . . yeah, definitely before I'd met Gabriel. I slowly turned the brass knob that opened the closet where my dad had kept his clothes. About a year after he'd died, with the help of Laycee and her mom, I'd bagged up nearly everything and taken it to Goodwill. But I couldn't bring myself to part with his work shirts or his heavy winter jacket. I think most people who've lost someone they love keep mementoes, things with a strong emotional attachment.

Reaching for the shirt closest to me, I took comfort in the feel of the heavyweight fabric in my hand. The cuff was frayed, and each elbow showed signs of wear. A loose thread on the second button down threatened to release its charge. I took a mental inventory of the contents of my sewing box, searching for dark blue thread, and my vision blurred. My dad wasn't going to care if the button was missing. Sometimes the most ordinary things can elicit a memory, especially if the need is great enough. In this case, it was a button on a washed-out denim shirt.

I pulled the shirt off the hanger and slipped it on. It was too big, of course. My dad was long and lean. Rangy I think is the word best used to describe his build. His shirts didn't swim on me the way Gabriel's did, but the sleeves still reached my fingertips, and the hem fell below my hips. Turning my head into the collar, I sniffed, but any scent of my dad had faded long before. It made no difference. Knowing he had been the last person to wear it was enough. It brought me closer to him.

"I'm here for you, Baby Girl," my father's voice whispered in my head, "and you can always talk to me."

So I did.

Although my dad was very easy to talk to, I think we were both grateful that he'd never had to have *The Talk* with me. Sex Ed classes in my high school were fairly comprehensive and covered a whole lot more than anything offered when he was a teenager. Any additional questions Laycee's mom was more than willing to answer. She also took me bra shopping, and as luck would have it, my first period began during a sleepover with Laycee. The sudden appearance of a box of tampons in the bathroom reassured my dad that I was developing normally.

But getting a free pass on the physical stuff didn't mean my dad was off the hook entirely. He got the joy of dealing with pimples, emotional meltdowns, and more angst than any teenage girl should be allowed to express. My hormonal outbursts were always dealt with on the porch swing, and always began with my dad saying, "Tell me what happened, Baby Girl."

And so I'd pour out my heart to him, and he would listen solemnly to whatever foolishness guaranteed an Oscar-worthy performance in histrionics. It didn't matter if my melodramatic outburst made absolutely no sense. I just needed to vent about the injustices of my life, both real and imagined, while seeking assurance there existed on the planet one adult who would always be on my side. No matter what. And my dad was smart enough to know this. Even when the subject matter was a bewildering catalog of events he couldn't possibly be expected to navigate, his actions told me that my hurt feelings were all that mattered.

Not being picked for the cheerleading squad. *Lacking overall gymnastic skill. I never asked to be the top of the pyramid, okay?*

Failing my driver's test the first time. *Seriously? How many sixteen-year-olds actually parallel park?*

Steve Barnett admitting he only kissed me because of a dare. *Shit! And to think I also let him put his hand inside my shirt and cop a feel.*

My dad offered his opinion only when it was asked for, which wasn't often because, let's be honest, teenagers don't want answers. All their problems have implications that are way beyond the grasp and understanding of anyone outside their peer group. How could any adult, especially a parent, empathize?

But one look at my face after the crushing Steve Barnett humiliation had been enough. Arms around me, my dad had comforted me as only a father can—with the absolute belief that Mr. Barnett was raising a complete asshole who would never be good enough for me.

"How will I know, Daddy," I sobbed, "when it *is* the right guy?"

"Because you won't need to ask me," he'd said, his large calloused thumb wiping away my tears. "You won't need to ask anybody. Your heart will tell you he's the right one. Always trust your heart."

Now, lying on the same bed where my father had once loved my mother, and where I had possibly been conceived, I wondered what advice my dad would have given me about Gabriel. The conversation inside my head seemed very real.

Do you love him, Baby Girl?

I don't know, Daddy.

Yeah you do, but it's okay. We can let that pass. Tell me, do you like him?

I thought so, but now I'm not so sure.

What's your heart saying, Rowan?

It's not saying anything.

Yeah it is, Baby Girl, you're just not listening.

I am listening, Daddy, but I don't think . . . he can't be the right one!

Why not?

Because Mr. Right isn't supposed to have a set of choppers that could shame a pit bull.

Oh, Baby Girl, that's just your head talking, not your heart. You have to listen more closely. What does your heart say, Rowan?

That . . . it wants what it wants.

You bet it does. Listen to me, Rowan, every sentient being has the capacity to love, but we don't always get to decide who our heart chooses. We can only decide whether or not we're going to trust that choice.

So you're saying the decision is mine?

It always has been, Rowan. Now, tell me all about this vampire of yours . . .

Emerging from a cocoon of memories, my face wet with tears I hadn't realized I'd cried, I was absolutely certain of one thing. Vampire or not, my father would have liked Gabriel very much.

Of course, there was still one troubling aspect that his ghostly presence couldn't help me with. This belief that Gabriel and I were bound to each other through some archaic ritual. That I was promised to him. What was it he'd told me?

You are a Vampire's Promise . . . given by word . . . accepted by deed . . . bound by ritual to keep safe that which has been surrendered.

I had no idea what any of it meant. Perhaps breaking it down, line by line, I might get a better insight.

You are a Vampire's Promise.

Okay, this was easy enough. Gabriel was the vampire, therefore I was the Promise. Although how a promise can be an actual person was something I didn't quite grasp. Still, the only vampires I knew all believed it was so, as did Anasztaizia, who was human.

Given by word.

Whose word? If it was mine, then I had pledged myself unintentionally and with no idea of what the consequences might be. And going on the assumption that I had given my word to Gabriel, it was hard to recall any conversation between us in which anything I said could be misconstrued for a solemn vow. Surely I couldn't be held responsible for what I murmured, and sometimes yelled, in the throes of passion. My brain and vocal cords had a hard enough time working in sync around him when he wasn't trying to turn me on.

Accepted by deed.

Now this was tricky. The only action that could possibly account for this would be when I bit Gabriel. That definitely classified as a deed, and it was one that still mortified me because I had no way to explain my bizarre behavior. And in light of Gabriel's recent coming out of the coffin, his wish to carry a permanent reminder of the event now took on a strange, and mildly troubling, significance for me.

And bound by ritual to keep safe that which has been surrendered.

This was the part that had me completely bewildered. Both the ritual and the surrendered parts. Unless I had been drugged with something that had a very selective amnesiac effect, I was fairly certain I would remember taking part in any ceremonial rite. Unless of course it had happened when I was a baby, although my mother, for reasons my dad never told me—assuming he even knew himself—had been dead set against my being christened or baptized.

As for the surrendered part . . . I was going to give myself a headache if I kept chasing that one. If it was something that belonged to Gabriel, why would he give it to me to keep safe? And, more important, *when* would he have given it to me?

I recalled a moment not long after he'd come back into my life when he tried to give me a gift. Inside the black jeweler's box he slid across the kitchen table was the most exquisite bracelet. Embedded in links of heavy gold were the most amazing chocolate-colored pearls. I'm not a fan of gold or pearls or jewelry in general, but this was unlike anything I had ever seen before. It was exotically beautiful, and my fingers itched to lift it from the nest of pale satin and feel the weight around my wrist. But, hard as it was, I closed the lid and slid the box back across the table to him.

With a look of curious resignation, Gabriel picked it up. He didn't ask for a reason, and I never offered one, but he knew. It was too much, too soon. Although he later proposed replacing the POS—my piece of shit car—with a new Hummer, an offer I didn't take seriously, he never tried to give me another gift. So far. What could I have that might belong to him? And why would he trust its safekeeping to me?

Trying to come up with a plausible explanation was starting to give me a headache. Closing my eyes, I ordered my brain to stop asking questions I couldn't answer.

CHAPTER 9

My body's expectation of sex was Gabriel's calling card to me. Even in my dreams. An all-too-familiar heat roused me to the edge of wakefulness, making me scissor my legs as I kicked the quilt off. I felt feverish, and my forehead and upper lip were both dotted with beads of sweat. Searching for relief, I pulled up my T-shirt and offered my flushed skin to the cooler air above the rumpled covers. It made little difference. My heart could compete with a jackhammer, it was beating so fast, and I pressed the heel of my hand against my breastbone, as if somehow that would slow the frenetic pace. All I accomplished was the release of a sound trapped in my throat, a groan of frustration carried on a wave of need that was unlike anything I'd felt before.

I swept my hand over my breast, and my nipple erupted at the contact. I couldn't remember ever being so aroused. I was needy, achy, and wet between my thighs. Whatever I'd been dreaming about must have bordered on the pornographic. Too bad all I could recall was the feel of skin on skin, the silky brush of hair, and the taste of a sinful tongue.

I made myself take a couple of long, slow breaths, realizing, as my heart decided not to send me into cardiac arrest, that my mouth was dry. It was the same parched feeling I got whenever I was trying to catch my breath, like right before Gabriel tipped me over the edge and I climaxed. I licked my lips . . . and heard a very different sound. One that wasn't supposed to be in my bedroom in the middle of the night. At least not right now.

My hand went to snap on the bedside lamp that wasn't there. Sleep-fuddled, I stared at the nightstand, looking for the missing light a few moments longer before waking up enough to grasp that this wasn't my bedroom. I'd fallen asleep on my dad's bed. The fact that I'd had an erotic dream while sleeping on his bed struck me as indecent. I sat up, my feelings of guilt amplified by the sight of Gabriel standing in the doorway.

I tried telling myself he was a figment of my imagination, conjured up by an overactive libido. But then I caught his scent—a familiar blend of winter forest and snow, all mixed together with a mystifying something else I couldn't name but recognized as being uniquely Gabriel. And I knew he was no mirage.

"W-what are you doing here?" I asked, the dryness in my throat making my voice husky.

He stepped toward me, and I scuttled back up the bed until I felt the headboard against my back. The sight of him transported me back to the monstrous mansion Katja had taken me to, and I was standing once again inside that awful room, a room bathed in candlelight and boasting a bed with erotically carved posts and black satin sheets. A bed not meant for resting tired muscles or relaxing a weary mind. If ever a bed was made for one specific purpose, it had been that one. It was a bed made for fucking and nothing else. And so was the woman who came with it.

A picture of carnal lust with long blond hair, she gave her voluptuous figure to Gabriel without hesitation. Or so I assumed. All I could see in my mind right now was the sudden spray of arterial blood that arced from the wound in her neck, and the frozen look of fear on her face. How quickly her expression had changed from anticipated pleasure to horrified panic as she realized what had been done to her. The promise of ecstasy had been a lie, and now the life force was flowing out of her with each frantic beat of her heart. And she was helpless to prevent it. With her blood staining his chest and mouth, a mouth I once thought I would never get tired of kissing, Gabriel had held my gaze and admitted the truth about himself.

You know what I am . . . you have always known . . .

And this was also true.

Here, in my dad's bedroom in the middle of the night, I finally accepted that. The man I had given myself to, the man I had secretly fantasized a future with, the man I wanted to grow old with . . . wasn't really a man at all. And somewhere, deep in a forgotten corner of my mind, a memory struggled to break free. It urged me to accept the truth about Gabriel. And as I did so, another truth was revealed. It didn't change a thing, God help me! I'd loved him before consciously knowing he was a vampire . . . and I still did.

Stepping slowly into the room, he held a glass of water in his hand. Carefully he placed it on the nightstand before turning to look at me. His expression conveyed how hurt he felt by my need to put physical distance between us. I watched as he parted his lips, not enough to smile but enough for me to see the tips of his fangs, and I saw his normally smooth brow furrow slightly. I could tell myself all night long that I had nothing to fear from him, but somewhere deep inside my intellect, the message hadn't been received. My innate sense of survival saw only a predator and was trying to protect me in the best way it knew how.

"You are afraid of me," Gabriel said in a voice that did nothing to indicate his mood.

"You st-startled me," I stammered. "I wasn't expecting to see you."

"No? You surprise me."

My heart had revved itself back up to jackhammer mode. Thanks to my newly acquired knowledge of vampires, I knew Gabriel would have no difficulty detecting the accelerated rhythm. I tried calming myself, silently pleading with my heart to slow down. But it ignored me as usual. If my brain wasn't excited about seeing Gabriel, my body definitely was. I took a deep breath, and looked at him. God— he was magnificent!

"What I meant to say was, I didn't expect to see you tonight. If I'd known you were coming, I wouldn't have gone to bed."

"Why are you sleeping in your father's room?" he asked, his glance taking in the rumpled bed covers.

I shrugged, unsure of how to explain my need in a way that wouldn't hurt his feelings any more than I already had. I opened my mouth and then closed it again. No matter how I put it, it was going to come out wrong. Gabriel shrugged and moved back to stand in the open doorway.

"It doesn't matter. Your reasons are your own." There was a reserve to his manner, an aloofness I didn't like, and then he surprised me by saying, "I should go."

"I think we need to talk," I said, speaking quickly before I lost my nerve. His offer to leave was the last thing I expected. "Only not in here."

"Of course."

I waited until he stepped out of the room before moving. Getting up, I hastily straightened the quilt I'd kicked off and picked up my dad's shirt from the floor. I must have shucked it off during my erotic dream. Still mortified by my fantasy, I felt my face burn with shame. It didn't matter that I couldn't control what I dreamed about. It had happened and I was going to have to live with it. Picking up the glass of water Gabriel had brought me, I eased my parched throat.

It was my intention to have this conversation in the kitchen or living room, but Gabriel stood at the top of the stairs, effectively blocking the way. He was challenging me, daring me to admit I didn't have enough control over my feelings to risk talking to him in the intimacy of my bedroom. It struck me that I had no idea how long he'd been watching me in my dad's bed. Had he heard me moan? Did he know the reason why? I refused to be intimidated by him and decided to call his bluff. I turned and walked directly into my bedroom, feeling his gaze on me as I went.

I switched on the lamp on my night table and turned around to see Gabriel had made no effort to come any farther than the doorway. He leaned up against one side of the doorframe, looking at me. I sat on the edge of my bed and saw him glance at the clock next to the lamp.

"I'm sorry," he said, "I didn't realize how late it was."

"No matter," I said, dismissing his concern.

"Did you find Aleksei helpful?"

I don't know why his question threw me off track. I should have expected it. "Yes. He was very nice to me." A warning flashed in Gabriel's eyes, and I recalled Anasztaizia's caution about the possessive nature of vampires. Male vampires in particular. I needed to make sure there was absolutely no misunderstanding what Aleksei had been doing while inside my house. "He answered my questions, Gabriel, nothing else."

"Did he answer all of them to your satisfaction?"

"No," I admitted, "some of them he couldn't answer, and some of them he wouldn't answer." I waited for his reaction and watched as the glow in his eyes began to diminish. "He did nothing wrong, and if you thought it was going to be a problem, then you shouldn't have sent him to me."

"If I didn't trust him, I wouldn't have," Gabriel said in a low voice.

"Then what's the problem?"

"It's difficult for me . . . knowing you were with someone else."

"But I was not *with* anyone else!" I protested hotly. "Besides, Anasztaizia was here."

"She was?" He seemed both surprised and relieved by this news.

"Yes, and I'd appreciate it if you didn't give her a hard time about it. I don't think I could have dealt with Aleksei by myself."

"Oh, I didn't realize." He was humbled by the unexpected tartness of my tone. "You must know I have never questioned your fidelity."

Gabriel might not have been questioning my fidelity, but he sure needed reassurance about something. Still, it was nice to know he didn't think I was a bed-hopping slut. Shifting position, I sat cross-legged and pulled a pillow into my lap. I needed something to do with my hands, and fussing with the decorative edge of the pillowcase seemed a good way to occupy them.

I stared at him. He was here for something besides conversation, and it wasn't that difficult to work out what. The strain each bicep was putting on the sleeves of his T-shirt told me his body was zinging as much as mine. It made me wonder whose self-control was in question. Asking about Aleksei was ridiculous. I was certain he was fully aware of every question I'd posed, along with every scrap of information Aleksei had given me. But his surprise over Anasztaizia's presence had seemed genuine enough, so maybe the big guy hadn't told him everything.

Keeping his voice low, and his expression absolutely neutral, he asked, "Is there anything you want to tell me?"

I took a moment or two to gather my thoughts, needing to make sure I was completely awake and not sleep-muddled in any way. I certainly hadn't been expecting my face-to-face with Gabriel to happen this soon, not when I was still reeling from the effects of a highly erotic dream. I might not remember any details, but I had no doubt whom I'd been dreaming about. And my present condition may not have been consciously orchestrated by Gabriel, but he would have no qualms about taking advantage of it if I let him.

"I'm not afraid of you," I said.

God knows I ought to be, but I wasn't. Gabriel was a supernatural creature, one who, by design, preyed on humans. But he had never once tried to harm me—unless almost making me pass out from multiple orgasms counted. In truth, he'd had plenty of opportunities to hurt, maim, or even kill me, and I'd never once felt even mildly threatened by him. If anything, I was the one who'd laid some pretty damaging physical trauma on him. And he still had the scar to prove it, much to my chagrin.

And knowing he was a vampire? Frankly I'd been more frightened seeing Aleksei on my doorstep than I was right now. Although, in all fairness, that might be because I'd not had sex with the Russian.

"That's good to know," Gabriel murmured quietly from the open doorway. "I never want you be afraid of me, Rowan."

"Oh, don't misunderstand me. I'm terrified by what I now know you're capable of"—thanks to my current enrollment in Professor Aleksei's Vampire 101 class—"but I'm not afraid of you. There is a difference."

Frowning slightly, he considered my words, and then, appreciating the rationale, graced me with a truly relaxed smile. It lit up his face, and his dimple winked sexily at me. "So . . . what do you want to ask me?"

I thought it important to deal with the obvious first. "I guess you really are a vampire, huh?" I said.

"Yes, I really am."

From his tone of voice he could just as easily have been admitting he was a Seventh Day Adventist, or had been born in Latvia, or only ate meat the third Sunday after the vernal equinox. It was strangely deflating, and I felt a little let down. Truthfully, I'd been expecting something *more* with his admission. Lightning, peals of thunder, and demonic laughter from outside the window would not have been amiss.

Gabriel was a creature that could take a life as easily as drawing breath. I know, I'd seen him do it, but all I could focus on at this precise moment was the fact he was also the lover I'd been waiting for. And I think that said more about me than it did him.

"You must believe me, Rowan, this was not how I imagined you finding out. What Katja did was unforgivable."

"Then why didn't you tell me?"

"Truthfully?"

"Of course!"

"I actually thought you might work it out for yourself." How the hell was I supposed to do that? I stared at him in bewilderment. "When I realized," he continued, "that you didn't consider me anything other than human, I wanted you to keep thinking that for as long as possible. I knew that eventually the time would come when hiding the truth from you would no longer be possible, but I hoped by then I would have had time to prepare you."

I didn't want to disillusion him, but I couldn't see how he would have prepared me for this. It's not like confessing he belonged to some weird religious cult that worshipped a potato shaped like the baby Jesus.

"You just didn't figure Katja into the equation."

Sighing, Gabriel scrubbed a hand over his face. "I seriously underestimated her feelings about you."

"No, Gabriel—you seriously underestimated her feelings about *you*."

The stricken look on his face said he really had had no idea the psycho bitch was in love with him. Guess human males weren't the only ones with a stranglehold on the stupid gene.

"No, I had no idea." He sighed. It was one of those I-just-got-kicked-in-the-balls type of sighs. "But if you recall, I did tell you that once you knew, it would change things."

CHAPTER 10

Gabriel was right about that. He had warned me this would happen, and I wasn't going to lie to him. It did change things. But when he'd told me that, I'd been imagining having to deal with a life that involved the Russian mob or drug dealers or prison. Not vampires.

"Yes, I can see how you might think that," Gabriel conceded after hearing my theories.

The muscle in his jaw tightened. I told myself it was more amusement than dismay over the foolishness of my assumptions. And I'd be lying if I didn't say a part of me wished Gabriel was involved with a gang. No matter the brutality that was customary with such a lifestyle, it remained a reality of my world. Not the supernatural. And thinking about it suddenly brought something else to mind.

"Let me see your back," I asked.

Without saying a word, he gripped the bottom of his T-shirt and pulled it slowly over his head. Any other time I would have been reduced to a pool of wantonness, and although I was impatient for him to strip, my reason now had nothing to do with lust. I did my best to ignore the vaguely insolent smile on his face as he balled up the garment and tossed it on the end of my bed.

Turning around, he pulled his hair to one side and gave me an unrestricted view. It was difficult not to be distracted by the show of heavy muscle moving beneath his skin as he raised his arms. I stared. It hadn't been my imagination—he was both tattooed and scarred.

A bizarre, yet oddly familiar, series of glyphs ran down the length of his spine. Their beauty was strangely enhanced by the thick twist of scar tissue defacing both of his shoulder blades. I could feel my eyebrows pull together as I stared at them. The tattooing I could understand, but what type of mutilation would leave such a cruel disfigurement? My hands began to tremble.

"How could I not have known about that?" I asked him. "How could I not have felt your scars?"

"You thought me perfect. I did not want to disillusion you."

"Yeah, but . . . *how?*"

Turning back to face me, Gabriel folded his arms. My heart did its usual dance at seeing his biceps flex. He made no effort to retrieve his T-shirt, and I'm not ashamed to admit redressing him wasn't my number-one priority. "It was a simple matter of letting you see only what you wanted to."

"Were you messing with my head? Some sort of auto-suggestion thing?"

"No. The manipulation was only over my own body." He turned back around and as I stared, open-mouthed, both the tattooing and the scars disappeared, leaving his back smooth and, well . . . perfect. He faced me again. "But now that you know the truth, I cannot maintain the illusion for very long."

"That's okay, I can deal with it." I wasn't going to admit that the perfection of his body had actually been a little intimidating. It was on the tip of my tongue to ask what else he was hiding from me, but common sense said I might be better off not knowing. Not until I absolutely had to. However, there was something I wasn't going to ignore. "But why did you lie about my tattoo? Why wouldn't you tell me what it meant? That it matched yours?"

"Rowan—you had just given me your virginity! Do you really think that was the appropriate time to explain you had my name tattooed on your ass? Besides," he continued, "I thought you were the one who was being deceptive until I realized you thought it was nothing more than a pretty design."

His argument had merit, and in all honesty, I probably would have done the same thing in his place. Blowing out an impatient breath, I jabbed the air with my finger, indicating his own inking. "So what does it all mean?"

"It tells how I came to be."

Great, now he was being cryptic. "And how was that?"

He gave me an odd look. "It is a story for another time."

"And the scars? Are they also for another time?"

He shrugged nonchalantly. "It is the same story."

Well, that sucked. If I'd thought that everything I'd been through those past twenty-four hours now qualified me for an all-access pass to the world of vampires, I'd figured wrong. There were still some pretty big areas of uncharted territory. There was, however, one subject that had to be discussed, and if Gabriel thought it was off-limits, tough shit. I was prepared to go all pit bull on him.

I looked at him; wanting to be sure I had his full attention before asking, "Why did you kill that woman? Please don't tell me it was an accident," I said, keeping my voice as level as I could. "I saw your face. You meant to take her life."

"Yes, I did." Matching my tone for evenness, he apologized, "And you will never know how much I wished you'd been spared having to see that."

Any remorse he felt had nothing to do with the woman or even his own participation in such a violent act. It was all focused on me. I had witnessed a side of him I wasn't meant to see, and he regretted that. I wasn't sure whether to be comforted or appalled by his concern, but if Gabriel showed no repentance for having taken a life, then he showed no pleasure in it either. And I knew exactly how I felt about this. Reassured.

"Was she a vampire too?" I asked him.

"No, she was human."

Somehow I'd suspected as much. "So why did you kill her?"

"It was necessary."

The brevity of his explanation shocked me almost as much as its cold delivery. I waited for him to expound on his answer, but he remained silent, indifferent almost.

"You ripped her throat out!" I didn't yell, but it was close.

His eyes glittered with an inhuman light that sent skeletal fingers skittering down my spine. It crossed my mind that Gabriel was not in the habit of being asked to explain his actions. If I was determined to pursue this, I had best tread carefully.

"You're exaggerating, Rowan," he said, his tone still cold. "A wild animal rips out throats. What I did was use my skill to guarantee a quick death."

"It was brutal—"

"It was better than she deserved!" The icy demeanor was quickly replaced by hot temper. I watched as he drew in a deep breath, his massive chest rising and falling with the effort to cool his rage. "This was not a random murder, Rowan. It was an execution—and it was *necessary*."

There was that word again. He said it like it was an answer in itself, and I shouldn't need to ask anything else. But what gave Gabriel the right to be anyone's judge, jury, and executioner?

"What did she do?"

At first I didn't think he was going to answer me, but he must have sensed that if there was any chance of our going forward together, then I needed to know. No matter how awful the truth might be, if he didn't tell me all of it, it would stand between us. Always.

"She was guilty of a great many things." His voice changed again. It now became curiously resigned. "All of them forbidden by your legal system, but the offense I held her accountable for was the selling of children."

"A-are you s-sure?" I stammered.

His eyes became hard, the bright blue turning a shade of gray I'd never seen before. It was how I imagined the sea would look during a violent winter storm.

"I am always sure. Trust me, Rowan, she wasn't trying to help troubled teens get their high school diplomas. She enjoyed the reputation of being able to procure any child for any purpose—a reputation she worked hard to maintain." He sighed and ran his fingers through the thick white waterfall of hair that cascaded over his shoulders. It shimmered brightly, even in the pale glow from my bedside lamp. "In your talk with Aleksei, did he discuss our laws with you?"

I recalled some remark about the superiority of all things vampire, including a form of checks and balances. "Yes," I answered, "but he didn't go into specifics." And at the time I'd been too pissed by his condescending attitude to want to know.

"Well, we don't have many," Gabriel allowed, "but the most important is the protection of those who are truly innocent. Children. If a vampire harms a child in any way, the punishment is death." He gave me a hard look. "And you should know there are never any *mitigating circumstances*. Our law is absolute. To harm a child is forbidden."

"But you said she wasn't a vampire," I countered.

"She wasn't. As a species, you prey viciously on your own kind, especially those most in need of protection. As a result, it was decided centuries ago to extend our law to include human offenders, and thereby protect those who are unable to protect themselves."

"And she was selling children?"

He nodded and my stomach rolled, sending a wave of nausea washing through me. This changed everything, as I'm sure Gabriel knew it would. My hands began shaking again, only this time it was as if I was afflicted with some type of debilitating tremor. I didn't doubt his words, but it was difficult for me to imagine the woman with the moonlight hair committing such despicable acts.

"But couldn't you have turned her over to the police?"

The faintly mocking smile that curled Gabriel's mouth said he found my faith in human law enforcement, and the judicial system, naïve. "I usually do," he told me, "once I am assured the evidence is strong enough to guarantee a lengthy incarceration. Unfortunately, her lawyer was able to get my evidence thrown out. On a *technicality*."

I didn't know it was possible to articulate a single word with such contempt.

"So you took matters into your own hands because her lawyer found a loophole?"

"It was the only course left open to me. Sadly, your legal system continually proves itself incompetent to punish the truly guilty."

I wish I could have said I was outraged by his words, but I wasn't. I'm not as naïve about our legal system as Gabriel might have thought. Seriously flawed, the process is, in my mind, most definitely not equitable. Whoever can afford the better attorney will, more often than not, win the day. So hearing that critical evidence was not admitted due to a technicality did not surprise me. I just wondered how much the woman's attorney had charged her for that. I was beginning to understand Gabriel's brand of vampire justice. The countless young lives he'd saved from future misery weighed heavily in the balance.

"What else is troubling you?" he said quietly from the doorway. I flashed him a look, and he lifted his shoulders slightly. "I know you well enough to tell when you are distraught."

He was right. I was distraught, only this was something a little more personal. Heat rushed up from below the neckline of my T-shirt and slapped me in the face. "I understand your reasons for doing what you did, but couldn't you have just offed her while she still had her clothes on?"

"Offed her?" Now I knew he was struggling not to laugh. "Yes, I suppose I could have, but then the message I wanted to send might not have been as effective."

"Message? What message?"

He sighed and went back to being serious. I think it was at this moment that I realized just how big a deal explaining himself to me was. "There's a certain degree of trust that comes with being naked. Even if you're not consciously aware of it, you need to feel safe before undressing, but sometimes safety is nothing but an illusion." Gabriel paused, and I picked up the pillow in my lap, hugging it to my chest. "Executing her in such an intimate setting also served as a warning."

"To whom?"

"Whoever takes her place."

"And what was the warning?"

"That I will always exact payment in full."

A number of random questions began bouncing around inside my head. "What did you do with the . . . um . . ."

"Body?" I nodded and Gabriel shrugged. "Nothing. I am sure by now it has been discovered by the authorities."

"So that wasn't your house then?" I don't know if his appalled expression was because I had thought he lived in such an architectural nightmare, or because I assumed he would have no problem committing murder under his roof. I decided to move on. "But the police will know how she died, right?"

All the episodes of CSI I'd watched on TV came back to haunt me. How would the wounds in her neck not be thought suspicious?

"Forensics will show her throat was cut, nothing more." He gave me a look that said he appreciated my concern, even if that wasn't my intent. "Manipulating evidence isn't so difficult."

"I'll keep that in mind," I murmured.

Understanding the bigger picture helped . . . and it didn't. I was still unhappy about the woman being naked, mostly because I didn't know what had happened before my untimely entry into the room. Had Gabriel already slept with her? I didn't need to ask him; my complete lack of a poker face relayed my insecurities.

"I didn't have sex with her, if that's what you're thinking," Gabriel continued. "I told you I would have no other but you. Making her think it would happen was simply a way of increasing her heart rate. Nothing else."

Now why hadn't that occurred to me? Increased heart rate equaled increased blood flow, and I could certainly vouch for the effectiveness of such a strategy. My heart went into a full gallop whenever Gabriel aroused me. I opened my mouth to ask another question, and then snapped it shut decisively. The look on Gabriel's face said I had pushed him about as far as he was willing to go on this particular subject.

So I asked a different question.

"Do you really believe I'm promised to you in some way?"

"Of course." He frowned and looked troubled. "Do you truly not feel the connection between us?"

"Not in the way you do apparently," I muttered more to myself than him.

"Think back to the very first time you saw me in the bar. What was the first thought that came into your head?"

"That I knew you, that we'd met before—but it isn't possible!"

"Why not?"

"Because I would remember it—I know I would!"

"And you will."

Anasztaizia had told me vampires could move quickly, but I hadn't really understood what she'd meant. One minute Gabriel was filling the doorway, and the next he was standing by the bed. I swear to God all I did was blink. I never saw him move.

Taking my chin in his hand, he raised my head. The feel of his fingers stroking my jaw was electric, and, thirsting for his touch, I leaned into his palm. I'm ashamed to say it took a moment before my eyes met his, because I was too busy reacquainting myself with his torso. But when I did look up, it was a glorious moment.

Framed by thick dark lashes, his eyes had changed. The familiar hypnotic blue was now shot through with a gold iridescence, and they stared back with an intensity that scared me. Gabriel was the absolute carnal experience—a thousand and one encounters that I could not name but wanted to experience in the worst possible way. Whether he was vampire or human, I couldn't shut off my feelings for him. I wasn't a faucet, for God's sake!

"A bond already exists between us," Gabriel said, his voice raw with emotion. "It was created a long time ago, and is one that cannot be broken by either human or vampire law. I gave myself to you then, completely and without hesitation, and I do so again."

As he stroked my cheek, I felt a faint tremble in his fingers. Words filled my head, words he had spoken to me the last time I'd been in his arms.

I am a Vampire's Promise . . . given by word . . . accepted by deed . . . and bound by ritual to keep safe that which has been surrendered.

"Yes," he murmured, "indeed you are."

"But I don't understand what it means."

"And I cannot tell you." A flash of pain flared in his eyes. "The memory must return of its own accord or it will carry no weight."

I punched the pillow in frustration. "Shit! Why can't I remember any of it?"

"You will," Gabriel promised. "Now that you truly know who I am, it will come back to you." I searched his face, wishing I could be as certain. "Perhaps," he said with a smile, "you just need the right incentive."

Leaning down, he kissed me.

His tongue was a magnificent distraction inside my mouth. Teasing and tasting, it filled me with a sensual longing as he took all I had to give. Slowly pulling back, I felt Gabriel draw my lower lip into his mouth, scraping the swollen inner skin with his teeth. It wasn't until I felt a sharp prick that I realized he'd dropped his fangs. Blood welled up, and I gasped as Gabriel's tongue swept over the puncture as he lapped up my blood. He made a noise deep in the back of his throat, a sound that was definitely more purr than growl, and it sent a wave of unimaginable pleasure rippling through me.

My hands reached out and gripped his upper arms. My head was spinning, and I felt dizzy. I tried opening my eyes, but my eyelashes seemed to have locked themselves together. Gabriel released my mouth, pressing his lips lightly against my forehead as he laid me down on the pillows. I let go of my hold on him, but caught his hand and entwined our fingers.

I was looking down a dark tunnel. One that was filled with secrets and answers. One that I had to walk through, trusting there would be a light at the other end to guide me. I felt an awareness course through me, like nothing I had ever felt before. It filled me with a different type of desire. Something far beyond physical craving. The hunger I felt for Gabriel now had a different taste. It was richer and went far deeper. I couldn't articulate what I was feeling, but as I opened my eyes, I could see Gabriel felt it too. In his face I saw an understanding that had not been there before. Whatever it was that existed between us had taken a pivotal step forward.

Loosening his fingers from my grasp, Gabriel took my hand and held it against his chest. His skin was hot, almost feverish, but as my fingers laid over his breastbone I felt a warmth enter them—a warmth that sparked and glowed, moving through my hand, spiraling down my arm, and entering my body. It infused every muscle, every nerve ending, and every pore of my being with a sense of belonging. I was saturated with the essence of him, joined in such a way that any meaningful separation would bring nothing less than complete and utter desolation.

Being linked to another living, breathing individual had never felt so *right,* and with that realization came a moment of absolute clarity. I *was* bound to Gabriel by word and deed and ritual, but there was something else I was aware of. I was also bound to Gabriel by choice. *My choice.*

I had designated him as the only male I would ever give myself to.

I couldn't say how or when it had happened, but I knew with an unshakable certainty that it had. In a sudden intuitive leap I saw the threads of my life entwined with his, as they always had been, for as far back down that dark tunnel as I could see. And somewhere in there was the reason why. Like two halves of anything, we were complete only when brought together. As opposites, we had found a way to bridge the dark between us. I didn't know how such a thing was possible, but I wasn't going to deny it had happened.

Like a brain freeze that comes from eating ice cream too quickly, the revelation made me gasp. "The bond between us—it happened before you were made a vampire, didn't it?"

Gripping his hand, I held on for all I was worth, but he didn't need to answer me. I could read the answer in his eyes. This was what he'd been waiting for. This was the start of what he needed me to remember, the first step in the journey that would bring me all the way back to him.

Gabriel's voice in my head had been right when it had told me I'd always known he was a vampire. I *had* always known because I was there when it had happened. The depth of feeling that bound us to each other had been declared *before* he was changed.

And there was more. Something important that I'd locked away in a forgotten corner of my mind. I just needed to find the key that would release the memory.

What was I keeping safe?

What had Gabriel surrendered?

"I think perhaps you will remember now," he said in a husky voice.

And then he was gone.

CHAPTER 11

A week passed with no further nocturnal visits from Gabriel, although that wasn't technically true. Better to say there were no visits where I was an active participant. Gabriel visited me every night while I slept. I knew this because each morning the bed covers bore the impression of his body where he'd lain beside me, and the pillow was filled with his scent. Also the pot of freshly brewed coffee and vase of flowers on the kitchen table were a dead giveaway.

No matter how long I tried to stay awake, I never caught him slipping into my bedroom. After the second night, I tried setting my alarm clock so it would go off around three in the morning, but it mysteriously got reset to my usual wake-up time. Gabriel evidently was not ready to have another conversation with me but was content to watch me sleep. I just hoped I didn't catch a cold, because a stuffed-up nose would result in some major snoring. Still, I couldn't deny the coffee and flowers were a nice touch.

The first bouquet I assumed was an apology for nipping my lip with his fang, but when subsequent ones appeared, I started to think he was on some weird guilt trip. I mean just watching me visit the land of REM was a little strange. But the more I thought about it, the less likely it seemed. Gabriel wasn't the kind of guy who would regard his voyeurism as needing an apology. I was pretty sure the motive behind his visits, coffee, and flowers was much simpler. He just wanted to remind me he was in my life and not about to go anywhere. And I was okay with that. I just wished he'd wake me up so I could tell him. Another week of his generosity and my house was going to look like a florist shop. Or a cemetery.

Unfortunately, I couldn't deny the feeling that we were stuck in a kind of no-man's-land, unable to move forward until I remembered whatever it was I'd forgotten. Despite Gabriel's unwavering belief that we belonged together, I would be lying if I didn't say I still had some doubts. No matter how intense the feeling of being connected to him was, it did not eradicate the everyday difficulties that existed between us—difficulties that I thought glaringly obvious, but that my vampire lover seemed content to ignore.

I had no difficulty admitting that I loved Gabriel (if he'd wake me up, I'd tell him to his face), and a part of me said that was more than most people ever got to experience. So why wasn't it enough? Somewhere deep inside me I knew I'd been *in love* with Gabriel since the very first time I saw him. So what if I couldn't remember when that was exactly? It didn't make it any less true.

Lying down, I smoothed my hand across the empty half of my bed, imagining what it would be like to always have another body next to me. The idea of having someone to share my life was something I had always assumed would happen one day. All I had to do was find the right guy. It never crossed my mind that he might not be, well . . . *human*. And in the cold light of morning, I couldn't pretend this difference between us didn't matter.

What type of a future could I have with Gabriel? The problem, as I saw it, wasn't so much with Gabriel being a vampire . . . it was with me being a non-vampire. The physical part of our relationship, the absolutely mind-blowing sex, was not going to last forever, and even though it might seem shallow of me to fixate on such a thing, I couldn't pretend it wasn't important. I was going to get old. My future came with sagging boobs, cellulite dimples, and gray hair. It was inevitable, and if I was with any other guy, it wouldn't be an issue. A normal guy's body would break down along with mine. Gabriel, however, was anything but normal.

He was not going to age as I did. When my boobs were trying to hide in my armpits every time I lay down, or my butt wanted to kiss the back of my knees, and age spots were spreading faster than kudzu, Gabriel would still look like a really hot thirtysomething able to bounce quarters off his abs. It didn't matter that a voice in my head said how I looked made no difference to him. It made a difference to me.

I rolled over and punched the pillow, my mood becoming a mix of anger and despair at the thought that any life I had with Gabriel would be over before it had a chance to begin. How depressing was that? I told myself I was fully prepared to take whatever time I had with him and live it to the fullest, and I did a damn good job of almost convincing myself I could pull it off. Except, somewhere deep inside me, I knew it wasn't going to be enough.

So . . . what was I supposed to do? Breaking things off between us was not an option, even if it were still possible, which it wasn't. The bond that joined us was a powerful one. I might not feel its pull as strongly as Gabriel did, but I did feel it.

Throwing back the covers, I headed for the bathroom and a shower. I still had to go to work. Christmas was only a few days away, and it was already a nightmare for anyone working retail. But I always try to look for the silver lining. Dealing with holiday shoppers might be just the thing to numb a few brain cells, but as the scent of pomegranate body wash filled my nose, I realized I was done with thinking. What I needed was a sign. I didn't care if it was a flashing neon strip or a simple Forrest Gump feather. I wasn't asking to be planted on the yellow brick road, but I really did want to avoid getting stranded on the fuck-up highway. All I wanted was a hint from an unbiased third party that spending the rest of my life with a vampire was exactly what the cosmic wheel of fate had planned for me all along.

"Dear God, give me *something!*" I implored beneath the shower spray.

As it turned out, what I got was a pretty hefty kick in the ass from a totally unexpected source. And it came with a side order of you-gotta-be-kidding. But before that, I had to cope with everything in my screwed-up corner of the world going just a little farther sideways.

* * *

I had not seen Laycee since the day we went shopping in the mall together, and although I missed seeing her, I was also kind of thankful. With each passing day, the possibility of my blurting out something about the existence of vampires lessened. Our avoidance of each other was not deliberate. Because she was a hairdresser, this time of year was always crazy hectic for Laycee. Being on her feet all day, and trying to diplomatically remind her clients she was a beautician, not a magician, was exhausting. I couldn't blame her for wanting to spend her down time with Jake. He could deal with her stress in ways that I could not, no matter how much I loved her.

"Are you and Eye Candy going to the blonde's tonight?" Laycee asked during my morning-drive-to-work phone call. Not seeing each other didn't mean we weren't communicating. "You know, the one we met in the coffee shop?" she added, in case I wasn't sure who she was talking about. Laycee never forgot a name, and not using Anasztaizia's was deliberate on her part. It meant she hadn't made up her mind whether she liked the striking Magyar.

"I'm not sure," I told her. In truth, I'd forgotten about the invite, which, considering all that had happened since then, wasn't so surprising. "Gabriel hasn't said one way or the other, but it's probably safe to assume we'll be going. He's very fond of Anasztaizia."

Laycee gave a rude snort. "What about Christmas? Will you spend it with Gabriel?"

Traditionally, I spent the day with Laycee's family.

"Don't worry," she said with a laugh, "my mom's gonna have her hands full with Jake and his kids."

"They're not going to be with their mom?" I asked, surprised by this unexpected turn of events.

"Nope. I think they're going to be spending a lot of time with us from now on. Suellen has a new boyfriend."

We exchanged a few comments that other people might have called catty but I preferred to think of as wise and insightful before saying good-bye. Laycee had a cut and color waiting for her, and I'd just reached work. Unfortunately, the rest of the day pretty much went downhill from there. It was, hands down, the absolute worst workday ever. Every customer I came in contact with was rude and nasty, with a big dose of bad attitude. Whatever idiot said people were a lot nicer during the Christmas season had never worked retail, and if it were up to me, there'd be an awful lot of stockings getting stuffed with coal come December twenty-fifth. I don't think I'd ever been so relieved to be able to flip the OPEN sign to CLOSED, engage the dead bolt, and turn off the main lights.

Although it was dark enough for vampires to be about their business, and I really didn't want to speculate on what that might actually entail, I felt safe enough walking to the POS. There were plenty of exterior lights in the parking lot, and other nearby stores were still brightly lit, with people moving about inside. Katja was smart. She wouldn't risk attacking me with the possibility of an audience. But it didn't stop me from having a mild attack of the heebie-jeebies when a Hummer with heavily tinted windows slid in behind me as I was driving through town. Stopping at a traffic light, I gave a sigh of relief when the car's interior was suddenly illuminated. Even though she was pretty, the girl driving wasn't stunning enough to be a vampire.

I didn't relax until I'd turned back on the county highway heading for home. I like the drive because the scenery is nice, even at night. The woods flanking either side of the road are for the most part still undeveloped, so any traffic I had to contend with usually had fur and four legs. I'd seen deer, foxes, and coyotes, but never anything like the creature I caught sight of now.

I try to be aware of my speed because I know the damage a deer can do when it collides with a moving vehicle. This, however, was no deer. I was unconsciously tracking the animal's movement and already braking when it emerged from the trees. I told myself it was a dog, someone's pet that had jumped the fence, determined to reconnect with its inner wolf. And then I thought it might be a coyote, except the coat was much too dark, and the way it moved said there was nothing canine about this animal.

Feline through and through, this was a creature that was very much at home hunting down its next meal. I hit the brake with a little more urgency, wincing as the tires screeched in protest. The cat must have realized it wasn't going to able to clear the front of the car at the same time I knew I wasn't going to be able to stop in time. It leaped in the air, twisting its body in a graceful arc, and landed on the hood of the POS.

I put both feet on the wide brake pedal, pushing it all the way to the floor. My elbows locked, and my not-so-efficient seat belt snapped open. Forward momentum did the rest, making certain I smacked my forehead against the top of the steering wheel. Shit! That was gonna leave a bruise. Cautiously, I opened my eyes and peered through the windshield. A pair of orange eyes looked back at me.

It felt like forever until I was able to move again, although in reality I doubt it was more than a few seconds. Not wanting to make any sudden, startling moves, I pushed myself slowly upright. The animal watched me intently but didn't move. I had a few problems convincing my fingers to relax their death-grip at the ten and two positions on the steering wheel, but eventually they did comply, allowing me to grasp the column shift and slide it into park. It took a little longer before my brain was able to reassure my foot that removing itself from the brake pedal would be a good thing.

I let out a breath.

Watching my movements was the most magnificent predator I had ever seen. I had absolutely no idea where it had come from or what it was doing on this particular stretch of rural highway, but I felt confident it wasn't indigenous to this hemisphere. My brain began to run through all the possibilities it could come up with to explain why such an animal would be running loose in the woods. Maybe there was a private zoo nearby, or one of those exotic animal rescue places, and it had escaped. Or—God forbid—it was the status symbol of some idiot with too much money and too few brains.

I don't know much about cats, except that I like them. If I was ever tempted to get a pet, then I would definitely go for a cat over a dog. Not that dogs don't have their good points, but dogs are pack animals and, as such, are needy. It's not their fault. It's the whole wolfy thing in their DNA. Dogs crave company And it doesn't matter to them if the company comes with two legs or four, just as long as someone's there. Cats, on the other hand, are perfectly fine being alone. Their aloof nature is one of the things I like the most about them. Of course, what I was looking at now wasn't going to curl up in my lap and let me scratch it behind the ear.

As if wanting to emphasize the point, the animal snarled at me through the windshield. It was a loud, ferocious noise that probably warned everything in a five-mile radius that it was here and not to be messed with. I shuddered and white-knuckled the steering wheel again as bright orange eyes glared at me. A shockingly pink tongue unfurled from between rows of very sharp-looking teeth. It had incisors as big as . . . well, they were bigger than Gabriel's. Midnight black from muzzle to tail, the animal looked strangely like it was pondering a problem.

It never crossed my mind to wonder why it didn't simply run back into the woods now that I had stopped. Or why I didn't shift into drive and start forward, slowly. The cat probably would have jumped gracefully off the hood once it felt the POS begin to move. Then again, maybe the sound of the still-running engine was familiar, a little like purring. Falling under the creature's spell, I was completely dazzled. I wondered if the animal was a hybrid, one of those designer breeds that seem to be popular these days. Or maybe it was a mutated throwback because this leopard, if that's what it actually was, was the size of a small pony. Not that anyone was going to throw a saddle on its back. If the leopards I'd seen in the zoo shared DNA with the creature now posing as a hood ornament, then I was looking at a Paleolithic ancestor.

The leopard—I couldn't think of it as anything else—opened its mouth and yawned. Whatever problem it had been struggling with had apparently been resolved. I just hoped it wasn't anything along the lines of getting fresh meat out of a can with no opener handy. It made a noise, but something a lot softer this time—a deep rumble coming from its chest, a definite purr. Raising a paw, it patted the glass separating us a few times before resting its pads against the windshield. I stared. The thing was the size of a dinner plate.

Shifting position, the cat rolled so it was now lying instead of crouching on the hood. I watched its tail drop down over the front of the hood and swish gently from side to side. The long tongue unfurled and licked the windshield. And then it batted the wet spot with its paw. I released the death-grip I had on the steering wheel and stretched my arm forward. Pressing my palm against the inside of the windshield, I high-fived the velvet black paw.

The big cat began to pant. Its muzzle twitched, its sides heaved, and its tail began swishing a little more rapidly. Its eyes now took on the color of ripe summer peaches, the kind you buy in small baskets from stands alongside the road. I spread my fingers, opening my hand on my side of the glass. It felt warm, as if the animal was radiating its body heat directly through its paw. And then the rumbling sound came again. Deep in its throat, it now sounded like a warning, and the same feeling of déjà vu that I'd felt when I first saw Gabriel suddenly came over me.

I had heard, and seen, this creature before. Not another animal that looked similar, but *this* actual leopard. It had been a long time ago, but it *had* happened, and all I needed to do now was remember when.

"What are you?" I murmured.

I don't know if it heard me or could understand what I was saying, but I'll go to my grave positive the damn thing grinned at me.

CHAPTER 12

I don't remember much about the drive home. Truthfully I don't remember driving home at all, but I must have done so because when I next got out of the POS, it was in the driveway in front of my house. So if I didn't drive home . . . who did?

I'm not sure what happened to the leopard. I think it jumped down off the hood and sort of melted into the tree line, but that was when my recollection of events started to get fuzzy. It might have vanished while it was still sitting on the hood of the car, looking at me—no, make that grinning at me—through the windshield. I do know my palm, the one I had pressed against the leopard's paw through the glass, still tingled. The animal was linked to Gabriel . . . who was linked to me. Or was I linked to both of them? Either way, I didn't think it made much difference.

And that's when I began crying.

Sitting in the POS with my head resting against my arm on the steering wheel, I let the tears flow. An internal wall, one I hadn't even realized I had built, imploded in spectacular fashion. The strain of dealing with revelations I barely knew how to make sense of proved too much for it. Guess I was using the wrong type of mortar. In any case, that internal wall collapsed and, in a torrent of tears, washed away brick by brick, until there was nothing left.

I don't cry pretty. I'm not one of those girls who can make their eyes glisten with moisture and only need to dab at them with the edge of a lace hanky. I'm more a roll of toilet paper type of person. When I really let go, my eyes get puffy and swollen, my mascara runs, and I need to blow my nose. Now, after what was probably no more than a few minutes of tear duct aerobics, I was positively exhausted. Crying—real gut-wrenching, shoulder-shuddering sobbing—is very tiring. With no toilet paper or tissues at hand, I wiped my eyes with the heel of my hand. Who cared if I gave myself raccoon eyes? My sleeved forearm took care of my nose—nasty, I know—but there wasn't much else I could do.

Crying may be exhausting, but it's also very therapeutic. I won't say I was feeling better, but the wave of desperation that had been quietly haunting me ever since I'd been forced to confront Gabriel's nature was now gone. Feeling like I was at least eighty years old, I got out of the car, wearily climbed the front porch stairs, and went straight up to bed. Too tired to get out of my clothes, I just managed to kick my shoes off, pull the quilt over me, and close my eyes. I'd never been so tired.

As I drifted off, I made a mental reminder to tell Gabriel about the leopard. He would know what its appearance meant. Only a voice in my head said it wasn't necessary.

Who do you think sent it to you in the first place?

Oh, right, who else would it be? I burrowed deeper under the covers and sighed. Seeing the leopard had been significant, and on the cusp of falling asleep I could have sworn I heard the sound of thunder. Or maybe it was a big cat purring. I fell asleep . . .

. . . and I dreamed . . .

The cold cut through me like a knife. It was the kind of chill that went beyond teeth-chattering and shivering. This cold penetrated so deep it made my muscles ache and had me seriously wondering if it was possible for the marrow in my bones to freeze while I was still alive. As in most dreams, I was dressed inappropriately.

This was my first indication that something was off. In other dreams I could be frolicking with a penguin in a bikini—me, not the penguin—and I wouldn't even notice that it was below freezing.

Now, I realized that if I didn't want to succumb to hyperthermia, I needed to start moving. But I had no idea where I was, and even less where I was supposed to go. Stuffing my hands in my armpits, I looked around.

Great. It was night.

Generally speaking, I'm not afraid of the dark, but there was something unnatural about the inky blackness surrounding me here. It seemed a little too black, if that was possible. I tried to get my bearings as I peered into the darkness. What little ambient light there was revealed I was in a forest of some sort. At first I thought it might be the stand of trees on the other side of my property line, but what I was seeing weren't pines. In fact, they looked more like something that belonged in a Salvador Dali painting. But I had the sense they had been here for a very, very long time.

A sound behind me signaled something was moving through the undergrowth. I gasped and fell to my knees. Cold air hit my lungs like a razor slicing my chest. Clutching my arms, I doubled over, waiting for the pain to pass. Whatever was behind me had stopped moving, but I could feel its eyes on me as I struggled to my feet. Perhaps it was surprised by my frailty. Perhaps it was surprised by my determination to go on. In any case, it had just lost a golden opportunity to attack.

A bitter wind now added to my misery. And with it came snow. A curtain of white flurries obscured what little view I had of my surroundings, effectively blinding me. Stumbling over a tree root, I came to the conclusion that a twisted ankle would be the same as being staked out like a sacrificial offering. I hugged my upper body, rocking back and forth in order to conserve what little body heat I still had. As I was trying to decide whether I should continue on or simply lie on the ground and wait until I woke up, the wind dropped. The absence of its howl was startling.

My stalker was also surprised by the sudden quiet. No longer able to hide the sound of its movements inside the wind's whine, it now crashed noisily behind me. I didn't bother looking. If the creature wanted to attack me, I had given it ample opportunity. Whatever it was seemed content to follow in my wake. Getting to my feet, I pushed the hair out of my face with numb fingers and stared at a glow in the distance. A light was shining, one that promised warmth and an end to this dreadful journey. And I wasn't the only one who saw it. A low rumbling growl told me that the light was a welcome beacon for both of us.

The predator behind me—and I knew it was a predator—moved out of the shadows and stopped a few feet behind me. I didn't see it— I was too afraid to look—but I *knew* it was there, the same way I knew it had slashing razor claws and multiple rows of sharp teeth. I couldn't outrun it, even if I wanted to. I was now so cold I couldn't do more than shuffle along like a zombie. All my muscles were stiff, my thigh muscles especially, and my gait was now reduced to something that wouldn't even get me a tryout at the Senior Olympics. But I needed the animal behind me to know I wasn't a pushover.

"I promise you this," I muttered through lips that had to be blue by now, "if you take me on, I'm not going down easy. I'll make sure you lose at least one eye before I'm done."

There came a whuff of air, like a deep breath on an exhale. I took it to mean that my companion not only understood what I had said, but somehow approved of my willingness to put up a fight. With this understanding between us, we headed toward the light. I stumbled two more times over roots hidden by the snowfall, and both times my fall elicited a series of growls from behind me. I found myself apologizing. If my progress was halted, then so was the animal's, and it didn't like being cold any more than I did.

I don't know how long we walked because I had lost all sense of time almost the moment I entered this strange place. In my head I tried counting out a minute, but my brain couldn't seem to make it past fifteen-Mississippi, so I gave up. We could have been walking for more than an hour or only ten minutes. I also stopped cataloging the physical toll being inflicted on my body. I'm quite sure it was still suffering, but my brain no longer bothered keeping track of the details. Or maybe my nerve endings were so cold they could no longer transmit information. However, my brain was lucid enough to let me know when my companion abandoned me. The sudden silence was deafening, and despite a voice in my head telling me maybe it wasn't such a good idea, I turned and looked behind me.

I don't know what I was expecting, but all I saw was more of the same unnatural blackness, broken up by huge tree limbs. The sense that I was now alone was heartbreaking. How could the creature have abandoned me without so much as a warning? I cursed myself for my timidity. If I had been brave enough to look sooner, what might I have seen? Of course, it was also probable that my lack of curiosity was precisely what had kept me alive. That, however, was scant comfort. My sense of loss was very real, as was my sudden fear at knowing I was alone.

I was surprised to find the pocket of light was now much closer, although I should have realized that time wasn't the only thing that becomes distorted in a dream, even a dream that felt as real as this one did. No doubt my companion had far superior eyesight and had already found whatever had brought it to this place. I needed to do the same. Answers lay within the pocket of light. Even if I didn't know the questions.

I stepped forward into a pool of warmth and screamed in agony. Going from one physical extreme to another is a shock to the system even under the best of circumstances, and this was nowhere near the best. In the space of a heartbeat I'd been kicked out of the arctic and shoved head first into a tropical heat wave, with no warm-up in between. My legs gave way, and my hands, responding instinctively, automatically braced against the fall. I felt as if I had landed on broken glass. The pain that shot up my arms to my shoulders was excruciating, flaying me open every inch of the way.

It was also the moment I knew beyond any doubt that this was no dream. I might still be lying in my bed, quilt pulled up to my chin, but whatever was going on inside my head owed nothing to REM sleep. A door was opening, a door to long-forgotten memories.

Clutching my hands to my chest, I rolled into a ball. Squeezing my eyes shut, I choked back the screams that threatened to erupt with every pain-filled spasm ricocheting through me. It was pure torture—even my eyelashes hurt—and then, just when I was certain I couldn't take any more, the pain ceased. A switch in my central nervous system had been mercifully flipped off.

Slowly I uncurled myself and rolled over onto my back. It took a few moments for me to catch my breath and make sure this wasn't only a temporary respite. I stretched out my limbs, grateful to find them pliant and responsive. Inside my shoes, my toes wiggled, and I could feel dirt as I scrunched up my fingers. Good. My extremities worked. I opened my eyes slowly, not wanting to risk getting my retinas fried in the brilliant, dazzling light that now bathed me. I had the sense that everything I had ever known in my life that was pure and good had been captured inside that soft radiance.

My struggle to get to this place had taken its toll, and getting to my feet was an awkward process. As I pushed myself upright, I felt the intensity of the light surrounding me diminish. Pushing the hair out of my eyes with one hand, I looked about me. I stood on the outer edge of a clearing, a circle where nothing grew save the cruelest-looking tree I'd ever seen. I felt a ridge forming between my brows as I stared at it. Instead of leaves, its branches bore vicious-looking thorns, the smallest of which was at least as thick as my forearm and longer than the distance between my wrist and elbow. And yet this was the origin of the glorious luminosity that filled the circle. I was at a loss to explain how such warmth and life could be emitted by something so awful. And then I saw. The light wasn't coming from the tree . . . it came from what was hanging in the tree.

My hand to flew to my mouth, and I gasped. Impaled on the thorny branches in an obscene crucifixion was Gabriel. His body was leaner, less muscular, but the white hair that I so loved was the same, although it now fell well past his hips. And he was younger somehow. The Gabriel I knew carried with him the experience of the life he had lived. It showed in his manner, his speech, his bearing. Some of it good . . . some of it bad, but it all made the man I knew. This Gabriel was different. It was as if he had yet to live those experiences. And I couldn't explain why I knew that any more than I could explain the light that came from him. The light that had brought me here.

"Gabriel!" I called his name, but he gave no sign he had heard me or even knew I was there. I hoped he was unconscious because it would be a respite from the pain he had to be feeling. I moved forward, stumbling as I made my way to the base of the tree. Any hope I had of rescuing him was immediately dashed. He was positioned too high up for me to reach, but I could see the strain the unnatural position of his body was placing on his arms and shoulders. How long had he been here? How much longer was he going to be able to suffer this torture? Tears flowed from my eyes as a sense of helplessness washed over me.

"Gabriel . . . ?" I spoke his name more softly this time, praying that he would not open his eyes, but wanting him to know he was not alone.

Blood washed over my shoes, blood . . . and something else. I bent down and plucked a feather out of the rust-colored liquid. It was longer than my arm, and the edges, where it was not stained with blood, were a shade of blue I had never seen before. A chill went through me as I slowly turned the feather over in my hand. The Gabriel I knew might be a vampire, but once he had been something else. Something very different.

CHAPTER 13

"It appears your angel has had his wings clipped," a harsh, raspy voice said from behind me.

I spun around and saw a figure standing at the edge of the clearing. Dressed in a hooded robe similar to those worn by medieval monks, the figure had pulled the hood forward in order to obscure his face. All that was revealed was a shock of coal-black hair against an unnaturally pale forehead. I stared and said nothing.

"Your angel has had his wings clipped," the robed figure repeated. The voice was male, but the rough tone made me think the owner had suffered a recent trauma to his vocal cords.

"Who are you?" I asked, making no response to his comment.

"I am the Wraith, and you are in my domain."

"Bullshit!" I snapped out. "This *domain* is inside my head."

The hood nodded in agreement. "True, but that does not change the fact that this is still my domain."

I felt a cold shiver as he came toward me. There was a sense of wrongness to him that I couldn't explain. He was everything Gabriel was not, and being in his presence made me uneasy. I watched as he moved closer, the hem of his robe gliding unnaturally over the ground.

"Did you do that to him?" I demanded, pointing to the feathers scattered over the ground.

The hood shook from side to side. "It is not within my power to punish one such as him."

"What's that supposed to mean?"

Tilting his head, he appeared to be staring at me, a move made all the more unnerving as I couldn't see his face. "Do you really not know who I am?"

"Let's assume I don't." Ordinarily I wouldn't have been so flippant, but whatever was happening here had gone beyond ordinary.

A long sleeve moved in Gabriel's direction. "If he is of the Light . . . then I am of the Dark."

"Meaning what? You're not capable of such torture?"

"Even one such as I must respect the balance that exists between all living things. An act such as this has . . . consequences."

Whatever was inside that robe, and I really didn't want to know, I felt it was speaking the truth. "Why are you here?" I asked.

"For the same reason as you." The huskiness got a little deeper. "Gabriel has summoned me also. It would seem he has need of us both."

I had absolutely no idea what he was talking about, but before I could start figuring it out, the Wraith moved past me to stand closer to the tree. "Look, Gabriel," he rasped, "Here is the one who has answered your call. Let us see if she has the courage to be your Promise."

For the first time, Gabriel looked at me. He raised his head, and his eyes roamed hungrily over me. As I stared into those blue-gold depths with the thick lashes framing them, I knew with every fiber of my being that this was the only male who would ever claim my heart. That it had always been his. From the beginning of time.

"Tell me . . . do you know what he is?"

I wasn't sure what answer the Wraith was looking for, but I was in no mood to play riddles. I wanted to get Gabriel down from that damn tree. And while the Wraith, or whatever it wanted to call itself, might tell me it wasn't responsible for putting Gabriel up there, I was damn sure it could get him down.

"What do you want from me?" I asked in a voice that could match the coldness of the dark forest beyond the circle.

"I want to know what you are willing to do to save him."

"Anything."

"Why?"

"He is everything to me." I spoke without hesitation.

A laugh came from deep inside the hood, a sound that filled me with terrors I couldn't begin to name. "We shall see . . . we shall see."

At the edge of the circle, between the stand of misshapen, gnarled trees that stood as silent guardians, pockets of air began to shimmer. At first, I thought it was a hallucination, but as I watched, I saw the air take form, become corporeal until each pocket birthed an animal. They were all predators, natural hunters armed with razor-sharp claws and slashing teeth. But they were bigger and more savage-looking than any animal I had ever seen. It was as if I were seeing the living blueprint of every predatory hunter graced with four legs. I remained as still as I possibly could, even though I was sure every one of them already knew how many strides were needed to reach me. Had one of them been my companion in the forest? I couldn't be sure, and then I knew.

A much larger version of the same black leopard I'd last seen gracing the hood of my car stepped forward into the circle of light. It stared at me with orange eyes, and a savage chorus broke out. The uproar of snarls and growls made me want to cover my ears with my hands. But as I listened, I was able to discern a sense of order amid the chaos of snarls. The great beasts were talking to each other, communicating in a way that was beyond my understanding, but true nevertheless. I watched in fascination as growls were punctuated with flashing teeth and claws. Remaining in constant motion, they continued to circle each other as well as the outer edge of the clearing. And I noticed they kept me in sight. Always.

I had almost forgotten the other figure standing with me until a grating rasp close to my ear reminded me. "Do you know what he is?" the Wraith repeated.

"He is Gabriel," I said, unsure what answer was required of me.

"Do not try my patience!" The voice was so close, all I would need to do was turn my head slightly and I would be able to see what else went with the pale skin and dark hair. But a voice in my head warned me that some beings were not meant to be seen. "I will not ask again, Rowan—*do you know what he is?*"

Why was I not surprised it knew my name? I turned away from the figure and looked at the crucified angel I was in love with. Did I know what he was? No, not truly. I could guess, make wild speculations, but truthfully, I had no name for what I thought he might be.

I shook my head. I wasn't going to play games. Not when Gabriel's life might be in the balance. "No, in truth, I don't know what he is."

"Then behold one whose fall from grace no longer permits him to walk in its radiance."

"So . . . he is Fallen?"

I could feel Gabriel looking at me, wanting to apologize for whatever he had done to bring me here. My eyes met his, and I gave him my reassurance that he had nothing to apologize for. Most certainly not for what he was. Not ever. He was the reason I was here. He had always been the reason. If an apology was needed, it would be mine for taking so long to come to him.

"Yes, he is Fallen." Dropping my eyes, I saw the dark folds of the robe sweep the ground by my feet. The Wraith was now standing next to me. "An angel who turned against his own in a misguided attempt to save humanity," the voice continued, "and who was, in turn, betrayed by another such as he."

"Turn against his own? But why would he do such a thing?"

"Why indeed? Why would anyone want to save mankind when it is your nature to be the harbingers of your own destruction."

I shook my head, confused. He could have been talking to me in Swahili. "I don't understand," I said with a touch of impatience. "What did he do to deserve this punishment, and who would do this to him?"

"Listen and learn"—the voice became a hiss—"and perhaps you may yet be his salvation."

A stir of breath blew around the edge of the clearing, and I felt it enter my mind. Powerless to resist, I gave myself over and allowed the voice to consume me.

"At the last Armageddon, the fate of mankind hung in the balance, but it created a division among those who walked in the Light, a division that in turn became a chasm that could not be crossed." A sleeve was raised, and a long bony finger pointed at Gabriel. "On one side stood the angels who believed that humanity was worth saving; on the other stood those who decreed man was nothing but a pestilence to be eradicated. But in the end what either side believed made no difference.

"By choosing to turn against those who sought to help you, humanity proved it had no worth, and when the great battle began, humans who should have stood with Gabriel and his brothers did not."

"What happened?" I asked, no longer able to tell if the voice I was hearing was inside my head or not.

"Given the means to capture an angel, they brought him to this long forgotten place, cut off his wings, and left him thus—forgotten by all."

"But why would they do that?" I didn't care if it thought me weak for the tears that slipped from my eyes.

The robed figure shrugged, its voice filled with contempt. "Because, foolish child, mankind will always seek to destroy what it does not understand. And it allows the seed of suspicion to take root far too easily."

"But who would tell them how to do such a thing?"

"Even an angel can be deceived by one of his own."

The touch of fur beneath my palm made my heart lurch in my chest. The huge black leopard, having padded to my side on silent paws, now pressed its head against my thigh. Without thinking, I curled my fingers and scratched the sweet spot behind its ear. A low rumble, emanating from deep inside the animal's chest, reverberated around the clearing, and I could feel the heat of its breath through my clothes.

"Ahhh, you find favor with the lesser beasts," the Wraith said, noting the animal at my side. "It is good that they approve of you."

I had the feeling there was something more going on than my being passed over as the main course on tonight's menu. "What will become of him?" I asked, staring at Gabriel.

"Walking a path in the Dark is now his destiny, as well as his choice, and it is a path he must walk alone."

"This path he has chosen will not be walked as an angel, will it?" The lack of response was confirmation enough. "Will it always be that way for him?"

"That will be for you to decide . . . when the time comes."

"For me? I don't understand."

"Gabriel will be given what others who seek the Dark Realm are not—the chance to redeem himself. Should he be successful, he will find his salvation in your hands"—he paused—"should you choose to offer it to him."

Salvation in my hands? What did that mean? And then my eye fell on a bloody feather lying on the ground. If Gabriel redeemed himself, he would be able to return to his life as a celestial being, provided I played my part, whatever that might be. A shiver ran through me. It was a responsibility I was completely unprepared for, and I could feel threads of panic threatening to overwhelm me.

"Why me?" I asked.

The Wraith made a gesture that could have been a shrug. I told myself it was my imagination. Shrugging was too human a gesture, and I didn't think there was anything remotely human about the creature inhabiting the robe.

"Because you are the one who answered him. The responsibility for his deliverance is yours and yours alone. He has already bound himself to you. Will you do the same? Will you cleave yourself to him for an eternity, if necessary, or will you leave here with no memory of him, save for a shadow in a childish dream? The choice is yours, Rowan."

Leave Gabriel? The idea was preposterous. I couldn't leave him— I loved him! I had always loved him, even when I didn't know I loved him. There came a sudden howling from the edge of the clearing as several of the great beasts decided to offer me their advice.

"Time is waning, and the lesser beasts grow restless." There was a warning beneath the words. "Will you give yourself to him, and only him? Become his vessel and the Promise he will seek?"

Without thinking, I turned my head and found myself face-to-face with the Wraith. The dark hair fell across a white face. A face with hollow cheeks and empty sockets where eyes should have been. A face with only a savage slash for a mouth and no nose. Wisps of smoke now curled from beneath the hem and the sleeves of the robe, and I wrinkled my nose as the smell of sulfur tainted the air.

"You already know my answer," I said, in a voice that revealed nothing about my true feelings. "You knew it the moment I stepped into the light." The light that Gabriel had sent to guide me to him.

"Yes I know, but"—a skeletal hand waved at the animals surrounding us—"they do not."

A chorus of howls rose up behind me, reminding me that apparently I wasn't the only one who had an interest in these proceedings.

"Then I will be Gabriel's vessel, and the Promise he will seek."

A sound like thunder clapped overhead, and the air was filled with the smell of burning wood as the tree holding Gabriel prisoner split in half. Thrown free, he landed on the ground in a tangle of twisted limbs, his hair covering him like a shroud. I started forward, but the leopard at my side let loose a roar that tore the air with its savage purity.

"The choice has been made," the Wraith said.

Razor-sharp claws flicked up small explosions of earth as the animal moved away from me. Muzzle quivering and ears twitching, it seemed excited as it approached the inert figure lying on the ground. It opened its mouth, and I saw daggers on both the upper and lower jaw. A long pink tongue slipped out between a pair of huge incisors, flicking as it tasted the air. Muscles rippled smoothly beneath a black velvet pelt. The leopard's body held an untold promise of power and speed, and I knew I was looking at death. Deadly in intent, beautiful in delivery.

Turning its massive head, the leopard stared at me, a questioning look in its orange eyes. Was it asking for my approval? For what I had no idea. But it had come to me with one purpose: to make me remember. I nodded slowly, and the leopard turned away. Refocusing on Gabriel, it began to growl low in its chest, and then, with a quickness that defied the eye, it leaped forward and straddled the figure lying defenseless on the ground.

"No!" I shrieked. If the animal meant to harm Gabriel, then it would have to take me first. I tried to move forward, but felt long fingers around my wrist, holding me fast.

"You have made your choice," the gravelly voice hissed in my ear, "and the lesser beasts are pleased. Now they, too, have chosen. Watch and remember so you will know always what he was . . . and what he chose to become."

Blue-gold eyes turned toward me, blazing with an intensity that reached down into the core of my being. I knew that my fate was now joined to Gabriel's in ways I couldn't begin to understand. And then I watched as he turned his head and looked up at the creature straddling him. Something passed between them . . . something given, something taken. And the air, which had become heavy with its own silence, was torn open in a deafening bellow that threatened to split the heavens.

The bony fingers holding my wrist loosened their hold, and I fell to my knees, unable to tear my eyes away from the scene before me. Wickedly sharp fangs now pierced the soft flesh of Gabriel's throat, his blood overflowing the leopard's jaws, running in a frantic rush from the wound. Weak from so much blood loss already, Gabriel made no move to protect himself. With the weight of one massive paw holding him down, he passively accepted whatever fate was to be his.

I turned my head away, unable to watch the life force ebb out of the only love I would ever know. Everything was lost before it ever had a chance to begin. Did Gabriel even know I loved him?

"Watch!" a voice commanded from above me.

Raising my head, I looked at the beast. Muzzle and fangs stained with blood, it stared back at me with unblinking eyes that had changed from orange to a familiar blue-gold. Now I understood the need for my approval.

"Did you think you are the only ones who pray for deliverance?" the Wraith asked with a sneer in its voice.

Yes, I suppose I had. I was wrong about that, and so much else, it would seem. My head was suddenly filled with images that were not my own. Images that showed the natural order of life, the delicate balance among all living things, being unjustly tipped in mankind's favor by greed and deceit. Helpless at their inability to restore stability, the lesser beasts prayed to the Dark for help. Needing a champion of their own, they asked for . . . a reason to make men afraid of the Dark once more. Now eyes that flickered between orange and blue-gold gazed at me, telling me that I, too, was a part of that prayer.

And then I saw the beast lie down on top of Gabriel, covering him with its long, muscular body and blood-spattered paws. It sank inside him, and my breath caught in my throat. I knew better than to try and make sense of what I was seeing. It was beyond my comprehension. Understanding wasn't needed. Acceptance was.

The lesser beasts had made their choice. The strongest among them would sacrifice themselves in order to enhance Gabriel's own abilities. Now he would be able to call upon the leopard's lightning-quick reflexes, speed, and strength. Take the acute senses, razor-sharp fangs, and claws and use them as his own. The blending of fallen angel and savage animal would birth a new predator. One that was near invincible. One that was forged in blood.

A vampire. And I had witnessed its birth. I was there. And I re-membered.

CHAPTER 14

Filled with a mix of relief and sadness, I threw back the quilt and stumbled out of bed. I had just reached the bottom of the staircase when the front door burst open and Gabriel took me down in a move that would have made an NFL linebacker proud. We sailed about a dozen feet through the open kitchen doorway, but he made sure it was his back that hit the ground instead of mine. Cushioning me against his chest, he rolled over, pinning me beneath him on the braided floor rug. Somewhere in our flight I had automatically snaked an arm around his neck. I now put the hand of my free arm against his chest, feeling the accelerated beat of his heart.

"Rowan, are you all right? Are you hurt anywhere?"

His tone was frantic, and his hands were all over me, although what he was expecting to find, I couldn't imagine. I'm not sure he knew either. It wasn't until he pushed my T-shirt up and I felt cold air brushing across an exposed nipple that I found my voice.

"Gabriel!"

He froze, his expression as easy for me to read as a first-grade primer. Anxiety and worry screamed at me. He traced my cheek with his thumb and then put it to his mouth, sucking off the moisture.

"You've been crying . . . you still are."

He covered my naked breast with his hand, and my nipple hardened as it happily nudged his palm. Loosening my arm from around Gabriel's neck, I put my hands on either side of his face and looked up at him. Anxiety and worry now gave way to loving concern—concern that centered entirely around me—my well-being, my safety, my happiness. My dream had not been a dream. It was the memory Gabriel needed me to remember. The moment when I had first seen him, before he became a vampire, when he was still an angel, albeit a fallen one.

Now I struggled to recall the words the Wraith had said to me, telling me how and why Gabriel had been punished so cruelly. It was no good, they were gone, but the despair Gabriel had experienced had not left me. That I felt all too clearly. His sense of being forsaken, abandoned, was almost more than I could bear. I wanted to ask him how long he had been imprisoned. The Wraith had said something about the last Armageddon, but who knew when that had been. I was starting to believe time was a concept that could be adapted to suit many needs.

Gabriel had told me there was a bond between us, and now, for the first time, I truly felt it. It made no difference what he was. Vampire, angel, or man, he loved me. And I loved him. It really was that simple. Moisture trickled out the corner of my eye, sliding toward my ear as I lay on the floor.

"Please, don't cry," Gabriel begged, a deep furrow appearing between his brows.

"I remembered," I told him, trying to keep my voice as calm as I could with more than six feet six inches of vampire inadvertently flattening me. "My memory came back."

"You remembered?"

Somehow he didn't look as reassured by this news as I thought he might. The hand cupping my breast moved reflexively, his thumb brushing gently over my skin. I nodded and swallowed, trying not to draw any attention to what he was doing. If I did then he might stop, and I really didn't want him to do that.

"How much have you remembered?" Gabriel asked cautiously.

"It was in the clearing . . . when you were crucified."

My words had the same effect as a bucket of cold water. The color drained from his face. He took away his hand and pulled down my

T-shirt, disappointing my nipple. I knew he felt embarrassed to be copping a feel while I was dealing with something very profound. It was also kind of rude, and Gabriel now asked my forgiveness.

"It's all right," I said, stroking my fingers gently over his shoulder. "You couldn't have known when it was going to happen. No one could."

I gazed up at him, my attention diverted by the perfect shape of his mouth, especially the full bottom lip, a lip I desperately wanted to latch onto so I could suck it until I lost the strength in my jaw. Agreeing with this sentiment, my body let me know how delighted it was to find itself in such a familiar position. Lying beneath Gabriel, it went straight into sexual overdrive. My breasts became full and tight, and my nipples transformed themselves into bullets that threatened to do some serious damage if Gabriel leaned any farther forward. My spine melted, reforming itself as a puddle on the floor, and the heat that was dancing along my rib cage was approaching inferno level. Every muscle south of my belly button clenched.

And I wasn't the only one.

Gabriel was also on fire. I could feel the heat pulsating through his clothes and washing over me. His thigh was sandwiched between my legs, and I could feel his erection. Rock-hard and enormous, it poked at my belly through the pants I was still wearing. In a way it was gratifying to know that neither one of us had much control over our physical responses to the other.

The only sound filling the kitchen was our ragged breathing. We were both having difficulty dragging air into our lungs. Gabriel was a long cool glass of water, and I was a woman in the desert dying of thirst. Fuck sipping slowly; I wanted to guzzle him down. The mane of white hair I was so accustomed to see flowing over his shoulders was now fastened in a thick braid that fell forward and coiled on my chest. On any other man such a style would have looked seriously gay, but it made Gabriel look every inch the Viking warrior I was certain he had actually been at one time. I could almost see him wearing battle braids and leaping from a longboat ready to do battle.

The other advantage of having his hair pulled back, one I hadn't considered before, was the lack of visual interference. Nothing to get in the way of his wide forehead, high cheekbones, and angular jaw.

Eyes framed by thick lashes bored into me while the line of his nose divided the perfect symmetry of his face.

"What were you doing?" I asked, stroking a forefinger down his braid and raising my eyebrows.

"Working out."

"You need to do that?" I was surprised; I'd assumed all his muscle tone was natural, and required no upkeep.

"Not really, but I find it useful for dealing with stress."

His eyes were glowing, and I saw slivers of gold begin to distort the smooth field of blue.

"What types of stress?"

"The kind that comes with frustration."

He opened his mouth just enough for me to see the tips of his fangs. It was an absolute turn-on and my body moved into high-octane range. I needed Gabriel to either get in me or get off me, and soon! It was another moment or two before I realized that, no matter how aroused he was, my lover wasn't going to make the first move. Our physical desire for each other was mutual, but he would smother his own lust and walk away from me if he thought I wasn't ready. Grateful that I lacked such discipline, I let him know just how ready I was in the rush of breath that escaped me.

Shifting his weight slightly, Gabriel rubbed the hard length of himself across my pubic bone. It was enough to unleash everything I'd been holding inside since discovering he was a vampire. Like a dam bursting, I chose to express my feelings on a purely carnal level. We couldn't get our clothes off fast enough. Somehow, I was already naked before I'd even managed to tug Gabriel's muscle shirt out of the pants he was wearing. I cursed under my breath at the uncooperative fabric, making him grin as he took over. Jumping to his feet, he stood over me, and stripped off his clothes. I think the offending shirt ended up in the sink. Lying back down on top of me, he lifted his hips, allowing me to slide my hand between us and close it around his cock. I felt him shudder as I took the heavy weight of him in my palm, opening and closing my fingers as I massaged him.

Neither one of us was in the mood for gentle seduction. Gabriel kissed me hard and fast. His mouth was demanding, possessive, and I wanted everything he was prepared to give me. Greedily I pushed my tongue into his mouth, feeling the sharp points of his fangs as I slid between them, right before he nipped my lower lip. It was the most incredible turn-on. He growled. The sound rumbled deep in his chest as he looked at me, and my spine clenched in anticipation. Kneading my breast with one hand, Gabriel busied his mouth with the other, suckling my flesh and scraping the taut nipple with his teeth. I almost came right then, but held back because what I wanted, what I needed, was more.

I was drenched, my core hot and swollen, desperate to feel Gabriel muscle his way inside me. I wanted him to stretch me open, make me take him deep. With a will of their own, my legs wrapped themselves around his waist. He raised his head and looked down at me. My aching breasts and the torturous pleasure he been administering were forgotten. I grabbed the thick braid that hung over his shoulder and wrapped the rope of hair around my hand.

"Now," I gasped in a voice thick with hunger, "I need you in me now!"

He knew how to follow directions. With one hard thrust he was all the way in, slanting his mouth over mine so he could swallow my shriek of pleasure. He was thick, hard, and just as hungry for me. And he felt bigger than before. My body took everything he had as he pounded into me. He kept one hand braced on the floor while the other was curled around my waist, his fingers gripping my flesh with each thrust of his hips.

I climaxed almost at once. Awash in a sea of orgasmic relief, I came and came again, and with each release I could feel Gabriel's body getting tighter. Every muscle pushed to its breaking point until he finally released the roar trapped inside and emptied himself inside me.

Collapsing, Gabriel buried his face in the hollow between my neck and shoulder, his breath hot against my skin. I placed my hand against his neck. His pulse was pounding so hard it was like a seismic event. If we had had difficulty breathing before, it was almost impossible now. The muscles in my thighs and lower body were screaming in protest at the violence of his invasion, but I brushed it aside. I didn't know it was possible to feel like this. Ecstasy. Euphoria. Bliss. None of those words did justice to the wave of pleasure that was continuing to ripple through me. Gabriel's lips pressed against the curve of my neck, the tip of his tongue tracing small circles as he lapped up the sweat on my skin.

Lifting his head, he opened his eyes and smiled down at me. And I stiffened. It was a purely involuntary action, but an understandable one, considering it was the first time I had truly seen his eyes change. His brow became a troubled frown.

"Your . . . eyes . . ." It was all I could manage.

The hot electric blue of Gabriel's iris had bled out to cover the sclera, and his pupils were now a brilliant gold. I had seen the same thing happen that night in the diner, only I had assumed I was having some sort of sex fantasy. Now I knew the reason why. Anasztaizia had warned me that vampire eyes could transform in this way, especially when the need to feed or have sex was strong enough. Considering what we'd just done, and the fact Gabriel had been licking my jugular, I was pretty confident I knew which appetite had the upper hand right now.

"Do it!" I said, my fingers digging into the back of his thick neck. He stared down at me, the frown deepening as if he did not trust what he was hearing. Tightening my legs around his waist, I pushed my hips up and felt him move deep inside me. All that was important was to satisfy this other hunger in him. "I want you to do this; I need you to do this," I told him, my voice thick with emotion.

Pulling back, Gabriel broke my hold around his neck with ease. I watched his lips curl back as his fangs dropped. They seemed to go on forever. Pulling my hair to one side, I offered him free access to my neck. His pupils were now glowing twin suns.

"Are you sure?" The tip of his tongue darted out and he licked his lips. "You can still refuse me."

It was foolish to think he couldn't sense my anxiety and the way it was spiking, but I needed him to know the reason for it. I had to reassure him before he made any wrong assumptions. "I'm worried that I won't know what to do . . . and that it'll hurt," I admitted.

He grasped a loose curl and wound it around his forefinger, smiling down at me. "Giving yourself is all you have to do, and I promise, a bee sting feels worse."

"Then do—"

He struck before I was able to articulate the rest of my sentence, his fangs puncturing my skin with pinpoint precision. I don't know about bee stings, but I've had red ant bites that felt worse. The long incisors sliced effortlessly through my skin, honing in on the vein running beneath the flesh and piercing it. As his fangs withdrew, I could feel my blood being pulled up, like liquid drawn into a syringe.

My body freaked out. Going into full panic, my self-preservation mode kicked in. I had no idea what a potent asset Mother Nature had given us in adrenaline. Twisting and turning, I tried to squirm out of Gabriel's grasp and free myself from his mouth. I drummed my heels in the small of his back, but it made no difference, so I dropped my legs and tried wriggling my way free. Unfortunately, I'd forgotten he was still buried deep inside me. Feeling his cock move reminded me of my accommodating position. Curling my hands into fists, I pounded on his back, his upper arms, his ribs—anywhere that I thought would make him release me. It was all pathetically useless.

With his mouth firmly latched onto my neck, he caught hold of my hands, securing the two of them easily in his one. As my blood was drawn out of me in long, slow pulls, my rational mind shut down completely, allowing primal instinct to take over. I went limp, gathering myself for one last-ditch effort at freedom. But Gabriel now had free access to my emotional state and was able to anticipate my next move.

Rolling onto his back, he wrapped his free arm and both legs around me, immobilizing me with his superior strength. I ceased my pitiful railings against him and accepted the inevitable, relaxing enough to release my mind as I did so. The resulting effect was off-the-wall amazing. A barrier deep inside me shattered, releasing a tidal wave of passion that I had never felt before. Now that I had stopped trying to fight what was happening to me, I found myself drowning in a sea of erotic pleasure. It was the most singular mind-blowing experience I've ever had.

As if my consciousness were caught inside each mouthful of blood that Gabriel took, I could feel myself being drawn up, sliding over his teeth and tongue before slipping effortlessly down his throat. Every nerve ending I had expanded and contracted as the pleasure that washed through him also washed through me. The ecstasy I was feeling was part mine, part his; blended together, it was incredible.

He rolled over again so I was beneath him once more, and now I wrapped my legs firmly around his waist and surged upward with my hips. Needing no second invitation, Gabriel began to move. Each forward thrust synchronized itself with a draw of my blood, and I gave myself to him willingly and without any hesitation. As he pulled his mouth away, the rumble in his chest became a growl that rattled the window over the sink. I watched him shudder as his orgasm surged through him, feeling him explode inside me with a ferocious, final thrust. When the tremors finally subsided, he leaned forward and licked my neck. His tongue traced a path from my ear to my collar bone, sealing the open wound as he did so.

"I wish you didn't have to do that." I murmured with a sigh of absolute contentment.

"Why?"

"It would be nice to see your mark on me all the time."

He chuckled low in the back of his throat. "If I didn't seal it, you'd bleed out, love."

"Hmmm, well, I guess that wouldn't do."

"No"—he swept his tongue across my neck again—"it most certainly wouldn't."

I sniffed, and a wonderful fragrance tickled my nose, familiar yet different at the same time.

"What is it?" Gabriel asked, seeing my nostrils flare.

"I can smell your blood," I told him, "only it seems different this time." I didn't remember nipping him hard enough to draw blood, but perhaps I had.

"How so?" Locking his elbows, he held himself up on his arms.

I closed my eyes and drew in the scent, letting it fill me. "Hmmm, it still reminds me of pine trees and snow, but there's more of a citrus undertone now—and something sweeter. Like cloves and oranges."

Gabriel let out a laugh, a deep, rich sound that made me open my eyes and stare at him. His eyes still hadn't returned to normal, but I'd already gotten used to seeing the golden pupil awash in a sea of electric blue.

"That, love," he said, wearing the biggest shit-eating grin I'd ever seen, "is the scent of *your* blood."

CHAPTER 15

At some point Gabriel got up and closed the front door, then carried me back up to bed. Safe in the warmth of his arms, I told him everything I could remember about my dream-memory. He was curiously silent.

"Is it painful for you to remember?" I asked quietly, my head against his chest as I listened to the steady beat of his heart. I couldn't imagine him not being in my bed.

"No," he said, dropping a kiss on the top of my head. "I am reminded of it every day."

I felt like the biggest blundering idiot who ever walked the earth. He had already said his tattoos told how he came to be, a phrasing that I had taken to mean how he became a vampire. It had not occurred to me that they had been added at the same time his wings had been so savagely removed. "Gabriel, what happened to you?"

Putting a finger beneath my chin, he raised my head so I was looking into his eyes.

"I will tell you," he promised, "but not now. You have had more than enough to deal with this night."

Something in his voice didn't sound right.

"I'm missing something, aren't I?" I could see a glimmer of caution shine in the depth of his eyes. "I haven't remembered it all, and you won't tell me about your back until I do." I didn't mean it to sound like an accusation, but that's how it came out.

He stroked my cheek with his forefinger. "Rowan, be thankful for what you have already remembered. It has brought us to a point I wasn't certain we would ever reach."

"Really?" He'd had doubts? "You thought I wouldn't let you feed from me?"

"I wasn't sure you would take me to your bed again, much less give your blood to me."

Not just doubts, he'd been really worried.

"So, what would you have done if things hadn't worked out between us?"

"This time when I left you, I would not have come back."

The idea that I'd almost lost him sent a shiver through me. Holding me tightly, Gabriel pulled the comforter up around my shoulders.

"Don't force it, Rowan," he said gently above my head. "Let the memories return in their own time. It may be that every detail does not wish to be recalled."

I wanted to protest, but I could feel myself getting sleepy—a combination of a stressful workday, not enough sleep, incredible sex, and some blood loss. Regarding the latter, I had no idea how much Gabriel had taken, but I was hopeful my body would replenish it quickly because right now I was incredibly tired.

"Why would that be?" I mumbled against his chest, wanting to stay with the conversation.

"There are some reasons that are beyond our comprehension," Gabriel said gravely, "and now, love, I must leave you."

I muttered a half-hearted protest as he slipped out of bed and began dressing. When had he gotten our clothes from the kitchen? I decided it didn't matter and let myself enjoy the reverse striptease he was giving me. The mattress sagged as he sat down to put on his boots. Turning my head, I saw faint streaks of light splintering the night sky. The significance of dawn's arrival was completely different now. Gabriel was still leaving me, but it was only because I lacked an appropriate place for him to bed down for the day. It made his departure a little more bearable. I plumped up the pillow he had been using, releasing his familiar scent. I'd make a fortune if I could bottle it.

"I wish I could be with you," I said, knowing it was a completely irrational request.

"I wouldn't be much fun," he responded playfully.

"Why's that?"

"Because, love, daylight puts all vampires into a state of inertia until the sun sets again. Our bodies simply shut down during that time."

I frowned. "But you've called me at lunchtime before."

Sitting back down on the bed, he pulled me to him. I would never tire of being in his arms. "It's true I am able to be awake for longer than most with no ill effects, but I need my own surroundings to be sure I am protected. And even I must rest sometimes."

Being in his own surroundings made sense, and also made the possibility of him staying here highly unlikely. "Are you aware of anything that happens when you're asleep?"

"Only in a nebulous way. It is why I have a sentinel."

"What's that?"

"Someone who watches over me while I rest."

Aleksei hadn't said anything about this. "You mean like a body-guard?"

"I prefer to think of my sentinel as a personal assistant with re-fined skills."

"But it would be a man, right?" I gave him a sideways glance and saw mischief twinkling in his eyes.

"Not always, no. It actually arouses less suspicion to have a sen-tinel of the opposite sex, the presumption being they are either wife or husband, mistress or lover."

"But wouldn't a man be better at providing protection?"

"Not necessarily," Gabriel said with a chuckle.

I swallowed and fussed with the comforter before asking, "So, is your sentinel a man?"

The idea of a woman watching over Gabriel while he slept stirred up some pretty strong feelings in me, feelings I wasn't particularly proud of. My experience with Katja was still too fresh and raw, skew-ing my reasoning where Gabriel was concerned. The notion of an-other female being this close to him did not make me a happy camper, even if he was in a state of inertia—*especially* if he was in a state of inertia. I tried to curb my jealousy by telling myself whatever their relationship, it had begun long before he'd met me and was purely platonic.

Yeah, right—have you had a good look at your boy lately? Can you imagine any woman not wanting to sample that? My God, just look at those shoulders—

My inner bitch sometimes forgets whose psyche she lives in. Shoving her in a box, I slammed the lid shut. I didn't need to have my insecurities paraded around inside my head.

"Yes, Tomas is male," Gabriel said, relieving my fears.

"Ah, that's his name, is it, Tomas?"

Taking hold of my chin with his fingers, Gabriel turned my head and brushed my lips with his. "Yes . . . and he's going to adore you."

Happiness bloomed in my chest. "How long has he been with you?"

Gabriel wrinkled his forehead. "Five hundred years, give or take a decade."

I'm pretty sure my jaw dropped open. "But I thought a vampire couldn't watch over you?"

"Vampires are not the only supernatural creatures with an extended life span," he told me, tapping the end of my nose playfully.

Oh shit!

"Would I be able to see where you sleep?" I asked. "I'd really like to have a visual image of where you are during the daytime."

"I would like that very much."

"Great, then it's a date."

I tried to stifle a yawn as Gabriel glanced out the bedroom window. It was still dark, but he needed to go. Throwing back the comforter, I started to sit up and immediately felt dizzy.

"Whoa, is this going to happen every time I give you my blood?" I asked.

"No, but this was the first time. The more often I feed, the quicker your body will adjust."

I had a sudden vision of Oliver Twist holding out his bowl and asking for more. "How often is often?"

"Perhaps every two or three days." He flushed and looked a little guilty. "I will take only enough until you are comfortable with me."

I smiled. "Gabriel, I'm more than comfortable with you, and you can take a whole friggin' pint if you promise me one thing." He raised a querying eyebrow, and now I smiled slyly. "That you'll always be inside me every time you need to take my blood."

"I doubt I'll ever need to take so much from you as that, but I promise to do my best to meet your condition. Now, love, I must go," he paused and looked at me with concern. "I don't suppose I can persuade you not to go to work today?"

"You're kidding, right?" I don't think he even realized he growled. "You want Angela to spend Christmas in a padded cell?"

"I think it's time I met this Angela of yours. I feel certain we could find much to talk about."

I didn't want to tell him it wouldn't be much of a conversation, what with Angela drooling all over the place. But I did give him my reassurance that I wouldn't overdo it at work.

"I can't expect Angela to handle things by herself. It wouldn't be fair." I shut off any further protest with a kiss, which he returned with a spine-tingling, curl-your-toes deal that left me breathless and even more dizzy than I already was. I decided it wouldn't hurt to go to the health-food store and get some supplements—iron or B-12 or something.

"Will I see you later?" I asked, playfully tugging the end of his braid.

He shook his head. "I might have to be gone for a day or two."

Dismay washed through me. I was missing him already. "Where are you going?" I didn't care if I came off as needy.

"Canada."

"What's in Canada?" Other than moose and Mounties.

"Katja. She has a home there."

He really should have said house not home. In my mind the word home conjures up images of a Norman Rockwell painting. Miss Psycho was definitely not the Suzie Homemaker type. "Is that where you think she is?"

He made a noncommittal grunting sound and shrugged. "Possibly, either there or she might have returned to—" He said a name that I supposed was either a town or a city, but it was a place I'd never heard of. Like a lot of people these days, my knowledge of world geography is more than a little sketchy. I find it challenging enough keeping track of all fifty states. Seeing the blank look on my face, Gabriel explained "It's a small town, not too far south of Vladivostok."

Now that I had heard of. Wouldn't be able to find it on a map if my life depended on it, but it had been the answer to a question on *Jeopardy* about the Trans-Siberian Railway. Odd, the things you remember.

In my mind I could see Katja's face once more, see her hatred for me glowing like a neon sign. "Do you really think she wants to hurt me?"

"Your safety is more important to me than anything, Rowan." His expression was as close to anxious as I was ever going to see. "I promise I won't let anything happen to you."

I didn't doubt it, but he also hadn't really answered me. I figured it was just a matter of time before Katja made her move. "Call me when you get back."

"Of course," he said, now standing by the side of the bed.

I hated to add to his worry, but it couldn't be helped. Tilting my head to look up at him, I asked, "What was surrendered to me, Gabriel? Was it something you gave me?"

The expression on his face changed, becoming the most serious I'd ever seen. "If you don't remember, then I'm not going to tell you."

"But . . . why not?"

"Because just as you are bound by ritual, so am I. Besides"—his mouth lifted in a smile that wasn't quite as reassuring as he might have thought—"its return is no longer necessary, and taking it back will not change anything."

By the time I got home that night, I was so tired I could barely see straight. I grabbed a pint of rum raisin ice cream from the freezer and headed upstairs to soak in a hot tub and get into bed.

I came awake certain my cell phone was ringing, but it sat silently on the nightstand. I checked for missed calls anyway, but there weren't any. Despite my physical exhaustion, sleep hadn't come as easily as I had hoped, so I'd relied on an old friend to help me drift off. The last thing I remember was Jane Eyre being all torn up thinking Mr. Rochester was going to marry that bitch Blanche Ingram—as if!

The clock on the nightstand told me it was past midnight. Something had woken me up, and I lay quietly, straining my ears to catch any sound that shouldn't be there. I wondered if Aleksei was skulking about downstairs. I giggled at the image that popped up inside my head. The big guy was most definitely not the skulking type. Still, I wouldn't put it past Gabriel to ask Aleksei to check in on me, and having access to my house seemed to delight the Russian no end. I have no idea why, it's not like my house is that special, but I like it. Apparently so did Aleksei. Or so Gabriel said.

I heard nothing except a tree limb scratching at the window and the far-off sound of a dog barking. Perhaps that's what had woken me. I fluffed up my pillow and turned over, but after ten minutes of staring at the ceiling, I knew I wasn't going back to sleep anytime soon. Getting out of bed, I decided a cup of coffee would go well with poor Jane's convoluted path to finding true love. As I got the filters out of the cupboard, I wondered how cold it was in Canada, and if Gabriel had found Katja at home. The thought of him being there—with her—woke up the green-eyed monster in a big way.

You don't know that she's even there, my inner bitch chided. *She might be in Vladi-friggin-vostock or wherever.*

I hoped she was, because then Gabriel would return all the sooner.

As I was pouring water from the glass carafe into the coffeemaker's reservoir, something outside the window caught my attention. Leaning forward over the sink, I looked out and saw a dark shape moving across the porch. It took me three tries to get the carafe back under the brew basket.

My brain told me it was nothing more than an owl. Most likely the same bad boy I suspected spent his time spying on Gabriel and me whenever we had sex on the porch. If he was looking for a repeat performance tonight, he was out of luck. I've never seen an owl up close, and the possibility was tantalizing. Opening the back door as quietly as I could, I stepped outside. The porch was empty, but the swing seat was moving as if something pretty big had used it as a launching pad. Like maybe an owl.

I leaned over the railing to see if my visitor was in the yard, but all I saw were pockets of darkness. Places where neither the moon nor the light from my kitchen window reached. If my owl was down there, he was clever enough to keep himself hidden. I put out my hand to catch the edge of the swing and halt its movement . . . and noticed the book lying on the cushion.

Okay, not an owl but something a little bigger. I smiled to myself. It had to be Aleksei. Who else was going to sit outside in the middle of the night, reading? Obviously, Gabriel entering my home while I slept was okay, but for Aleksei, it would be the wrong thing to do. Still, if he had been told to keep an eye on me, I didn't see why he had to be uncomfortable doing it. Pleased that Aleksei was respecting my boundaries, I also realized it was past time to establish some ground rules.

Picking up the book, I turned the slim volume over and frowned. It had the look of something that had been passed through many hands, and a strange, uneasy feeling fluttered in my stomach. The pages rustled lightly beneath my fingers. They were thin, not translucent enough to be considered true onionskin, but close enough. I stared at the title page, and gave a sigh of frustration. A single word, written in a meticulous hand, was centered on the page. Unfortunately I had no idea what it said and couldn't begin to decipher what language it was written in. Still, if the book belonged to Aleksei, then it was possible the writing was a form of Cyrillic. Turning a few more of the delicate pages with care, I saw more of the same indecipherable words, all apparently written in the same hand. This was an heirloom, something beautiful and precious, and also very private.

"Aleksei?" I called his name over the railing but got no response. I called again, and then once more, louder this time, all to no avail. I wondered if he was turning a deliberate deaf ear. Perhaps he wasn't supposed to be here after all. My finger stroked the spine of the slender volume in my hands. How could he leave something so lovely to be exposed to the elements? With a shake of my head, I decided the best place for it was on my bookshelf. As I turned to go back inside, the hair on the nape of my neck stood up.

I wasn't alone.

CHAPTER 16

A figure materialized out of the shadows at the far end of the porch, eliciting an involuntary *gaaack* response from me. The only two people I would expect to see at this time of night were both vampires, and this was no vampire. I didn't know what he was, but thanks to the big red alert flag that popped up in my head, I knew he wasn't human. At least not entirely. No matter how deliciously yummy he looked.

Fear can provoke some unpredictable responses, depending on how an individual's fight-or-flight response is wired. Anything from paralyzed muscles to peeing your pants to complete and utter disbelief. Staring at the figure moving toward me, I discovered my own F-O-F response must have short-circuited somewhere because I was filled with the irresistible urge to giggle. Not what I would call the best reaction to finding myself in an unfamiliar and possibly dangerous situation. But there you have it. I was a hiccup away from hysterical laughter.

Standing in the circle of light spilling from the kitchen window, my visitor made sure I got a good look at him. Tall and slim, he had a face that looked like a Renaissance painting come to life. Dark brown hair, highlighted with streaks of gold, fell to his shoulders in soft waves. His eyes were the color of a tropical sunset, and stubble shadowed his jaw. The five o'clock shadow seemed out of place, almost as if he needed to reassure one of us of his masculinity. Instead of the robes that my brain said he ought to be wearing, he was dressed in faded jeans and a Charlie the Unicorn T-shirt. Though he was nowhere near as muscular as Gabriel, the definition of his chest and abdomen was clearly visible beneath Charlie's prancing hooves, and his jeans were snug enough that I could tell he dressed to the right. The idea that I was in any danger seemed absurd, so I made absolutely no effort to protect myself.

"May I?" he asked in a voice that was both hushed and awe-filled at the same time. It reminded me of the way you automatically lower your voice in a library . . . or church. He held out a hand, and I stared at his fingers. They were unnaturally long and malformed. It took me a moment to work out that each had an extra joint. Even the thumb.

"May you what?" I asked, jerking my eyes back up to his face.

"May I have my book back?"

I looked down at the slim volume in my hand, and then back up at him. Of course the book was his; who else's could it be? Shyly I held it out to him, watching his fingers curl around the spine. It was hard not to shudder.

"What is it?" I asked, trying to be polite. *Yeah, you do realize you might be standing next to a homicidal maniac, but make sure you're not being rude about it! Sheesh! You gonna invite him in for coffee, too?* "I couldn't understand the title."

"It says *Beowulf.*"

I remembered reading the poem in high school and getting an A on my report. I think that was because I was one of the few who actually did read it all the way through. Everyone else in my English class found it the most monumental bore, but I found it very romantic.

"What language is that?" I asked, pointing to the volume now almost hidden inside his palm.

"English."

I snorted. So much for manners. "It doesn't look like any English I've ever seen."

The smile that lit up his face was a thing of absolute beauty.

"Perhaps it would be more accurate to say it's the original Anglo-Saxon. Every translation I've read always fails to capture both Beowulf's despair and his hope."

He passed his hand over the volume and—*poof!*—it disappeared. My knees wobbled, but I didn't faint, although I probably would have if I'd known what else was coming.

The air around me grew noticeably warmer and was filled with an odd rustling sound. I looked at my unexpected visitor, and my mouth dropped open. I know it did. How could it not? I stared at him in disbelief. He had wings that couldn't possibly be real . . . could they? It occurred to me that perhaps I wasn't awake after all. Still lying in my bed, I was actively engaged in some fantastic dream conjured up by my exhausted brain. But in my dreams I'm never affected by the weather, and right now my nipples were standing at attention, a consequence that owed more to the cold night air than my visitor's handsome face. After all, the last time I thought I was dreaming and felt cold, it turned out to be something else.

If this wasn't a dream, or a wide-awake hallucination, then there could only be one other explanation. After taking my blood not a dozen steps from where I was now standing, Gabriel must have accidentally ruptured a vessel or caused me to throw a clot or something else equally fatal.

"Aw, fuck it—I'm dead, aren't I?" My visitor laughed, a deep sound that was a surprise coming from such a lithe frame. I'd been hanging out with vampires too much, forgetting that not every male had to be built like a brick outhouse. "No, that comes with a lot more bells and whistles."

"Oh, really?" That was good to know . . . I think.

"Yes, really. Think more Las Vegas. Besides I'm not an escort."

"You ought to be," I said in frank admiration. "I mean you've got it all going—" His slightly disapproving look cut me off in mid-sentence. Shit! Wrong type of escort! "Are you sure I'm not dead?"

"Would you like me to prove it?"

Curious to know what this might involve, I nodded. I didn't see him reach for me, but I felt his arms around me, pulling me in close. There came a whisper of air as feathers folded around me, and then his mouth was covering mine and he kissed me. And he knew how to kiss—oh boy, did he ever!

His lips were soft and warm. His tongue stole inside my mouth, filling me with honeyed ambrosia, and promising me things I didn't even know I could want. Part of my brain went all Jiminy Cricket on me, demanding to know why I wasn't stopping him, while another part was telling me to just enjoy it. I doubt there are many girls who can say they've been kissed by a vampire and an angel in one lifetime, and I could go one better. I'd been kissed by both in the same twenty-four hours. When he finally let me go, his expression said the experience hadn't been quite what he'd expected. Not bad exactly, just different.

In some ways he was more attractive than Gabriel, but I viewed his ethereal beauty with a peculiar sense of detachment, admiring him much as I would a really hot model in the pages of some glossy magazine. Oh, don't get me wrong, the kiss was spectacular, and one I'll never forget. My lips still tingled, but as I stared up into eyes that were a reflection of a perfect sunset, I felt absolutely nothing. My heartbeat kept the same steady rhythm, and everything south of my navel dozed. Even the feel of his erection through his jeans didn't provoke my interest—filled me with mild concern, yes, but didn't turn me on. My internal flame, now that it had been lit, was only going to ignite for one male on the planet. "Who the fuck are you?" Truthfully I didn't mean to swear, given what he was and all, and I was grateful he didn't seem bothered by my slip. I guess it wasn't the first time he'd heard the word.

I'd always been somewhat ambivalent regarding the existence of angels, and my recent recollection regarding Gabriel's origin had done nothing to change my mind. Pictures of rosy-cheeked cherubim resting on clouds disturb me. I think it's because behind the dimples and smiles, I suspect they're secretly pissed that they never got the chance to grow up—and fuck up—like the rest of us. I don't trust them, so I guess it's a good thing that if an angel had to show up on my back porch, it looked like the one standing in front of me now. A perfectly gorgeous guy with a pretty nice six-pack and a hard-on. If some naked, chubby Little Lord Fauntleroy look-alike showed up with wings a-fluttering, I'd probably run screaming.

I told myself I was handling things remarkably well, but actually my brain was simply compartmentalizing this latest phenomenon so I could process it later. Having an angel appear on my back porch didn't seem quite as unnerving as you might think. And I was fascinated by his wings. Not all angels have white ones, apparently. His were a breathtaking blend of reds and gold, matching his eyes perfectly. It was on the tip of my tongue to ask if the color had any significance when they suddenly disappeared. Like the copy of *Beowulf.* One minute they were wrapped around me, the next I could feel cool air along the backs of my arms. I bit the inside of my lip so I wouldn't ask what he'd done with them.

"Interesting," the angel said, taking a step away from me. Folding his arms across his chest, he gave me a questioning look. He had pretty good biceps, but nowhere near the definition I'd been used to seeing lately. "You didn't ask what I am or even if I'm real, both of which I would have expected. Instead you want to know *who* I am."

"Yeah, well, sorry to disappoint you," I said. "My view of the world has been expanded recently, and seeing you is just another curveball aimed at my head."

"How delightful you are, Rowan."

His voice took on a lovely, musical lilt that I imagine was very soothing in any number of situations. But lovely or not, it didn't explain how he knew my name.

"You still haven't answered my question," I said pointedly.

He sighed. "Forgive me. Knowing Gabriel, I should have expected you not to be surprised by my appearance."

"*You* know Gabriel?"

"Of course I do." He seemed both puzzled and surprised by my question.

"So, did he send you?" *And do you actually know he's a vampire?*

"No, he did not." Leaning forward, he dropped his voice to a conspiratorial whisper. "Given how possessive they can be, I would appreciate it if you didn't mention my being here."

"*They?*"

"Vampires."

Well, that answered that question. "If you know how possessive Gabriel is, why did you kiss me?" I asked him.

He gave me a sly grin. "Sometimes the reward is worth the risk."

I wondered just how well he knew Gabriel. Tucking a curl behind my ear, I repeated my initial question, but a little more politely this time. "So, who are you?"

"I am Sebastian." He tilted his head, and the light from the kitchen window caught his hair, making the highlights shimmer.

Frowning, I wracked my brain. I'd heard the name before but couldn't quite place it, and then it came to me. "You're not a football fan, are you?"

His grin could have lit up the entire eastern seaboard. "Ah, so Gabriel has told you about me!"

"He's mentioned you," I said. Didn't mention anything about wings, though. "And I'm guessing he told you about me?" How else would he know my name?

"Oh, Rowan, he didn't have to. I've always known about you."

Ever since Gabriel had come into my life, I'd been feeling like I was running a half-step behind everyone else, and now it was happening again. Gabriel had made a minor reference to Sebastian on the first date we had, mentioning a fondness for football that I shared, but he had never spoken of him again—something that struck me at this particular moment as very curious. Why wouldn't he mention being on first-name terms with an angel? I could understand his not wanting to hold a press conference to announce the fact, but he could have told me.

I shivered and rubbed my arms. An angel on my back porch should have been enough to make me forget any physical discomfort I might be feeling, but his arrival was just another facet of my newly expanding world. As fascinated as I was, it didn't stop my teeth from chattering. I wiggled my toes inside my slippers and then noticed Sebastian was barefoot.

"Aren't you cold?" I asked, pointing at his wonderfully perfect toes. The shake of his head didn't come as a surprise. He didn't feel the cold, and neither did vampires, now I thought about it. Whatever was behind this surprise visit, my celestial guest didn't seem to be in a hurry to get to the point, so I took it upon myself to move him along.

"So let me guess, you've come bearing tidings of great joy, right?"

He laughed again, and shook his head. "No, I missed that one, but I hear it was quite a show."

How could an angel miss the presentation to the world of God's only son? I would have thought attendance was mandatory. What was he doing—washing his fabulous hair? If Sebastian was concerned by the oversight, he didn't show it. Then again, he'd had some time to get over it.

"Look, I don't want to be rude or anything, Sebastian," I continued, seeing the cold air turn my breath to smoke, "but I'm freezing my ass off, so could you just cut to the chase and tell me what you want?"

He focused on my face, his expression becoming pensive. Was he hoping my nose was going to tell him who had built Stonehenge or something? He probably already knew that, but it was something *I'd* like to know. Maybe I should ask him.

The wind picked up, blowing my hair about my face. The angel's silent examination was starting to freak me out. Perhaps Sebastian wasn't trying to find the answer to anything complicated, perhaps he just wanted to know why I wasn't turned on by him. Save me from male ego! In all fairness, if he'd been my first supernatural contact, then I would have been all over him, but he wasn't, and I couldn't do a thing to change that.

Finally, he blew out an exasperated breath, saying, "I've come to ask why you have not fulfilled your part of the ritual, Rowan. Why are you unwilling to return what was surrendered?"

In a way, it was a comfort knowing that at least one angel inhabited Clueless Land. Of course, it stood to reason that he would be off-the-wall weird, even if he did have the requisite feathers. Whatever expression I was wearing inspired Sebastian to grace me with a beatific smile and recite, *"You are a Vampire's Promise... given by word... accepted by deed... and bound by ritual to keep safe that which has been surrendered."*

"So I've been told," I muttered under my breath. Unfortunately, angels and vampires both have excellent hearing. You really would think I'd know better.

"Then why...?" The radiant smile was replaced with a puzzled frown, and then a look that could only be described as stunned amazement. "You don't remember, do you?"

Ladies and Gentlemen, we have a winner! "Um, I guess not." I did my best not to sound completely idiotic.

My memory was coming back—in fits and starts. Ever since the dream that wasn't a dream, I'd been remembering all sorts of things at the oddest moments. Usually it was nothing more than a fragment—a single word whispered in my ear, a glimpse of hair, the lightest stroke of a hand across my skin, a scent both familiar and unknown at the same time. Sometimes, it was such a jumble of images that I knew a much larger span of events was being covered. However, I had no way of putting them in any context. No way of knowing if they took place before or after the incident in the clearing. The only thing I knew with any certainty was that Gabriel's taking my blood had been the catalyst that triggered the chain reaction inside my head. But there were still gaps, and whatever Sebastian was referring to now was one of them.

"So you are not refusing to complete the ritual?" he asked slowly, as a worried frown wrinkled his boyish brow.

"Not intentionally, no."

"And you're not unwilling?"

"That's kind of hard to answer when I'm not sure what it is I'm supposed to do, but no, I don't think I'd be unwilling."

He paced up and down a couple of times before coming to a stop in front of me. When he reached out a hand, the tips of his fingers unerringly went to the spot where Gabriel had punctured my vein. "You have given him your blood," he murmured softly. "This was also done willingly?" I nodded. "Then you have no choice, Rowan. You must complete the ritual."

"Why?" I moved his fingers from my neck, surprised at how warm they were. "How am I supposed to fix something when I don't know what it is, or how I broke it in the first place?"

"Something has been broken?" Sebastian asked, confused.

"I'm speaking metaphorically." We both sighed. Mine was an exhale of frustration, his one of thoughtful contemplation. "Look, my memory's been returning, but I haven't got it all back," I explained, "and I honestly don't know how to make any sense of what it is I am remembering." The look on his face encouraged me to continue. "I know Gabriel hasn't always been a vampire. I know he was once an angel, a fallen angel, and I know that he gave me something important to keep safe. Something I'm supposed to return to him." I glanced up at Sebastian's face and gave him an apologetic shrug. "I don't know why you're so concerned when it doesn't matter to Gabriel anymore."

"Why would you think it doesn't matter?"

"He told me."

"What did he say?"

"That he was bound by ritual and couldn't tell me what it was, but that it made no difference if I remembered, because returning whatever I had was no longer necessary. It wouldn't change anything."

I thought Sebastian was going to explode. His face went dark, and his eyes became pools of molten lava. His wings reappeared in a furious rustle, and muttering something completely unintelligible, he hid himself from me. I doubt if more than a minute passed, but it felt much longer. Making the wings vanish, the angel stepped forward, his face once more a perfect representation of a figure painted by one of the old masters.

"You know what it is, don't you?" I said. It was more of a statement than a real question, and I was filled with a mix of excitement and sheer, unmitigated terror at seeing him nod his head. Whatever I'd been given had been important. Something about Gabriel's casual dismissal had caused Sebastian to lose his cool. And it was something he was going to tell me. "I don't suppose it's the title to a garage full of antique cars, is it?"

His mouth became a grimace. "It's a little more important than that."

I closed my eyes, steeling myself for what I couldn't imagine. "Then perhaps you'd better tell me."

"Rowan . . ." He hesitated, and I opened my eyes to see his were now lakes of fire. A wave of nausea washed over me, and I began to tremble. Sebastian caught hold of my hands, his extra-jointed thumbs rubbing the inside of each wrist. Suddenly I didn't want to know what Gabriel had surrendered to me. I had the awful feeling that it was going to be so much worse than discovering the man I loved was a vampire. If Gabriel was okay with not getting it back, then who was Sebastian to force it on him?

"I don't want to know," I said, trying to pull my hands out of the angel's grasp. "Don't tell me!"

Panic was threading its way through me, and the feeling that I was going to throw up was so real I could taste bile in the back of my throat.

"Rowan . . . ," Sebastian drew me into him, pulling me close and wrapping an arm about my shoulders. "Rowan, you have to be told, and if Gabriel will not speak of it, then I must."

"No!" My voice rose to a shriek. "Gabriel doesn't want it! He says it doesn't matter!"

Speaking with just the right amount of calm, Sebastian made me think I wasn't the first hysterical female he'd ever dealt with. "Gabriel cannot make such a decision by himself. If he is bound by ritual, Rowan, then so are you, and this he knows. To allow you no voice in this outcome makes a mockery of you as his Promise, and belittles the vow you made to him."

The arm around my shoulder dropped, and he stepped back. I took a deep breath to calm myself, waiting until both the nausea and the hysteria subsided. Finally I spoke, though not as calmly as he had.

"What did Gabriel give me to keep safe for him?"

The angel looked as if he had the weight of the world on his shoulders. "His soul, Rowan. You have Gabriel's soul in your safe-keeping."

CHAPTER 17

I never really understood the phrase *you could hear a pin drop* until this exact moment. It was as if every living creature on the planet decided to hold its breath at exactly the same time because the earth had stopped spinning and we were all waiting to see if gravity was nothing more than a joke. My rib cage constricted, threatening to crush the lungs it was designed to protect. I opened my mouth, gasping for air, but there was none to be had. The beat of my heart slowed to the point that I could hear the blood moving sluggishly through each separate chamber. I felt strangely heavy, as if my muscles could no longer support my skin and bones.

I didn't know whether to laugh or cry, so I wound up trying to do both at the same time, spluttering and coughing. Not a good idea. Sebastian patted me on the back as he led me to the swing seat and sat me down. I looked at him with watery eyes, searching for a sign that this was some sort of celestial *gotcha*, but his face was so grave, so solemn, I knew he wasn't kidding.

I was in possession of Gabriel's soul.

How the hell did you pull that one off?

I had absolutely no idea. Ever since I'd first heard I was keeping something safe, I'd assumed it to be something tangible. It never crossed my mind that it might be anything . . . incorporeal.

"You're not messing with me, are you?" I asked. "You know, joking?" Sebastian shook his hair, revealing a red tint I hadn't noticed before. "How is such a thing possible? How can a person exist without their soul, and how can it be given to someone else? You're an angel—tell me how."

"You really don't remember, do you?"

Now it was my turn to shake my head. "No," I whispered. "I really don't."

Sebastian closed his eyes for a few moments, as if trying to make up his mind about something. When he raised his lids again, they seemed more orange than red, and I could see he had come to a decision. "Tell me everything you do remember."

It didn't take as long as I thought it might, and when I was done, I was filled with a strange sense of relief. Telling Gabriel had been one thing, but this was someone who hadn't been there, who didn't know. Surprisingly, he didn't laugh or think I was in need of some serious drugs. Getting to his feet, Sebastian extended his hand and gave me a blissfully radiant smile. It made me think he really should have been at Christ's birth.

"If you will permit it, Rowan, I can help you recover your lost memories."

"You're not going to kiss me again, are you?" Allowing him the same catalyst as Gabriel to kick-start my recall process seemed a lot like being unfaithful.

"No, I already know that won't work." He actually sounded disappointed. "But there is another way I can restore what has been forgotten, only I need your complete trust. Do I have it?"

I doubt there were many women who had ever responded no to that question from Sebastian, and I wasn't about to join their lonely ranks. Instead I placed my fingers in his outstretched palm and allowed myself to be pulled against his body once more. I heard the rustle of his wings as he wrapped them around me, encasing me in a cocoon of fragrant warmth. The scent reminded me of incense and made me think of being in church. A softness brushed against my bare arms.

"Rowan?"

Sebastian's free arm encircled my waist, but it was the gentle tug on my hand that made me look up. I gasped. His eyes were once again lakes of molten fire. It took all I had not to try to free myself from his embrace, but the arm around my waist was now a band of steel.

"Do you trust me, Rowan?" he asked.

I hesitated a moment before nodding my head. I trusted Sebastian, but not my own voice. The wings at my back tightened, his long fingers curled around my hand, and the fire in his eyes intensified. And then . . . I fell.

The Void.

The source from which all that enters the Dark Realm is reborn. The repository of both life and death, hope and despair, dark and more darkness. A knife's edge balance of all that was, all that is, and all that is still to be.

She feels him move behind her, his hands on her shoulders, his breath stirring her hair. Following the gentle pressure of his fingers, she turns and looks up at him. Staring into blue-gold eyes, her hand flutters against his naked chest, where the rapid beat of his heart pounds against her palm. In the clearing she gave her word, and the time has come for the ritual to be completed.

"I am your vessel," she tells him, "let me keep safe what you can no longer possess."

His hands move, and her dress slips from her shoulders, pooling like a silken cloud at her feet. The blood roars through her as his eyes roam hungrily over her pale flesh. She is not immune to him, and her tongue licks over parched lips as she touches him. Is it wrong to want him? She, who has yet to lie with a man, would give her soul to lie with him. Right here, right now.

Her breath catches as he cups her breast in his hand, his thumb awakening her nipple with a promise. His other hand, splayed in the small of her back, brings her in closer, allowing his thigh to split her legs. His hands move, spreading warmth from the tips of his fingers to a place hidden deep inside her. She is helpless to resist. The heat increases, searing her lungs and scorching her heart, and though she is afraid, she will do nothing to douse the flame that wants to consume her. This she knows will bind them, one to the other, for all time.

She follows him down to the ground, and he enters her body in one smooth stroke. There is a tearing deep inside, and the pain of him filling her makes her cry out. Biting her lip, she draws blood, but it does not stop her from riding the wave of his desire and permitting him to slake his lust with her. And as he soars on the crest of his need, she realizes it is not her soul that will be given up in this moment of oblivion. It is his.

Matching the intensity of his passion, she opens herself to him. Fully, completely, and with no reservation. Accepting, in a secret place deep inside her, what he can no longer possess. Swathing his soul with her own, she promises to keep it safe until the time when he can reclaim it from her.

"Never let go of me!" she commands, her palm once more covering his beating heart. "Keep me with you always."

They stand together at the edge of the chasm, knowing that the swirling darkness below will extinguish the last remnant of his angelic light forever. He will be reborn, becoming something else. Something other. Something it was never his destiny to be. But Fate is a fickle mistress, and her temper is not for the faint of heart. Reincarnated as the perfect predator, he will be a slayer of men. Those he once sought to protect will now become his prey. He turns and takes her in his arms. With one last desperate kiss, he bruises her mouth, making her eyes fill with tears. And that is why she does not see him step over the edge and give himself to the darkness below. And she is better for it.

Now she waits. Leaning over the lip of the chasm, she searches the black river below her, looking for any sign of him. She knows he will be returned to the lesser beasts. He must be taught how to use the skills they have so generously bestowed, and while he fulfills this part of the bargain he has struck, he must forget her. He will seek her out, but not until his temper, skill, and appetites are as natural to him as breathing. Only then will he come to her, only then will it be safe, and find her he will.

For she is his redemption . . . his hope . . . his Promise.

She peers anxiously into the dark, and calls his name. Leaning perilously over the precipice, she reaches forward, stretching out her arm. His voice ricochets off the walls of the abyss as he calls to her.

She can feel his newly dark presence, feel the violence stirring within him as he searches blindly for her. She cares not that he is now some thing else. All that matters is that he is hers, and she is his.

"GABRIEL!"

Her cry is sucked down into the vat that would swallow him whole, and is returned to her on an echo that becomes a thunderclap in the night. She leans farther forward. In danger of falling herself, she stretches her arm out from her body, willing him to find her, to seize her hand and hold on.

And then, when she has almost given up hope, she feels the cold strength of his fingers grasping hers. The brutal pull on her arm and shoulder as he clings to the lifeline she offers threatens the limit of her endurance. But with a strength only the mad possess, she pulls him from the Void. His body is coated with the slime and filth that is his afterbirth, and it oozes down his newly enhanced frame.

She sloughs off the muck, committing the feel of this new form to her hands as she does so. He looks down at her with eyes now turned to molten gold and leans down to lap at the blood on her bruised lip. Immediately his teeth lengthen, and she understands what he needs from her. Her throat is the offering, and as he strikes, he brings her to ecstasy on a wave of unimaginable yearning. Knowing her blood will make him strong, she denies him nothing of herself.

"I am yours to do with as you will," he whispers in her ear when it is done, and as he presses his cold lips to her burning ones, they bind themselves to each other.

By word. By deed. By ritual . . . and by choice.

CHAPTER 18

I blinked and found myself lying on the ground, with Sebastian looking down at me. He was wearing the most curious expression, and his head was bent so low his hair swirled around my face.

"What happened?" I groaned, struggling to sit up.

"I have no idea." Extending a hand, he helped me to my feet and then sat me back on the swing seat. "You just sort of fell over. From the way your eyes were rolling, I thought you might be having a seizure. It was very impressive."

"Trust me, it wasn't meant to be," I told him, embarrassed by his account.

"Does that sort of thing happen to you often?"

I shook my head, wincing at the sudden bolt of pain that pierced the center of my forehead. Apparently I'd hit the deck face-first and was going to have a sizable goose egg for my trouble. Leaning back against the cushions, I ran my fingertips over the bruised area and grunted. A headache was already starting to thrum. Gingerly I pushed aside the pain. The memory was still there, as clear as day. Sebastian disappeared through the back door, returning a moment later with a glass of water and one of the blankets from my bed.

"What did you see?" He began, solicitously tucking the blanket around me.

I drained half the glass before saying, "Me, pulling Gabriel from the Void."

I wasn't about to share the rest of my vision or hallucination or whatever it was with him. I didn't care if he was an angel. Some things were private. Sebastian's expression said he accepted my explanation exactly as I'd told him, no more, no less. "Tell me what I'm missing," I asked him as I placed the now-empty glass on the deck and tucked my hands beneath the blanket. "Fill in the blanks for me, Sebastian."

Sitting down next to me, he slipped a hand beneath the blanket and pried apart my palms with his long fingers. Slipping his hand between mine, he sighed.

"Entering the Dark Realm is perilous and never free of charge. Whether those wishing admittance walk on two legs or crawl on their bellies, the cost is always their soul."

"Crawl on their bellies?" I sounded dubious even to my ears.

"Have you forgotten who prayed for the creation of a vampire? You think only humankind is worthy of having a soul?"

"Sorry, I guess I never really . . ."

"An angel is created from the light, the purest that exists," Sebastian continued. "An angel can never give his soul to the Dark Realm, nor can he enter such a place while still in possession of it."

"Why not?" I might have been pushing my luck, but it was worth the risk.

"To do so would upset the balance of all living things."

"Oh, I see." I didn't really, but now wasn't the right time to ask what he meant.

"When Gabriel accepted the offer made by the Wraith—"

"Who exactly is that?"

The look Sebastian gave me said he probably wasn't going to tolerate many more interruptions. "The keeper of the Dark Realm."

"You don't mean Satan, do you?" Technically I didn't regard this as an interruption.

"The Wraith is a powerful demon, but not Satan or Lucifer or the Devil. If that entity were to appear, there would be no doubt as to his identity. Besides," Sebastian sniffed, "he's prideful. He would not hide inside a hooded robe."

I shivered and squeezed the hand still encased between mine beneath the blanket, promising not to interrupt anymore.

"When dealing with the Wraith, one must expect a certain amount of trickery. He exists to mislead, misinform, and deceive. The soul of an angel is something to be coveted, but the law governing the Sanctity of Souls is an old one. It cannot be broken."

"So he needed to find a loophole," I murmured. Sebastian nodded in agreement. "What happened?"

"Each of the Fallen who accepted what was offered was granted the opportunity to seek a vessel into which his soul could be transferred. If the vessel could keep it safe until the appointed time, then it was to be returned, and the Fallen would be given—"

"—redemption at my hands!"

The look on Sebastian's face said he forgave my outburst. "Now do you understand how important you are?"

"Fuck me." I truly wished I'd been able to say something profound and insightful, but vulgarity was all I could manage. "What was the catch?" I would have frowned, but it hurt my forehead too much.

"The catch," Sebastian said in a grave tone, "was in the vessels themselves. Although able to possess an angel's soul, they were not governed by the same laws."

"Meaning?"

"They were not protected by the Sanctity of Souls." He looked downright miserable. "If the Wraith could get the vessel—the Promise—to release the soul prior to its being reclaimed . . ."

He didn't need to finish, and I understood the reason for his dismay. "How would that happen?"

"The same way it always does. With temptation . . . seduction . . . dark promises of things that will never be. Once a Promise has been identified, the assault is relentless. The Wraith will not cease until the soul has been acquired."

"How many Promises have surrendered?"

"It is unknown." Misery was replaced by utter grief.

It was something I really didn't want to think about, but how could I not? "Why hasn't the Wraith tried to get Gabriel's soul from me?"

Sebastian shook his head, and gave me a thoughtful look. "I don't know, but why do you suppose it is that you were unable to remember your past with Gabriel?"

It was something I hadn't thought about. "You think the Wraith made me forget?"

"It is a demon's nature to deceive," he repeated.

"Then why not just take Gabriel's soul from me?"

Sebastian blew out a breath. "A soul must be surrendered willingly. How can you surrender something you don't realize is in your possession? If the Wraith made you forget, then the unexpected result was ensuring your safety."

I wasn't sure if this was a good thing or not, and in my mind's eye I saw again the robed figure with the hood pulled forward, hiding its skeletal features. It didn't give me the warm fuzzies knowing I might owe a demon for keeping me safe so far.

"Tell me, Sebastian, how long was Gabriel crucified on that damn tree?"

My question took him by surprise, and I saw anger spark in his eyes. Frankly, I couldn't give a rat's ass. I figured some angel somewhere owed Gabriel big-time for what had been done to him, and if Sebastian didn't like my question, too bad. He shouldn't have offered to tell me anything.

"Time, as you know it in this existence, is just that," he said.

"Just what?"

"In this existence." I decided Sebastian had definitely been wandering around in Clueless Land by himself just a little too long. "Time is not fixed, Rowan," he continued, "it is fluid. Changing and adapting as necessary."

"It is, huh?"

The smile he wore wasn't exactly patronizing, but it made me feel the same way I had when my dad tried to explain the intricacies of a catalytic converter to me. Whoosh! Right over my head. But it was unreasonable of me not to consider what Sebastian was saying. Perhaps it was like the Old Testament. Do you really think Noah, swinging a hammer and building an ark, was actually six hundred years old?

"Humor me," I told him. "Surely you can take this fluidity and put it in terms even my puny brain can understand."

He gave me the kind of suffering look that elderly relatives are so good at. "The Armageddon for which Gabriel was punished occurred at least a hundred millennia before he was made a vampire, and he has been a vampire for more than three thousand of your years."

I opened my mouth to say something, and then shut it again. While I was willing to accept that his use of the word *Armageddon* was merely a reference to a battle, I decided Sebastian knew crap about putting time in a context that I could relate to. A hundred millennia—was he serious? I was better off trying to fathom infinity.

But what if he's telling the truth and his version of time is actually correct?

Holy crap! Just how old was Gabriel, and more to the point—how old was I? I had been with him in the clearing; I had been with him at the Void. Did that make *me* more than three thousand years old?

"Gabriel has been searching for you for an eternity," Sebastian said, as if reading my mind. "I think you mean more to him than he ever thought possible or had any right to expect. Through the passage of time, he has shared both your joys and your sorrows, watching as you grew and matured. Becoming so much more than the young girl who first came to him in the clearing, and yet . . ."

"What?" Pauses like this usually mean some form of criticism is coming.

"And yet you still retain that inner strength, that essence that drew you to him. It has not been diminished by the passing years. You are as strong now as you were when you first agreed to be his."

I wasn't sure how he would know this, but it didn't stop me from blushing at the compliment. We had now reached the point where I had to ask, "What will happen to Gabriel when he gets his soul back?"

Sebastian's eyes glowed like dying embers. "He will be restored to what he was always meant to be."

I'm fairly intelligent, some might even say bright, and I caught his meaning right away. "You mean he'll become an angel again. Like you."

"Not like me," Sebastian chuckled, "but an angel, yes."

"Why not like you?" Unable to help myself, I grinned at him. "I think your wings are real badass." Who wouldn't want to be an angel with wings the color of a hundred sunsets?

I don't know if angels are capable of blushing, but he did look pleased. "Thank you," he said, "but in your comprehension I'm near the bottom of the angelic food chain so to speak. Gabriel is far superior to me."

"So whatever he was being punished for has now been forgiven?"

"It has. Which is why he sought you out."

I didn't want to burst Sebastian's bubble, but I wasn't sure how forgiving Gabriel was going to be to those responsible for his punishment. Being crucified was bad enough, but his wings had also been cut off. The Gabriel I knew could do nothing to warrant such cruelty, and that was knowing him as a vampire.

"Rowan, I have to ask you something so I can be certain my understanding of the situation is perfectly clear."

"Okay, what do you want to know?" I was a little alarmed by his sudden seriousness.

His expression became grave. "Now that your memory is restored, would you be willing to fulfill the ritual, and return Gabriel's soul of your own accord?"

"Aren't you forgetting something? He told me its return was no longer necessary, and let's not kid ourselves, Sebastian, we both know exactly what he was referring to. Gabriel told me it wouldn't change anything, and I'm assuming he meant for him. I don't think it's up to me anymore. I can't return something he won't take back."

"But what if you could? What if it actually wasn't up to Gabriel but entirely in your hands? Would you return his soul then?"

This was completely different, and horribly unfair.

If I was being brutally honest, then the answer had to be a huge resounding *no*. I didn't want Gabriel to return to his former angelic glory because it would mean I would lose him. Angels and humans did not have long-term relationships and, I felt pretty sure, not casual ones involving sex either.

If I wanted to keep Gabriel with me, then I would keep him as a vampire. A human would be better, but I wouldn't quibble over details. Emotionally he made me feel things I'd never felt possible, opened me up to new experiences, challenged my way of thinking, and broadened my horizons. It all sounded incredibly corny, but it was true. And physically, well let's just say I've reached heights I never knew existed. I didn't want to give any of that up.

Selfishness in every ugly form imaginable swept over me as this realization hit home, whispering in my ear that it made no difference what I had agreed to eons ago. If Sebastian wanted the truth, then my answer would be no. God forgive me, but I didn't think I was capable of giving Gabriel up. But it was all so wrong, and deep down I knew it. Catching my chin in his long fingers, Sebastian tilted my head up until I was looking at him. I didn't realize my conflict was leaking out until his face blurred, and I felt hot, salty tears overspill my eyes and run down my cheeks. Leaning forward, he pressed his lips to each eye, drinking the moisture from my lashes.

"Rowan . . ."

"I know! I know!" I half-sobbed, jerking free of his hand.

I wiped my face on the sleeve of the T-shirt I was wearing, forgetting it was the one Gabriel had left behind. What little self-control I had remaining was almost destroyed as his scent enveloped me. Teetering on the edge, I was about to throw myself into a vat of self-pity when my inner bitch decided she'd seen just about enough of my pathetic show. It was time to man up. Fourth and long, with no timeouts left, the home team behind by four points. All the quarterback could do was throw a Hail Mary pass. Striding furiously through my misery, she came bearing one message.

Grow the fuck up, Rowan—this isn't about you! Hasn't Gabriel suffered enough? A vampire for more than three thousand years, something he was never meant to be. A victim of circumstance who took what was offered because the alternative was too awful to contemplate. Now he has been forgiven, and he needs you to release him from this purgatorial existence he's been enduring. Time to return what is rightfully his. To restore him to his true self.

And from somewhere deep inside me came a shattering luminescence.

If you love him, you will find a way to let him go . . . you must . . .

This vow I had made, the promise I had given, was what bound me to him. I was the guardian of his soul, swearing to keep it safe from all harm, no matter how long that might be. I had not been forced into this decision. I had given my word and pledged myself to him, freely. There had been a moment in the clearing right after the Wraith had asked if I would become Gabriel's Promise, a moment when I could have refused. I could have turned away and retraced my steps, and I would have been safe. The memories would have faded over time, becoming nothing more substantial than the ghost of a dream.

But I hadn't said no. Something had brought me to the clearing, something that would not be denied. Gabriel's faith in me. And my love for him was what enabled me to carry his most precious gift through the passage of time. Refusing to give it back was not an option. No matter the sacrifice I was asked to make . . . how could I not do this?

Well, what do you know—home team scores a touchdown!

"So, how do I get him to take it back from me?" I asked, wiping my eyes.

CHAPTER 19

Sebastian looked decidedly uncomfortable, which I found a little bewildering. Hadn't I given him the answer he was looking for? I said nothing, waiting for him to speak. The quiet stretched out for the space of a heartbeat, and then another, until I couldn't stand it anymore. Perhaps I needed to try a different approach?

"Sebastian, is there any reason Gabriel would not want his soul back? Surely he doesn't want to stay a vampire forever."

"Perhaps he does," came the morose reply.

"Bullshit!" I couldn't believe what I was hearing. "What the hell's wrong with him? What can he possibly be thinking?" The angel's face became a billboard for misery. "Has any other vampire done this?" He shook his head. "And you had no idea it was going to happen?"

"None. It was assumed he was being coerced in some way."

"What? By me?" He had the grace to look embarrassed. "Is that what you still think?"

"No, of course not," he replied hurriedly. "The fact that you weren't aware you even had Gabriel's soul definitely weighs in your favor. Also your apparent willingness to complete the ritual, even though . . ." His voice trailed off.

"Even though what?" I asked suspiciously.

"Even though it is now utterly hopeless."

"What do you mean, hopeless?" I could feel my temper rising. "You said if the matter was in my hands, would I be willing to go through with it? Are you saying it doesn't make any difference?"

"I had to be certain that Gabriel's decision was his alone . . . and I'm not entirely sure."

"About which part specifically?"

"Whether his decision can be nullified by you."

The expression on his face was that of an individual in wretched despair. Apparently this was beyond anything he'd ever had to deal with. "But you think there may be a possibility?"

He sighed. "I don't know, perhaps . . . who can say?"

It wasn't an outright no, and that was good enough for me. In the meantime, there was something else that had been nagging at me. "When did Gabriel first tell you he didn't want his soul back?"

"He never actually told me—"

"Well, he told someone!"

I thought from the way he narrowed his eyes that Sebastian wasn't going to answer me, but then I saw his lips moving and realized he was doing his time-in-this-existence calculations.

"It would be what you would call early summer," he said finally.

Aw, shit. That would be when Gabriel had dumped me. I suddenly recalled the conversation between us the night he'd come back into my life. I'd thought his reason for vanishing so abruptly nothing but a weak excuse. Hurt pride had made my tongue, if not caustic, then at the very least sarcastic. Now, I was appalled at the shameful way I'd treated him.

Gabriel had told me he needed to make a decision about the return of something that had been taken from him. No, not taken, something he'd been forced to give up. Something that, if it was returned to him, would change his life. But he had refused to accept it because it came at too high a price, a price the current holder would have to pay. I thought he was playing me, so I got angry, believing this so-called decision had nothing to do with me. I couldn't have been more wrong. It had *everything* to do with me. Holy Mary, Mother of Christ! What to do now?

"Did he say *why?*" I asked Sebastian.

"No, but I think it's obvious. He will not do anything that might put you in harm's way."

"How would I be in harm's way?"

He shrugged. "I can't say."

Yeah, he could, he just didn't want to, which meant I was going to have to pull it out of him piece by piece.

"Well, how is it done? Returning a soul?"

"It is a relatively simple matter of the correct invocation being recited while the Fallen maintains physical contact with the Promise. The supplication releases the vessel's hold and allows the soul to be returned."

"That doesn't sound so bad." I'd been expecting black candles, pentagrams, and an animal blood sacrifice at the very least. "So how would that put me in harm's way?"

The angel looked uncomfortable. "Ordinarily it wouldn't, but with you a complication has developed."

Which was just another way of saying "you are so screwed."

"What kind of complication?"

He glanced at me, and I saw his Adam's apple was working overtime, which only seemed to confirm my "screwed" theory. Whatever he needed to say involved me, and it wasn't good.

"The only way for a Promise to safeguard a soul is to link it with their own," he said, looking as if he'd just realized he was standing in the middle of a minefield. "The intent being to return it in a timely manner."

Having already received a lesson in Sebastian's explanation about the fluidity of time, I wasn't sure I liked where this was headed.

"What do you mean by *timely manner?*"

"It was always believed that the need for vampires would be short-lived. A thousand years at most. Humankind would learn the lesson or would no longer be a factor. Either way, balance would be restored."

"Only someone miscalculated, didn't they?"

" 'Yes." His nostrils flared, and his eyes turned fiery. "And it has proved to be a grave error, one that has resulted in a very different outcome. It was never imagined that the necessity for vampires would continue into this century . . . or possibly beyond."

Well, wasn't that just fine and dandy? The powers-that-be hadn't counted on mankind's overriding instinct for self-preservation, the will to survive at any cost.

"That Gabriel has adapted through the centuries," he continued, "is a testament not only to his strength of will, but also his desire to find you. Seeking his redemption has been paramount. It's just a shame it has taken so long to find it."

I know an accusation when I hear one, and I realized the angel was holding me entirely responsible for this turn of events. I don't mind taking my share of the blame when I'm guilty, but that wasn't the case here.

"Wait a minute," I said indignantly, "are you saying this complication wouldn't exist if he'd found me sooner?" I didn't need him to verbalize his answer; his eyes said it all. "For your information he *did*. I know for a fact we've met before, because he told me we had."

"That's true enough," Sebastian conceded, "but that's all it was. A single introduction, the briefest of meetings, a shared look across a room. You would not permit him the opportunity to form the necessary connection. And in the process of seeking you out, his vampire nature has grown stronger, thus allowing him to experience something he never could in his celestial form."

"What's that?"

"The chance to embrace emotional love."

"Angels can't feel love?"

"They feel love, but only in its more physical manifestation."

Which explained his earlier hard-on. "That," I said hating to disillusion him, "is lust, not love."

He looked somewhat crestfallen. "Then an angel truly cannot experience love the same way humans do."

"Or vampires."

"Or vampires."

This was really interesting shit, and something I wanted to discuss with him in depth. Unfortunately, it was a conversation for another time and place, and besides, it didn't change anything.

"So how is time a complication in my case?"

Shaking his head, Sebastian looked more pitiful than before. "The best way I can explain it is by saying Gabriel believes his soul has now become inextricably linked to yours. One cannot be released without the other."

I may not always be the sharpest knife in the drawer, but this wasn't one of those times. I understood all too well what the angel was telling me. There was only one way to release my soul that I knew of, and that was to . . . yeah, I got the picture. Gabriel didn't want his soul back because he wasn't going to take my life to do it. This was the price that, in his opinion, was too high for me to pay.

"Do you know for sure that our souls are linked like this? That there's no chance of my surviving the prayers and physical contact stuff?"

"Nothing is certain, Rowan. But it makes little difference now. Gabriel cannot undo his decision."

"He can't?" Sebastian shook his head. "So what's the point of telling me any of this?"

"A vampire has never made such a sacrifice to the Dark Realm. I had hoped you might be able to undo it."

"How?"

He shrugged. "I don't know . . . this dilemma is unprecedented."

Which meant we were groping in the dark and had nothing to guide us. I resumed pacing, going over in my head everything Sebastian had told me about being a Promise and what I could now remember. I walked up and down three times before coming to a stop in front of him. "What we need is a loophole."

"A loophole?" He sounded dubious.

"Yes." I nodded, feeling something coming together inside my head. "The Wraith is a—what did you call him—a trickster? Well, doesn't the other side know that?"

"The other . . ."

"Yeah, the Light?" I pointed to the sky. "Surely they know how he operates?"

"Of course."

"Then there has to be a loophole. I refuse to believe that Gabriel would make a decision like this without there being some sort of escape clause or way out. There has to be something, no matter how small a possibility." I demonstrated with my thumb and forefinger. "I refuse to believe it doesn't exist."

"But what if it doesn't?"

"Then my purpose as his Promise has been more than a mockery, Sebastian. It's been pointless. And I refuse to accept that. There has to be a way to undo this, and you're going to find it for me!"

"I am?" Now he looked worried.

"Who better? You know Gabriel, you know me, and you know what we're up against. Nothing is ever a hundred percent guaranteed. There is always a chance that something has been overlooked. We just need to find it. One chance, Sebastian, that's all we need."

There was silence as he thought through what I had just told him. "You truly believe an exemption might exist?"

"I do," I answered firmly. "I refuse to believe anything else." Sitting down next to him, I took his hands in mine. The feel of his long fingers overlapping themselves didn't seem so weird anymore. "If you can come up with another suggestion, I'm all ears."

"But . . . if I cannot find a loophole?"

"Then we'll do it the old-fashioned way, with candles and prayers and whatever else is needed—and you can damn well tie us together if that's what it takes to keep Gabriel connected to me."

Sometimes you just need to know another option exists, even if it's not a very good one. I didn't have much faith in the angel's bell, book, and candle routine, but it made him feel better to hear I was willing to consider it. Which was the whole point.

"I won't let Gabriel throw away his chance at redemption, Sebastian, not until I've tried everything."

His eyes made me think of blood oranges. "But Rowan, he loves you. He will never agree to any of this."

I nodded and gulped down the sudden lump in my throat. "Guess I'm just going to have to coerce him then. Don't you see, Sebastian, I love him too much to not do this. I couldn't live with myself, or him, if we didn't at least try."

"But what you are risking—"

"—is my risk to take, Sebastian, *mine*. We have no way of knowing what I may or may not lose, but we do know what Gabriel will lose. And that is something I'm not willing to give up. I don't care what some stubborn, possessive vampire says. Even if he is the love of my life. In the end, it will count for something. It has to." I paused and drew in a breath. "Never underestimate the power of positive thinking," I said, with what I hoped was a confident smile. "One way or the other Gabriel *will* get his chance at redemption. Now go find me that loophole!"

It was the only answer. I tugged on the neck of the T-shirt I was wearing and buried my nose in the fabric. Gabriel's scent infused every pore in my body, calming me, putting me at ease. I loved him too much not to do this, even if it meant, no matter which outcome came to pass, I would never see him again.

I would be all right with that because the decision had been made the moment I first set foot inside the clearing—and saw him hanging on that damn tree.

CHAPTER 20

The sound of my cell phone ringing startled both of us. Not only was it unexpected, it took a few flustered moments for me to work out that the ringtone was coming from the front pocket of the angel's jeans. I distinctly remembered leaving my cell phone in the company of Jane Eyre.

"I saw it when I got the blanket," Sebastian said, standing up and handing it to me with a totally unashamed look. "I didn't want you missing any calls."

Wondering what else those long fingers might have been poking around in, I took the phone from him, checked caller ID, and frowned. Why would Laycee be calling me at nearly two in the morning? Was she sick? Had there been an accident—oh God, was Jake hurt?

I was about to put the phone to my ear when a new sound told me I had a text message.

"What the hell?" I muttered, pulling up the screen and reading.

"What is it?" Sebastian asked, seeing my expression.

"It's Laycee," I told him, still undecided how I felt about my phone being in his pants. "She says she's out front with a surprise for me."

"You don't like surprises?"

I love surprises, but the kind that come in the early hours of the morning aren't normally the ones you want to get. Something was definitely wrong. If Laycee was in my driveway, then it wasn't good news that had gotten her out of bed in the middle of the night.

"I like surprises," Sebastian murmured in my ear.

I turned my head to see an expression of almost childlike delight on his face. I didn't care how much he liked surprises; this was one he was going to have to miss. If Laycee saw him, it would lead to the mother of all question-and-answer sessions.

"You have to go," I said firmly. "Laycee can't see you here with me."

"Why not? Just tell her I'm an old friend of Gabriel's come for a visit. It's the truth," he added in an aggrieved tone.

"That may be, but it's two in the morning, and Gabriel isn't here." Sebastian didn't know much about the dynamics of human relationships, I decided.

"Why haven't you told her about Gabriel? I thought she was your best friend."

"She is," I said, wondering how he knew that, and knowing now wasn't the time to ask him. Maybe he was a little more intuitive than I gave him credit for. "And she does know about Gabriel," I corrected, "she just doesn't *know* about him." The look he gave me said he didn't understand the difference. "It's complicated, Sebastian. Something like this has to be handled a certain way. You can't just blurt it out, and honestly, I'm not sure how to tell her."

"That Gabriel's a vampire?"

"No, that you're an angel."

The way my life was going right now, it wasn't too far-fetched to think I'd have better luck getting Laycee to accept a vampire in my bed than an angel on my swing seat.

My phone chimed again. The words WHERE R U? IM W8ING! lit up the screen. I turned, ready to ask Sebastian to leave again—get on my knees and beg if necessary—but I didn't have to. Getting to his feet, he smiled, and simply . . . vanished. Like the book. And his wings. I was too relieved to be unnerved. Hopefully he'd gone loophole hunting.

The text chime went off two more times as I walked through the kitchen and down the hall. The messages were the same as before, the only difference being the number of question and exclamation marks used.

"This better be the best surprise in the world or I'm so gonna kick your ass," I yelled as I opened the door and stepped out onto the porch.

From my top step I could see Laycee standing in the driveway. She was dressed in leggings, a sweatshirt that had to be Jake's, judging from the fit, and ballet flats. It was a grab-what-you-can-and-throw-it-on outfit. She was a mess, and also not wearing makeup. It might have been two in the morning, but Laycee was the kind of girl who didn't go to the mailbox without making sure her hair was tidy and she had on lip gloss. Whatever was going on was bad—a feeling that was reinforced by the fact that she made absolutely no effort to move. A fire alarm siren went off inside my head.

"Laycee, what's wrong? Has something happened to Jake?" She shook her head, which I took to be a good thing. Okay, not Jake, who then? "Is it your mom or dad?" More frantic shaking. I frowned, trying to think of what else could be responsible for her unkempt appearance. "Jake's . . . kids?"

This time she shook her head so vigorously the scrunchie that was holding her hair back from her face fell out. Ignoring it, she rapped her knuckles on the roof of the car she was standing next to. The alarm in my head wailed a little louder. I hadn't even noticed the car.

Instead of the white, beat-up nondescript sedan Laycee usually drove, she had apparently arrived in a shiny black BMW, which was now parked next to the POS. My knowledge of cars might be pretty dismal, but even I recognized the distinct logo embedded in the hood. If this was the surprise she wanted to show me, it might explain her appearance, but this was no surprise gift from her beau. I had my doubts that a small-town sheriff's salary would cover the payments on a new BMW.

I came down the porch steps and walked toward her. She remained frozen to the spot, and although there were still a few feet between us, I could feel the anxiety rolling off her in waves. She didn't say anything; instead she began waving her hands in front of her, as if her nail polish was wet. This was Laycee's distress signal.

Now her anxiety was mixed with something else. Fear. Closing the distance between us, I caught hold of her hands, needing to halt their frantic fluttering more than anything else. I also wondered if it had been a mistake asking Sebastian to leave.

"Laycee, where's Jake?"

Pulling a hand free, she swiped at her eyes with the heel. "With his kids. They're having an early Christmas with his folks."

I don't know why, but it was a relief knowing Jake wasn't involved in whatever was going on. And then Laycee said something that made my stomach churn.

"I'm so sorry, Rowan. I should have known the bitch was lying."

The cold night air was nothing compared to the icy shiver that ran down my spine.

"Who was lying?"

She hiccupped back a sob, her fingers beginning another anxious dance in the air. "I didn't want to believe her, but it was kind of obvious that she knew Gabriel, and so I-I-I- . . ."

"Shhhhh." I pulled her in close, and the avalanche of tears fell. I didn't need Laycee to tell me who had upset her. I already knew. "It's okay. She's had a lot of practice telling lies," I told her, my hand rubbing soothing circles on her back. "You mustn't blame yourself. I would have done the same thing."

Now that I knew who I was dealing with, the details didn't matter. It wouldn't change anything, but I was curious to know which one of us had been the bait. "Was it me or Gabriel?" I asked softly. The shrug of Laycee's shoulders told me it made no difference. She would have come for either one of us. "It's okay. She didn't hurt you, did she?"

Laycee gulped a mouthful of air, and I watched her fight to put her emotions under control. Stepping out of my embrace, she kept a firm grip on my hand as she shook her head. And then I saw her eyes widen as something behind me caught her attention, and the expression on her face changed. No one likes to be made a fool of, and definitely not when it comes at the expense of someone you love. Realizing she had been duped, Laycee was now angry. Whatever story had been fabricated must have been very believable to get my best friend out in the middle of the night. I wasn't kidding about

Katja. She'd literally had centuries to perfect her skill at being deceitful. It was too bad Laycee had no idea what she was dealing with, and it was going to be up to me to protect her from the truth as best as I could.

"I can't believe I was so stupid!" she hissed in a low voice.

"Laycee, don't."

"Does she really know Eye Candy?"

I nodded, grateful I wasn't the only one who thought Katja was all wrong for him. "Yeah, unfortunately she does."

"What is she, an ex-girlfriend or something?"

"Worse," I said with a tight smile. "A never-was." It was reassuring to have Laycee return my smile.

"Why is it some women think every dick is just dying to get in their panties?"

"I got no idea, Layce."

Narrowing her eyes, she flicked her gaze over my shoulder, and murmured, "She's behind you."

"I know." I reached for her hand and squeezed it. "Be careful what you say from now on," I warned. "She can hear everything, and I do mean everything, and trust me when I tell you she's a lot stronger than she looks."

"Yeah?" Laycee gave a disbelieving glance over my shoulder.

I squeezed her hand—hard. "Yes," I insisted. "Trust me. I know."

My words, and the seriousness of my tone, were enough. Laycee nodded.

"Hello, Little One, have you missed me?"

The husky sound of Katja's voice, and the condescending form of address, did nothing but piss me off. She must have been hiding in the shadows by the side of the house. If I'd turned my head as I came down the steps I probably would have seen her, but I'd been so focused on Laycee, it never crossed my mind to look for anyone else.

Unable to come in, and knowing an invite from me wasn't in her future, Katja had used my best friend to get me out of my house. It went without saying that this was a bad situation, one that I could pretty much guarantee was going to get a lot worse. The psycho vampire bitch was crazy-scary, but right now I couldn't focus on that. I had to find a way of making sure Laycee was safe, and the only thing I could think of was getting her inside the house. She would be safe there because Katja couldn't cross the threshold.

I turned around to face my nemesis, surprised to see she had changed her wardrobe. I'd imagined the long black leather coat and thigh-high boots were something of a signature look for her, but apparently not. Tonight she had on a dress that barely covered her ass. Red leather, laced up each side corset-style, and advertising, among other things, its wearer's aversion to underwear. Completing the slut look were impossibly high stilettos. Katja's choice of wardrobe may have been better suited to the red light district in any major capital of the world, but it also allowed me to see she bore no aftereffects from her altercation with Gabriel.

All of her limbs seemed to be depressingly hale and hearty, without so much as a fading bruise to mark the beat-down my boyfriend had given her. Having witnessed the brawl between them, I knew I would be no match for Katja's physical strength, even if she did look as if a heavy breeze would snap her in two. All I could hope for was to get inside her head and rattle her enough so she'd make a mistake. Perhaps use her arrogance against her. Of course, the downside to my plan was the fact that Katja wasn't what you would call mentally stable. The anxieties I would have had dealing with a human who was a whack job were amplified a hundred times because Katja was a vampire.

"I'd like to say it's nice to see you, but we both know that would be a lie," I told her with my very best smile.

"She really should get some pointers from *What Not to Wear*," Laycee murmured behind me.

I thought for a minute that she'd forgotten my warning about people with exceptional hearing, but the look on Laycee's face said the statement was a deliberate dig. Guess I wasn't the only one who thought rattling Katja's cage was a good idea. At least it got Laycee off her weepy roller-coaster ride.

"I don't think *subtle* is in her vocabulary," I said.

"It's not in her closet either," Laycee snapped back, "but I'll admit she's definitely got *in your face* working for her."

Looking at Katja, I addressed her directly. "I'm going to take a stab in the dark and guess you never were in Canada, were you?"

She made an ugly sound that might have been a laugh. "You have no idea how disappointed I am in Gabriel. One tiny little alarm goes off, and he rushes out to see what I'm up to." She came toward me, amethyst eyes sparkling and hip-length black hair swinging. Placing a hand on my shoulder, she squeezed until I was sure she was going to snap my collarbone. "Are you so sure he wants you, Little One? He seems very anxious to find me."

"Yeah, right, like you really think Gabriel's interested in you? Keep telling yourself that if it makes you feel better, but we both know if you really believed it, you wouldn't be here."

Her eyes glittered with temper, and her mouth became a crimson slash. The pressure from her fingers tightened, and I felt the sting of tears in my eyes. Damn it! I absolutely was not going to cry in front of her.

"You should watch your manners, Little One."

Tossing her hair over her shoulder, she made her way to the BMW, her stiletto heels tapping loudly on the concrete slabs that made up my driveway. I felt Laycee squeeze my hand. As far as she was concerned, Katja was just some nut job with an obsessive crush on my boyfriend, something the two of us could deal with easily. Unfortunately, I knew just how much danger we were actually in.

The sound of Katja slamming the beemer's trunk made both of us jump. The Goth Queen was no longer alone. I can't say for certain, because I didn't actually see, but I'm pretty sure the guy who was now standing next to her had climbed out of the trunk. I watched as he offered the exotic beauty his arm.

"Who the hell is that?" Laycee asked, tightening her grip on my arm.

Oh crap, this night just kept getting better and better.

CHAPTER 21

The arm Katja was hanging on to seemed familiar, but I couldn't place the man at first. I was too busy trying to work out why he would have been in the trunk of the car, and I got the feeling that riding there had not been his idea. I could only surmise that, for whatever reason, Katja hadn't wanted Laycee—and, by extension, me—to know about him.

"I've brought an old friend to see you, Little One," she said, smiling at me.

An old friend? What old friend? The only people Katja and I had in common were Aleksei and Gabriel, and the person at her side wasn't either of them. But there was something familiar about him, only at first I couldn't place it. And then it came to me. On our first date Gabriel had taken me to the movies, and afterward Aleksei and Katja and another guy had been waiting for us in the parking lot. Aleksei had needed to talk with Gabriel, and Katja had put the moves on me. The only thing that saved me from complete humiliation had been the other guy. I remembered thinking at the time he had the wholesome all-American look that clothing designers love to use in their advertising campaigns. But he didn't look anything like that now.

"Oh my god!" I gasped, putting a hand to my mouth as he came closer. Laycee went one better and covered her nose as well.

It was the middle of the night, and the temperature had dropped enough that frost was already making the POS look like it had been attacked by a bunch of ten-year-old girls armed with glitter sticks. It should also have been cold enough to mask the smell of rot and decay. I've driven the county highway enough times to recognize the stench of decomp when I smell it, and the pathetic creature shambling alongside Katja reeked of it. He was rotting on the inside. My stomach churned, but despite feeling nauseous, I forced myself to look at him.

The Kansas farm boy had been replaced by a shadow of his former self. Sunken eyes and sallow skin were exaggerated by weeping sores at the corners of his mouth. The World War Two pilot's jacket was now torn and smeared with filth, as were his pants. I had thought his uneven, stumbling gait was due to some sort of injury, but it was because he wore only one boot. His other foot was bare and looked as if something had been chewing on it. Surely not him?

I think he recognized me because as he came closer, he raised a hand to smooth back his hair. The soft brown mop that had once brushed against my cheek was now a clump of greasy, matted strands, and I could see bald patches on his skull where it had fallen out. As his hand continued to move, I saw his nails were long and encrusted with filth. They reminded me of talons.

The ripe, fetid odor grew stronger the closer he came and, unable to fight it any longer, Laycee leaned over and decorated a freshly planted tub of red and white chrysanthemums with what had probably been her supper.

"Sorry," she said, her hands shaking as she wiped her mouth with a tissue she'd pulled from somewhere. I risked a glance in her direction, and the look she gave me said she was okay. Needless to say, Katja was not affected in the slightest. She could have been out for a stroll in the park with her beau.

Oscar . . . his name was Oscar.

They both stopped moving a few feet away from us, and Katja whispered something in Oscar's ear. It wasn't until I saw him struggling to open his mouth that I realized what she had told him to do. Without thinking, I grabbed Laycee by the shoulders and pulled her around so she faced me.

"For the love of God, Layce, do not look at him!"

An order such as that would set off a knee-jerk reaction in most people. It was an open invitation to do exactly what they were being told not to do. Laycee, however, could have given Lot's wife a lesson in disobedience.

Behind her, Oscar had managed to get his mouth open and drop his fangs. It had been a struggle and I could only imagine the difficulty was due to his terrible condition. Staring at him over Laycee's head, I could see his fangs were as diseased at the rest of him. The tips had been broken off, leaving ragged points; these and the remainder of his teeth were a sickening yellowish brown. His mouth reminded me of a wall that has broken glass set in the concrete to deter people from climbing over it. With his fangs in such an awful state, making a smooth strike into a vein would be pretty much impossible for him. He would need to chew through flesh and muscle in order to find what he needed. I knew, because I'd asked. Curious about the mechanics of how Gabriel's fangs dropped and retracted, he'd run the tip of my forefinger lightly over his gum, letting me feel the slight swelling where his fangs were housed.

"But how do they come out?" I'd asked, looking up at him from my still euphoric post-sex position on the kitchen floor.

He'd been more than happy to demonstrate, and I watched the razor sharp points slice through the gum tissue to create an opening through which each fang could descend.

"Doesn't it hurt?"

Gabriel smiled, somehow more satisfied, it seemed to me. Even his dimple looked pleased with itself. Was this what taking my blood had done to him?

"No," he said, looking down at me. "As with any incision, my body starts to heal itself almost at once, so there's no open wound, no chance of infection, no pain."

Amused by my fascination, he'd demonstrated again . . . and again.

Seeing Oscar's jagged fangs, I could only imagine how painful it had to be for him to drop them. Trying to make an opening in his gum line with uneven, broken-off tips had to feel like he was cutting his mouth with a dull, rusty knife.

"What's he doing?" Laycee asked, looking up at me. She took her hand from my arm and made a crude gesture. I nodded. Better to have her think Oscar had his cock out and was jerking off than to see what he really had out.

Leaning toward him, Katja whispered in his ear. He nodded, a movement that was filled with the most incredible weariness. I had no idea how ill he was, but he looked like he was sinking fast. As I watched him begin the painful process of trying to retract his fangs, I wondered what was wrong with him. Did he have the vampire equivalent of AIDS or something? I sifted through all the information I had stored away from my Vampire 101 lesson with Aleksei and Anasztaizia, recalling a discussion about the pivotal role blood played in a vampire's development.

The beautiful Magyar had told me that blood was necessary to ensure a vampire's health and overall well-being. It ensured that the regeneration factor in their bodies kept working and protected them from disease, which explained why so many vampires were able to survive both the Black Death in the Middle Ages and the Great Plague of London in 1665.

The open sores and chewed foot, coupled with the overall condition of his mouth, all led me to the same terrible conclusion. Oscar hadn't been feeding. He had once been handsome and strong. Now he was a pathetic shadow of his previous self. I didn't care that Katja was capable of tearing me limb from limb with no provocation whatsoever. My gut told me she was responsible for his pitiful condition.

"Oh my God—you've been starving him, haven't you?"

I flung the accusation at her, almost daring her to deny it. She didn't. Instead she acted as if I had never spoken.

"Do you want to know how I met Oscar?" she asked, flicking her hair over her shoulder.

"You really are a sadistic bitch," I told her, furious with her complete disregard for the vampire next to her.

"It was in Hawaii right before the bombing of Pearl Harbor," she continued. "He was a pilot in your military. You wouldn't believe how handsome he was then, and you can imagine my delight when I discovered he could be turned." She sounded positively gleeful.

"So why do this to him, Katja?"

"Hmmm, what?" She raised an eyebrow and looked at me, and then spared a glance for the once handsome pilot. "He broke the rules and had to be punished."

"What rules?"

She began examining her nails. I swear I've never seen a female so obsessed with the state of her cuticles.

"My rules. You caught too much of his interest, Little One."

I was stunned by her words. Oscar and I had met only that one time, and I doubt we were in each other's company for more than ten minutes. Hardly enough time to make an impression, unless you were Scarlett Johansson, which I most assuredly am not. I wondered which had pricked Katja's vanity more—the fact Oscar had spoken to me or that he'd put his hands on me. With her ego, just his looking in my direction might have been enough.

"Of course," Katja said, holding her hands before her and checking the polished perfection of each nail, "his deterioration has progressed somewhat faster than I anticipated."

"What's wrong with him?" Laycee asked, surprising both of us by joining in the conversation.

It had been my intention to warn Laycee not to say anything, but I was gratified to see the fear in her eyes now reduced to a more general wariness. Besides, telling Laycee to ignore a conversation was pointless. She had a tendency to speak her mind and the consequences be damned. I held my breath as Katja reached out and caught a handful of Laycee's platinum hair, running her fingers over the tresses. She dropped it with a look of distaste, rubbing the tips of her fingers together, as if she'd touched something dirty. It was a deliberate insult, designed to provoke Laycee's temper, but my girl was smart enough to recognize she was being taunted. Keeping her thoughts to herself and her mouth shut was proof enough fear wasn't going to make her do anything stupid.

"Oscar is still considered to be a new vampire," Katja said conversationally. "He needs to feed at least once or twice a month. If not"—she paused, and waved a hand in his general direction—"this is what happens."

I thought, for a moment, that everything was going to be okay. Laycee, I was certain, would form the opinion that illegal substances

had Swiss-cheesed Katja's brain. The word *vampire* was a eu-
phemism for something more offensive, something that I would be
able to explain to her later, when this was over. But the minute I saw
the look on her face, I knew that wasn't going to happen.

"A vampire? You're fucking with me, right?"

Looking like Trailer Park Barbie is one thing, behaving like other
people's idea of Trailer Park Barbie is another. And that includes
using vulgarity. Laycee only ever uses the F-bomb when she is se-
verely stressed. A frown marred Katja's smooth brow, quickly followed by a look of disbelief.

"She doesn't know about Gabriel?" she asked, directing her question at me.

I shook my head. First Sebastian and now Katja. Why did everyone question my ability to keep a secret? Had Lois Lane told anyone
that Clark Kent was really Superman? And don't tell me she didn't
know. She wouldn't be much of a reporter—or girlfriend—if she
couldn't work that one out!

It was a waste of time lying.

"Is that why you had her turn her back?"

"Yeah, that's why."

"And you never told her about Gabriel?" The idea seemed to
amuse her more than anything else.

Laycee interrupted in a pissed-off tone. Like most people, she
hates being talked about as if she isn't in the same room. "What's
going on, Rowan, what don't I know about Gabriel, and is Euro-
Trash on something?"

I was so used to hearing her refer to Gabriel as Eye Candy, that
the use of his first name threw me. It sounded so strange hearing it in
her voice that I thought for a moment she was talking about someone
else. I opened my mouth to speak even though I had no idea what I
was going to say, but before I could utter a syllable, Katja's banshee-
like shriek drowned out everything. I clapped my hands over my ears,
staring at the dumbfounded look on Laycee's face.

"No! I'm not *on something*," Katja snarled, grabbing hold of
Laycee's wrist, "but I am going to let you in on a secret your wonderful friend has been keeping from you."

Giving Laycee's arm a sharp jerk, Katja began dragging her to where Oscar stood. I stared, horrified, as he opened his mouth, amped-up salivary glands making him drool on himself. Realizing Katja's intention, I screamed at her.

"No, Katja—don't do it!"

It was enough to make her stop, and Laycee, taking advantage of the momentary halt, began trying to jerk herself out of Katja's iron grip. It was useless, of course, but that didn't mean Laycee was going to give up. Unable to break free of her grasp, she turned her attention to Katja's vise-like fingers and tried prying them open. A furrow appeared between the exotic vampire's perfect eyebrows. I had to stop Laycee before Katja got pissed enough to really hurt her.

"Laycee, stop it! Remember what I said about being stronger than she looks? Believe me, you'll end up hurting yourself before you hurt her."

Turning her head, Katja gave Laycee a smile that was all shiny white teeth. My screaming had been in vain. Instead of compelling Oscar to drop his fangs, Katja now dropped hers. I watched the color leach out of Laycee's face and saw her eyes become huge blue saucers of incomprehensible fear. I wished more than ever that I hadn't made Sebastian leave. Not because I thought he could overpower Katja. I doubted angels were physically stronger than vampires, but he might have been able to give me some idea of what to do next. And if not, I was reasonably sure we'd reached the point where seeing his wings would be a lot less shocking than seeing a vampire's fangs. And infinitely preferable. Whether Laycee would have believed her eyes was another matter, but I think she would have enjoyed looking at Sebastian. Yeah, I'm sure she would.

"Katja, you've gone to a lot of trouble tonight, so what's the game plan?" I spoke fast, hoping to penetrate her brain and turn her focus back on me. "We both know why you needed to get me out of my house, and now that's happened, what are you going to do next?" She turned her head and looked at me. The expression on her face was a little nonplussed, as if my asking was the last thing she expected. "You do have a plan, don't you?"

Laycee suddenly fell to her knees and began screaming. From the way she was beating at the hand holding her wrist, Katja must have been squeezing hard enough to break bones, if she hadn't already.

"Katja, please! I'll do whatever you want, but leave Laycee out of this. She doesn't need to be involved. She's already done what you wanted, and you know she can't hurt you."

Trying to strike a bargain with someone who's a hundred percent whack job is a really bad idea. Actually it's more than a bad idea, it's lunacy. Didn't stop me from trying, though, even if I knew deep down it was a lost cause.

I felt myself being impaled by dark violet eyes while Katja considered my proposal. She took her time, keeping hold of Laycee's wrist as she did so, and I saw the subtle movement of her fingers. In my head I could hear small bones grinding against each other. Beads of perspiration broke out across Laycee's forehead, and her face tuned a sickly shade of gray. I could only imagine the pain she was in, but she refused to let Katja see. She bowed her head so her hair hid her face. Launching myself at Katja would only guarantee Laycee more than a broken wrist. I needed to keep a clear head and find a way out of this nightmare. Broken bones could always be mended.

Coming to a decision, Katja opened her hand, and Laycee crumpled to the ground like a rag doll, her hand cradled against her chest.

"You know Gabriel will not come to save you," Katja cooed triumphantly.

It was nauseating knowing the trip to Canada had been nothing more than a ploy orchestrated by Katja's twisted mind. But Gabriel wasn't the only vampire I knew.

"Don't count on Aleksei to rescue you either," Katja added, reading my mind. "He has other concerns to deal with."

Despair couldn't describe the feeling that welled up inside me. Misery, hopelessness, dismay.

"What have you done to Aleksei?" It was foolishness to ask, but I was fond of the big guy and needed to know if he had been put in harm's way.

"He's at the hospital at his girlfriend's bedside, no doubt wringing his hands." Hunching her shoulders, she pantomimed the action.

"What's wrong with Anasztaizia?"

I fought hard not to let my panic show. It never crossed my mind that Anasztaizia might also be in danger. Katja curled her crimson lips as she approached me. The smile was one, I felt certain, that had been seen by many. No doubt right before she completely ruined their lives.

"A restaurant can be such a dangerous place, and who knew hot grease could do so much damage. Especially to such a pretty face." Katja tilted her head to one side. "Of course, Aleksei will get the very best doctor and, who knows, maybe he can save her sight, but"—she shrugged her shoulders before adding maliciously—"her face will never look the same. Too bad she is not vampire, yes?"

My fingers itched to grab a fistful of long black hair and yank it out by the roots before slapping the smug look off Katja's porcelain face. Anything to make her hurt the way I knew Aleksei was hurting right now. The big guy wouldn't care about Anasztaizia's face. His concern would be to make certain she survived Katja's vicious attack. But the beautiful Magyar would care. I knew Anasztaizia well enough to know that she enjoyed the admiring glances she received. If her situation turned as awful as Katja was suggesting, then Aleksei was going to have his work cut out for him. Anasztaizia would not want him to stay with her out of a sense of guilt or pity. Convincing her he felt otherwise would be quite a task.

Beyond Katja's shoulder I watched Laycee trying to get up from the ground. Bracing herself with her good arm, she struggled first to her knees and then to her feet. It took some effort, and by the time she was standing, her face was horribly pale. Her forehead shone with perspiration, and her upper lip glistened. She winced when she accidentally jostled her bad hand. It didn't silence her tongue, however.

"You do know . . . ," She paused, catching her breath and waiting for Katja to look at her, "you're one fucked-up bitch, right?"

Goading Katja with sarcasm was not the smartest move to make, and Laycee knew it. But she wasn't going to allow herself to be bullied either. Not even by a raven-haired vampire wearing a dress better suited to a hooker. Wearing expensive shoes with red soles just made her a high-priced hooker. I was so proud of my friend, I felt a lump in my throat.

"And you are like cockroach," Katja said in a voice that was like ice.

"Oh, you mean when the dust has cleared and you're all toast, I'll still be standing?"

"No," Katja snarled, "you are like something I can crush under my foot."

Moving fast, Katja grabbed a fistful of Jake's sweatshirt and swung Laycee up off the ground, holding her a few feet in the air at arm's length.

"Katja, stop!" I yelled, panic spilling into my voice. "Your fight is with me, not her." I punched her in the upper arm and damn near broke my hand. Her arm felt like a piece of iron pipe. "I'll do whatever you want," I repeated, "but only if you let Laycee go."

Opening her fist, Katja dropped Laycee to the ground. She landed awkwardly, stifling a whimper of pain as she protected her damaged hand. The sound brought a smile to Katja's face. I needed to end this, and now. Miss Psycho might be smiling, but it wasn't reaching her eyes. Whatever string was winding her up was close to snapping, which meant if I was going to save Laycee, it had to happen fast.

I took a deep breath, and forced myself to be calm. "Katja, what do you want?"

"I want you to give yourself to Oscar," she said, laughing maliciously.

CHAPTER 22

Laycee struggled to her knees again. "This is a joke, right?" she asked Katja.

Getting nothing but a cold stare in return, Laycee looked to me for confirmation. I wanted to agree with her, but I was busy processing the implications of Katja's demand.

"If you're thinking about blackmail, I gotta tell you that ain't gonna work," Laycee said. "Anyone who knows Rowan will tell you she's not the cheating kind, but if she was, you'd have to be out of your mind to think she'd fool around on Eye Candy. I mean, have you *seen* him?" She glanced at Oscar, and shuddered. "And you think she'd prefer that? Just not gonna happen," she added with a slow shake of her head.

"Oh, it's going to happen, I can assure you of that," Katja told her with chilling conviction.

"Lady, you're not just crazy, you're completely certifiable!"

"If you don't want your other wrist broken, I suggest you hold your tongue."

The menace in Katja's tone brought me wheeling back into their conversation, and I gave Laycee a warning look. Provoking Katja wasn't going to help anything, and, as grateful as I was for the defense of my honor, I had no way to explain to Laycee that in this particular instance *giving* didn't mean what she thought it did. Satisfied that Laycee wasn't going to let her tongue run away with her, at least not for the next few minutes, I turned my attention to the pathetic creature that had once been a handsome, vibrant vampire. Oscar's gait seemed to be worsening. He stumbled around the parked BMW, bouncing off the side a couple of times and almost losing his balance. It was difficult to know if he was losing muscle control in his legs or his eyesight was failing. Either was a possibility. He must have sensed me watching him because he stopped moving and turned around to stare back at me. Knowing his present condition was not his own doing didn't stop revulsion from rising in me. His off-focus gaze and the long, glistening strands of saliva falling from his slack jaw brought to mind an incident from my childhood. One involving a rabid dog.

I was young, no more than six or seven, when the dog slunk into our yard through a loose fence slat. I didn't see it at first because it stood in the middle of my dad's prize hydrangeas, shaking from head to tail. When I did notice it, I told it to shoo and called it a bad doggie, knowing how cross my dad would be if it started digging. The dog didn't dig, but neither did it go away. It didn't have the look of an animal that was used to fending for itself. This had, until recently, been someone's family pet. Now it had gotten itself caught at the wrong end of a bite, and it was suffering. I watched, wide-eyed, as it began to stagger about, snapping and growling at the big pink blossoms. White foam slathered its muzzle and fell in long viscous strands. It became a moment filled with firsts for me. My first rabid dog, my first awareness of firearms, and my first experience with death.

I never realized my dad was there until he moved past me carrying the rifle. As young as I was, I knew what he was going to do, and so did the dog. It didn't try to run, it didn't move at all. It just stood there, as still as its trembling limbs would allow, whimpering softly and waiting for my dad to put an end to its misery. And for a moment, no more than a heartbeat or two, the madness brought about by the awful disease disappeared. A look of sorrow mixed with gratitude filled its big brown eyes as my dad squeezed the trigger.

A similar look now filled Oscar's eyes. Just like the rabid dog, he had no control over the impulses that were driving his behavior, impulses I was certain would only get worse as his downward spiral progressed. What functioning reason still remained would soon be stripped away, leaving only primal instinct driving his will to survive. Unfortunately, I didn't have a handy machete in my back pocket to take his head off with, and I'm not sure I could have done it even if I had.

"Don't you mean you want me to feed Oscar?" I asked Katja.

She shrugged her shoulders. "If you prefer."

"Ro?" I could hear fear threading itself back through Laycee's voice. "What's she talking about?"

"Your super best friend is going to give him her blood," Katja said, turning to Laycee with a malicious grin.

I think, on some level, I'd known this was what Katja had in mind ever since I'd seen Oscar's pitiful condition. Still, hearing her actually admit it sent an icy chill through me. My brain began scrambling through everything both Anasztaizia and Aleksei had told me about vampire feeding. Oscar was in such a bad way, it was a good bet he wouldn't be able to stop until I was dead or pretty close to it. Which, for Katja, was the whole point.

"You know Gabriel will never forgive you for this," I told her coldly.

"Too bad he's not here to stop me then, isn't it?" She closed the distance between us and put a hand beneath my chin. "Since we last saw each other I've been busy, Little One, learning about what you are. Did you know the first time a Promise gives their blood, it can only be to the vampire they are intended for? It's physically impossible for any other to feed from them before this has happened. Do you know why?" Without waiting for my response, she leaned in closer and put her lips next to my ear. "To make sure the wrong vampire doesn't accidentally drain them. Now tell me, Little One, why would that be so important? What makes you so special that only a Fallen can have you the first time?"

She leaned back, and her nails scraped lightly along either side of my jaw. I wasn't sure if I believed her, although it made sense in a weird way. Maybe it was more than dumb luck that had prevented me from crossing paths with any vampires before I met Gabriel. Then again, maybe I had and just didn't know it.

"Of course, once you have allowed a feeding to happen, your protection is gone. You are just like cow waiting to become steak on plate . . ." She trailed off, her fingers scraping lightly down my throat before stopping at the juncture of my neck and shoulder. "What is this hold that you have over him, hmmm?"

"We like the same movies," I said dryly.

Katja's information, whatever the source, had not gone far enough. If she had any idea that I possessed Gabriel's soul, she wouldn't have been able to resist flaunting the extent of her knowledge. She said nothing because she didn't know. She had only scratched the surface of what a Promise was.

Dropping her hand from my shoulder, she made a half-turn away from me, snapped back, and bitch-slapped me across the face. Her strength was incredible. I think I actually went a little bit airborne before falling back against the side of the POS. I banged my head on the driver's-side door hard enough to almost make me black out. Everything went blurry for a few moments, spots of light dancing behind my eyelids. I think it was a full minute before I could focus again.

"Stop fucking with me," Katja snarled, glaring at me. The rage in her eyes was now simmering over into a full, roiling boil. I thought for a moment that she might just end it here and now. I wouldn't put it beyond her capability to yank my heart out through my chest if she wanted to. But that would leave Laycee vulnerable, and I still had to find a way to get her to the safety of my house.

The sound of retching coming from behind the beemer pulled Katja's attention away from me. She hurried back toward the vehicle, presumably to tend to Oscar. He had been leaning against the car but now seemed to have either slid or fallen to the ground. Taking advantage of this momentary respite, Laycee hustled to my side. Bewildered, angry, and scared to death, she did her best to hide those feelings. Things were happening that she couldn't explain, and I knew her well enough to know that part of her anger was directed at me. It was obvious I knew more than I was letting on, and I understood exactly where she was coming from. I'd felt the same way only a short while ago when I'd learned the truth about Gabriel. Sadly, I couldn't change anything, couldn't turn the clock back and make everything the way it was before. I reached for her hand and squeezed it, grateful that she didn't pull away.

"What's going on, Rowan? Who *are* these people?"

Katja had disappeared behind the BMW and was now out of sight. I might not be able to see her, but the cold night air carried her voice clearly enough. She was murmuring something to Oscar in a low, soothing tone. The words were foreign, but the melodic cadence sounded almost like it belonged in a baby's nursery—an idea that repulsed me more than the prospect of having Oscar slobber all over me.

"Laycee, do you trust me?" I kept my own voice as low as possible.

The sound of more retching cut off Katja's voice, followed by a moan of pain. It sounded as if Oscar had just vomited up something vital, and Laycee wrinkled her nose in distaste. I squeezed her fingers until she turned and looked at me.

"Do you trust me?" I repeated.

A worried frown appeared. "Of course I trust you—why, what are you going to do?" In an instant she looked more confused than worried. "What the fuck's going on, Rowan?"

"Later. I promise I'll tell you everything later, but right now I have to get you to a safe place." I gave what I hoped was a reassuring smile. "You need to get inside the house. You'll be safe there. Neither of them can cross the threshold and you mustn't invite them in, even if they say they can compel you to."

I was desperately counting on Laycee to call for help. I was certain all three of the sheriff's office vehicles descending on my property with sirens wailing and lights flashing would be too many witnesses for any vampire to deal with.

"Can't cross a threshold?" Laycee's eyes had become huge blue saucers. "Are you saying they're . . . they're—oh my god! *You mean her teeth are for real?*"

"Hush!" Her voice was rising, and I couldn't afford to underestimate Katja's audible range.

"You can't be serious!" she hissed at me.

"It doesn't matter what you believe, but you've got to trust me when I say the shit's about to hit the fan. And it's going to make everything so much worse if you don't get inside the house." I jerked on her good hand to make sure I had her full attention. "Do you understand what I'm saying?"

She nodded. "Yeah, sure . . . get inside the house . . . don't invite them in." A single tear unexpectedly rolled down the side of her nose. "Why do I need to be in the house again?"

I took a breath. Despite her question, Laycee really was handling this so much better than I could have hoped. "You'll be safe there," I told her.

"But . . . what about you?"

"I know how to deal with them." That was stretching the truth, but I wasn't about to tell her anything different. "Katja is going to try to use us against each other, and we can't let that happen."

"What do you want me to do?" she asked, blinking furiously in an effort to hide her tears.

"When I give the signal, I want you to run as fast as you can." I couldn't risk Laycee's making a dash for it now because I needed to be close enough to Katja to be a problem she would be forced to deal with. I might be able to buy Laycee only a few extra seconds, but sometimes that's all you need. "Do not, under any circumstances, stop or look back until you are through the front door. Understand?" She nodded. "I'm really sorry I didn't tell you about, well, things that were going on. I promise when this is all over, we're going to have a very long conversation."

She started to say something, hesitated, and then decided to ask it anyway. "Is Eye Candy . . . ?"

There was no way I could lie to her now, not after what she'd seen. "Yeah, he is."

"Really? Oh wow, guess that explains why the sex is so good!"

The only thing that stopped me from bursting into tears was the sudden silence from behind the BMW. Katja's murmuring voice no longer reached us.

Moving away from the POS, I looked for the weakened vampire but didn't see him and took this as a sign he was no longer able to stand. A definite check mark in my favor.

"What's wrong with Oscar?" I asked Katja, taking a casual step toward her. Behind me, Laycee took her own step—in the opposite direction. "He sounds pretty bad."

"Nothing that you can't make right," the psycho vampire sneered at me.

"Yeah, about that"—I took another couple of steps and casually moved to my left, hopefully blocking Katja's line of sight. Her arrogance in assuming Laycee was paralyzed with fear would, I prayed, be my ace in the hole. With a hand on her hip, Katja pivoted and followed my lead. "I don't think Gabriel's going to stand for me feeding another vampire, what with him being so possessive and all."

Her amethyst eyes narrowed as she considered what I'd said. I knew she wouldn't be surprised by my refusal, and agreeing right away would have sent up red warning flags of suspicion. I took a few more baby steps in her direction, hopping from foot to foot as if I was trying to stop my toes from cramping. Still having my slippers on helped with the illusion. Katja was now about an arm's length away. I had no idea how close to the house Laycee was, and I couldn't risk looking over my shoulder, but I could sense she was closer to the porch steps than she was to me.

Blowing out an impatient breath, Katja took her own step toward me, but one of her stiletto heels got caught in the gap between the driveway paving stones, throwing her off-balance. I couldn't have planned it any better. It was the only chance I would get and I took it.

"LAYCEEEEE—RUUUUUUUNNNN!"

I launched myself at the Goth Queen, head-butting her in the midsection and wrapping my arms around her in a bear hug. Watching all those football games on TV had finally come in useful. I'd sacked the quarterback, popping her off her expensive high heels and putting her on the ground. There was a gratifying *whuff* of breath as I landed on top of her. She definitely had not expected me to attack her.

That's what you get for being such an arrogant bitch!

The element of surprise lasted only as long as it took Katja to catch a breath. It was like trying to hold on to a giant eel. I had barely a moment to gloat before a sharp pain in my side had me sucking in air, and I was being flipped over onto my back. Straddling me, Katja started screaming something completely unintelligible as she banged my head on the ground a couple of times. Then she dropped her fangs. For a moment I thought she was going to bite me herself, but Laycee's sudden break for safety distracted her.

Seeing her guarantee of my cooperation making a run for it, Katja shrieked again. I turned my head and through watery eyes saw that Laycee had gone completely deer-in-the-headlights. She had stopped moving and was not as close to the porch steps as I had hoped. I'd told her not to look back, but I guess the shrieking banshee act had been too compelling. I didn't blame her. I would have done the same thing.

With Laycee frozen in place, Katja took hold of my face, her fingers digging in and squeezing my cheeks painfully. "You stupid bitch," she snarled, "you can't beat me! You're too weak!"

As she started to get off me, I saw one last chance to prove her wrong. "LAYCEE—RUN!" I screamed, launching myself upward and grabbing a fistful of long black hair.

There's a reason why, when girls fight, you see a lot of hair pulling. It damn well hurts, for one thing, and nothing is more devastating than seeing a chunk of your hair in your opponent's hand. I was banking on female vampires having the same reaction. Yanking really hard, I smiled at the feel of silken strands wrapped around my fingers.

Galvanized by my second yell, Laycee snapped out of her dazed state and took off like a jackrabbit. I watched her clear the steps in a single leap before throwing herself through the still-open front door. She hit the hallway carpet runner and, from the sound of it, went crashing into the narrow side table. I had put a planter of blooming amaryllis there, and the sound of Laycee's scream suggested she had momentarily forgotten about her broken wrist, and tried to catch the heavy container as it fell. The string of cursing was music to my ears.

Even the swiftest vampire can be slowed down if they have to drag an extra hundred and fifty pounds or so behind them. Katja was no exception. Her scream of rage at seeing Laycee sail through the front door nearly shattered my eardrums. Grabbing the hair at the nape of her neck, she twisted around and kicked off one of her high heels, catching it effortlessly in one hand and holding it above her head like a weapon. Certain I was about to get a four-inch stiletto heel buried in my skull, I let go of her hair, and covered my head with both hands. The sound of breaking glass made me look up. Katja had thrown her shoe through the windshield of the POS, breaking it.

Kicking off the other shoe, she bent over me. I could smell the anger and frustration coming off her. It reminded me of rotten eggs and sour milk. I looked up just in time to see five bright-red razors arcing down toward me, and turned my head to one side. I was fast, but not fast enough to escape vampire speed. I saved my eye, but her nails still managed to slice open my right cheek. My face exploded in a ball of flame as blood began gushing. I bit my tongue, refusing to give Katja the satisfaction of hearing me cry out. Things got a little fuzzy after that.

Katja vented her temper by kicking me. I curled into a ball, protecting myself as best I could. I felt something wet and sticky on the back of my head. It seemed the smack-down onto the concrete had been a little rougher than I had thought. With the back of my head bleeding, as well as my face, Oscar might be a few pints short by the time he got a shot at me. The giggle that spontaneously erupted at this thought earned me a vicious kick. I'm pretty sure Katja broke a rib . . . maybe two.

CHAPTER 23

I thought Katja might succeed in pulling my arm from the socket the way she yanked me to my feet. Stumbling, I followed her toward the BMW, where a starving vampire waited to feast on me. Blood was running from my slashed cheek and dripping off my chin. I guess Oscar's sense of smell was still working okay, because he suddenly crawled out from behind the POS. If he hadn't been so weak, I'm certain he could have vaulted over the roof of the car and been at my neck while Katja was still rearranging my ribs with her foot. I watched in horror as he dug his claw-like nails into the ground and hauled himself forward. To judge from the way his nostrils were flaring and the ribbons of drool overflowing his mouth, the smell of fresh blood was driving him ape-shit. Katja stopped moving. My midriff felt like it was on fire, and I wrapped my free arm around it as I stared at the pathetic creature on the ground. He was looking more and more like the rabid dog of my memory, and the thought of him being at my throat made me shudder in revulsion. It all seemed so unreal, like I was in a really bad slasher movie.

Thank God Laycee was safe.

Katja jerked on my arm, forcing me to look at her. The crimson lips twisted in a malevolent smile, and I knew she'd driven off the side of the road into crazy-land. She opened her mouth to say something, but whatever insight she wanted to share was suddenly drowned out by the sound of a car's engine as it roared up the driveway. Yanking me closer, the Goth Queen moved behind me.

"Coward," I told her, earning a punch in my side that doubled me over in agony.

Digging her hand into my shoulder, Katja pulled me upright as a big black vehicle came into view. It looked like something from one of those old movies they show on TV after midnight, the kind only true insomniacs watch. The passenger-side door opened while the car was still moving, and I saw Gabriel jump out. Landing on the balls of his feet, he straightened up and stared at me. I'd forgotten what a mess the right side of my face must have been until I saw him pull his brows together, his face turning as dark as thunder. He'd been pretty mad at the black eye Suellen DuPree had given me. I could only imagine how much worse I looked right now. Somehow I didn't think Katja was going to be able to crab-hop her way out of this one.

"Rowan, love? Are you all right?"

My heart literally tried to jump out of my chest at the sound of his voice. I don't know how, but I managed to put a wobbly smile on my face while I blinked back tears at the same time. Physically I was a wreck, and I'm pretty sure Gabriel could catalog each bruise and every scratch on me with one look. But his question had another purpose. Of course he needed reassurance about my welfare; that went without saying, but the sound of my voice would tell him how close I was to going over the edge of my mental cliff. I figured I had a ways to go yet.

"I've had better days," I told him. "How was moose country?"

"Didn't go."

"Ah. Change of plans?"

"Didn't seem much point in going without you, babe."

Behind me Katja shifted slightly. "You really should let me go," I murmured over my shoulder, knowing that every vampire in my front yard could hear me just fine. Her response was to tighten the grip she had on my arm and shoulder. My awkward shrug was for Gabriel's benefit. "Okay, it's your funeral," I murmured.

"No, Little One," she hissed in my ear, "I'm thinking it will be yours."

The sudden prick at the side of my neck told me she'd dropped her fangs, and a tendril of pure, undiluted fear released itself inside me.

I don't know how long it takes your garden-variety vampire to drain a human body of blood. I would imagine there are all sorts of variables that need to be taken into account—body weight, for example, the amount of force a vampire can exert with each sucking pull, the probable lack of cooperation of the victim, things like that. What I do know is that the average human body has between ten and twelve pints of blood and doesn't actually need to be drained for a fatality to occur. All Katja needed to do was make sure I lost enough blood to send me into traumatic shock, something I wouldn't be able to come back from without professional medical help—and a blood bank. Neither of which was currently in my front yard.

The big black car had come to a complete stop and the engine shut off. I think we all held our breath—well, all of us except Oscar. If he held his breath, he might not be able to get it going again. I didn't want to take my eyes from Gabriel's face, but I automatically looked over when the door opened. Just human nature, I guess. The driver got out, and I felt a strange twisting sensation in the center of my chest. It was Gabriel—or would have been if his hair was coal black and his eyes silver.

The new party crasher was dressed in black leather pants, but either hadn't had time to find a shirt or didn't think wearing one was necessary. Truthfully, he didn't need one. Shirtless was a good look for him. A very good look. Walking around to the front of the car, he stood next to Gabriel. Bad and badder, with a few minor differences. This guy's tats were across his chest, the glyphs similar to the ones down Gabriel's back. And I didn't need him to turn around to know that there would be two crescent-shaped scars on his back where he'd once had wings.

My gaze alternated between Gabriel and the newcomer. They could almost be twins, the physical similarity was so great. I also didn't need to be told the new addition to our playgroup was also a vampire. As if he read my mind, he ran out his fangs for show. They were, I noticed, much longer than Gabriel's.

I had momentarily forgotten about Katja because my attention had been completely focused on this new vampire. But now I could feel her shaking behind me. Whoever this new guy was, she was definitely afraid of him. More afraid, I would say, than when she had decided to take on Gabriel.

"Rowan, I'd like you to meet Ryiel." Using the honeyed tone of voice that could melt my spine, Gabriel introduced us.

Ryiel? I'd heard the name before, but couldn't for the life of me think where. And then it came to me. He was Katja's maker. The Original Vampire who'd changed her at the request of a Carpathian goat herder named Vladimir. I was about to speak when the most god-awful howl filled the air. It was a sound tempered with frustration and pain. With the unexpected arrival of Gabriel and Ryiel, Oscar had been forgotten. Two heads, one white, one black, turned to look at the ground behind them.

"What is *that?*" Ryiel asked, making no attempt to hide his disgust.

His voice was a deeper, rougher version of Gabriel's, and I was glad for the distinction. I don't think I would have survived two vampires who could make my insides perform cartwheels just by saying hello. There was also something in his tone that made me think Ryiel was a vampire of few words, but when he did speak, everyone listened. I held my breath as he slowly walked over to Oscar's prostrate form.

Having used the last of his reserves to pull himself past the parked cars, the vampire who had once hailed from the plains of Kansas collapsed in complete and utter exhaustion. Too weak to even lift his head, he began sobbing pitifully into the hard ground. Part of me was surprised he had enough moisture left in his body to produce tears, and, even though I was revolted by his condition, I couldn't help the swell of compassion that swept through me. As far as I was concerned, being nice to me didn't warrant this type of punishment.

"She starved him," I yelled at the two Original Vampires. "Deliberately."

Katja, not appreciating my comment, jabbed me viciously in my other side. A searing pain flared, making me suck in a breath, but I decided it was worth it. I wanted to be sure she couldn't make up some excuse to get out of being punished for this despicable deed, assuming she was even going to be allowed to speak in her own defense. The look on Gabriel's face was very expressive. It said *snowball* and *hell*.

Oscar was now whimpering, and I watched as Ryiel knelt by his side. The cold night air carried the low rumble of the Original Vampire's voice, and I hoped that whatever he was saying to Oscar, it was kind. And then I saw the muscles in Ryiel's back bunch and flex, and clearly heard the sound of a sharp retort, like the starting pistol for a race. Oscar fell silent.

Ryiel stood up and resumed his place next to Gabriel, and I became aware of two things. The first was, as I'd thought, he also carried scars on each shoulder blade similar to those Gabriel had, and the second was that Oscar no longer had his head. Actually, that wasn't strictly accurate. He did still have his head, only now it was on the ground by his feet instead of being attached to his neck. The world as I knew it began to tilt again. I almost laughed out loud because I realized that, if not for Katja's iron grip on my arm, I'd probably fall down. I felt certain it would be the last time I was going to be grateful to her for anything.

In my head I heard Gabriel's voice speaking to me.

Stay strong, Rowan . . . this is almost over . . .

It certainly was for Oscar, whose only crime that I knew of was being in the wrong place at the wrong time and hooking up with the wrong vampire. Why couldn't he have met Gabriel, like Aleksei did? The sudden thought of the big guy made me jerk my head up.

"Aleksei needs your help, Gabriel. I think Anasztaizia might be hurt."

A flash of anger crossed his face before he quickly smoothed it away. "It will all be taken care of," he promised, still using the same voice that now had my stomach doing a lazy roll.

I figured the stress of the situation was playing havoc with my hormones, because the sound of Gabriel's voice was making me aroused. I couldn't help it, but it felt horribly inappropriate under the circumstances.

Thankfully, Ryiel stepped forward, and I was able to focus my attention on him. His expression was stern as he stared at Katja, making me wonder how to judge their relationship. I knew he was the vampire who'd turned her, but did that mean he regarded her as his child? His offspring? His progeny? I made a mental note to ask Gabriel how vampires refer to the humans they have changed, and if there was any affectionate bond between them after the deed is done. From the look on Ryiel's face, it wouldn't seem so. He gave all the appearance of being one very pissed-off vampire, and I'd be lying if I didn't say I wanted him to punish Katja. At the very least snap her wrist just as she'd done to Laycee. But I kept quiet, trusting in Gabriel.

It will all be taken care of, I promise you.

I could live with that. It was enough to know Katja had stepped over a pretty significant line, and was hip-deep in trouble.

"Let the Promise go," Ryiel's voice boomed.

For a moment I didn't know who he was talking about. And then I realized it was me. The way he said the word *Promise*, it made me sound as if I was the most important thing in the whole world. Behind me Katja sucked in a breath. I could sense her hesitation, but it took a few more seconds before I understood the reason why. She was actually contemplating defying Ryiel, trying to decide whether disobedience was worth the risk. I couldn't believe she would even consider doing such a thing. Was she that stupid, or that crazy?

She shifted her weight from foot to foot, and I glanced down to see she was wearing her shoes again. How had she gotten them back, especially the one she'd thrown at the POS? I had no idea, but from the hoppy dance she was doing, I was tempted to ask if they were pinching her toes.

"Katja! I will not ask again." Ryiel's voice was now harsh and unforgiving. I got the impression he wasn't the most patient of vampires. "Let the Promise return to Gabriel."

The mention of my boyfriend's name jolted Katja out of whatever stupor she was in danger of sinking into. I also think it forced her to make up her mind, but I didn't think it was going to be a good decision on her part. Flexing her fingers, she repositioned her hands on my arm and shoulder, tightening her hold. Another sucking breath hissed like a snake next to my ear.

"Does she really mean more to you than I could ever be?" Katja asked Gabriel.

I honestly didn't know whether to laugh or cry. What was it going to take for her to accept that if she was the last female on the planet, Gabriel still wouldn't want her. He never had. Ever. I was always his, from that first moment in the clearing. And he was mine. Some hearts were just meant to be together, and that's what Katja refused to acknowledge and could never understand.

"It has always been Rowan," Gabriel answered in a husky voice, keeping his eyes fixed on me. "And it always will be."

I could feel my heart breaking because I loved him so much, and he didn't know I was going to give him up. Now, more than ever, I knew I could not allow him to refuse to take back his soul.

Behind me Katja shrugged, and I could feel something had changed. Had she finally recognized her romantic pursuit of Gabriel was a futile one? That she would never have a relationship with him of any kind? Better late than never . . . I guess.

"Then you had best enjoy her while you can," she said right before she sank her fangs into my neck and dragged her teeth along the length of my shoulder, flaying me open.

"GAAABRIELLLLL!"

The pain was indescribable and almost obliterated the searing burn from my broken ribs that screaming Gabriel's name produced. I couldn't move because Katja had clamped her hands on my arms, pinning them to my sides, effectively immobilizing me while she continued to wreak havoc on my neck.

When Gabriel took my blood I was able to feel what he felt, and assumed it was the bond between us that allowed such a personal link. Being able to feel a similar connection to Katja was almost as horrifying as being attacked by her in the first place. It was also disgustingly intimate. The first mouthful of my blood that she drew up was filled with the hatred and animosity she felt toward me; but then, after pushing past those destructive emotions, I got a glimpse of what had made her this way.

I saw her as a child, a beautiful young girl not yet in her teens, dressed in silks and satins, with ribbons adorning her lustrous dark hair. From the style of fashion, and the manner in which her hair was dressed, I'd guess Katja grew up in the mid-1600s. Her life, however, was appalling. A pretty doll used by those with power and money, she was passed from bed to bed to satisfy the most depraved of sexual appetites. I couldn't decide which was more horrifying—the abuse itself, or Katja's belief that being treated this way was acceptable. And reminding myself that these were different times didn't make it better.

Furious that she had inadvertently shared such intimacies with me, Katja used her fangs to rip and tear my skin. She now had another reason to hate me, though I doubt she needed one. I gasped, and whatever images I might have had of Katja's childhood were swallowed up by a black hole of excruciating pain. I had never experienced anything like this, and I could feel my chances of survival dwindling with each passing second. Katja's fangs were inflicting as much damage as possible in order to maximize my blood loss. The realization made me think of the woman Gabriel had executed. Bad luck for me Katja didn't possess the skill or finesse to make it happen in a controlled, efficient manner. This was going to be as messy as she could possibly make it, and I knew that was for Gabriel's benefit. By the time she was done, my neck was going to look like a pack of hyenas had been chewing on me.

I didn't know how much time had passed when I fell to my knees—three, maybe four seconds?—but everything was moving in slow motion. Gabriel must have been in shock because he hadn't made a move toward me. Surely one good smack alongside Katja's head and she'd be persuaded to let go of me. And if that smack resulted in an accidental decapitation, I'd give him my word I wouldn't lose any sleep over it. Lord knows I was going to cry more for poor Oscar than for the Goth Queen. And then I understood what was wrong. Gabriel couldn't make a move on Katja while Ryiel was here. It would be wrong of him. Ryiel was her maker, and it was his place to deal with her.

In the meantime . . . I was dying.

The shock of feeling Katja release her hold on my neck and arms at the same time was like a jolt of electricity through my system. I was too far out of it to even try and use my hands in an attempt to stanch the flow of blood. I knew it would be nothing but a wasted effort. I imagined I was doing a passable imitation of a blown Texas oil well, only the blood flow couldn't be capped.

Slumping over on my side, I saw Ryiel had his hand wrapped

around Katja's throat and he was holding her up off the ground. Letting go of me was not her choice, it would seem, and even though her face was turning blue and her eyes were bulging unattractively, she was fighting him with everything she had. Reluctantly, I had to admire her. Crazy or not, she wasn't going to go away peaceably. If she was a guy she'd have had a massive set of balls. Unfortunately for Katja, Ryiel was not as impressed as I was by her tenacious nature. With an angry snarl, he flicked his wrist, and Katja went completely limp in his grasp. He dropped her to the ground, where she landed like a rag doll. I could only assume he'd broken her neck, and I thought about how unfair that was. Katja would be up and running around in no time at all, while I was still gonna be deader than the proverbial doornail.

By now I could barely feel the blood running down my arm. How much had I lost? I was trying to remember how long it took me to fill a bag when I donated at the last Red Cross blood drive. Five minutes? Less? More? I didn't recall, but I was getting light-headed. There had to be at least a pint or more soaked into my pajamas, and I was fairly confident just as much had seeped into the ground by now. And it wasn't stopping. I was feeling shaky and cold and disoriented. I was becoming an expert at going into shock.

I couldn't seem to remember why I was outside, but I knew Gabriel was there. There was something I had to tell him, something important. I needed him to know how sorry I was . . . sorry that I wasn't strong enough . . . sorry that I'd failed him . . . and how very much I loved him. I was trying not to close my eyes. In all the movies I've seen, once the badly injured person closes their eyes, it's all over. I didn't want that, not yet, but it was really hard trying to keep them open. I'd never felt so tired. I reckoned I could sleep for a week, and I was feeling cold. Really cold.

You do know you're dying, right? my inner bitch informed me.

No shit! Good to know one of us still has a firm grasp on the obvious.

"ROWAN!"

I could hear the panic in Gabriel's voice, and I was getting a little miffed that it was taking him so long to reach me.

What's the point of all that speed vampires are famous for if they don't use it? But maybe he needs to take his time. He's got to be able to lie convincingly when I ask him how bad off I am. God knows, I'm a mess, and—oh shit!—he doesn't know Laycee's in the house. I've got to tell him that, and also tell him she knows he's a vampire. I think, under the circumstances, he'll forgive me. And for some reason I'm thinking about taking a trip to Kansas, except I can't remember what for. What's in Kansas except Dorothy and Toto, and why would I go for that? My most hated movie of all time was *The Wizard of Oz*. Maybe, if I just closed my eyes for a moment and rested, I'd remember what was so important about Kansas. Maybe, if I took a little nap, I'd remember a lot of other things when I woke up. And I really needed a nap because I was so tired I could sleep for a month . . .

"Rowan . . . Rowan . . ."

Jeez, I must have the absolute worst case of CRS in recorded history because I know I know that voice calling my name. I just can't place it.

"Rowan . . . open your eyes for me."

It's a great voice, warm and persuasive and kind of sexy, too. But it's not my type of sexy, and opening my eyes is going to take a whole lot more persuading than that. I can be quite stubborn when I set my mind to it.

"Don't want to," I mumbled petulantly, ". . . tired . . ."

"You can sleep later, Rowan."

Something was tickling my ear, which was annoying as hell. I tried to slap it away but instead I caught it in my fingers. It was long and silky, and despite my better judgment I opened my eyes. It was a feather. Red and gold, it shimmered in my hand, promising the most glorious sunrise. Or sunset.

"I've found your loophole," Sebastian whispered in my ear.

CHAPTER 24

I wasn't that surprised to find myself at the Void. It was, after all, where my life with Gabriel had truly begun. And it was fitting I should return, although I wasn't sure why Sebastian had brought me here. Getting to my feet, I looked around. The only light that I could see was coming from the Void itself, and as that was in constant motion, the light was also forever moving. Splashes of brightness randomly thrown against enormous cavern walls illuminated the dense blackness with a momentary brilliance. It reminded me of some kid going crazy with a paintball gun.

Tipping back my head, I looked up, but the light didn't reach that far, so all I could see was endless darkness. There was no sky because this place, wherever it was, was not above ground. It was deep within the bowels of the earth. I was standing on one side of a vast abyss. Was it really this big the last time I was here? I don't remember. Back then, all I was focused on was Gabriel. I paid no attention to my surroundings. The Void had served a purpose, and once it was accomplished, I thought no more about it.

Carefully I checked my neck, expecting to feel the butchery wrought by Katja's fangs. But my skin was surprisingly smooth, with not even a scratch to show for the attack. I moved the flat of my hand across my shoulder, but once again the skin was unbroken. Staring at my palm, I fully expected to see it stained with blood, but it was perfectly clean. I wasn't bleeding, which could only be a good thing, and I was able to stand without help, which was even better. I raised my arm, moving it experimentally above my head, flexing my elbow, wrist, and fingers. Everything seemed to be working just fine. Gingerly I took in a breath, and then a deeper one. My fingers made their way down my sides, pushing lightly against my ribs. They didn't hurt, so I took the deepest breath I could stand and exhaled slowly. I guess whoever fixed my neck also took care of my ribs.

I was almost too afraid to feel my face, but I knew I'd only torture myself if I didn't, so I raised a hand to my cheek and glided it over the skin. It was as smooth as the proverbial baby's backside. I was almost ashamed at the depth of the relief I felt.

Now I couldn't help the tears that trickled down my face. Certain earlier that I would be scarred for life, I couldn't believe how lucky I was to escape Katja's cruelty.

Of course, there was always another explanation.

"Am I dead?"

"Not quite, but it's not from lack of trying, I see." Sebastian actually sounded pissed.

"Sorry, I just wanted to be sure. It would be embarrassing to think I wasn't when I really was."

"Why, what do you think you would do?"

"I don't know," I told him with a shrug. "I just wanted to know."

"Well, you're not dead." His mouth curved in a sly smile. "Would you like me to prove it?"

Despite the infectiousness of his smile, I decided to pass. "As I recall, you were quite disappointed by the results the last time you did that."

"I'm willing to try again if you are. It might be different here."

"I don't think Gabriel would like it, no matter where we are."

"No," the angel agreed, reluctantly, "I don't suppose he would."

Vaguely I recalled Sebastian holding me in his arms and carrying me away. I could still hear Gabriel screaming my name and the sound of his boots pounding on the concrete slabs as he raced to reach my side, but it was too little too late, as the saying goes. Sebastian had already taken me away.

"He will forgive you," he reassured me. "When he knows what you have done for him, he will forgive you."

Dear God, I hope so.

I wondered if I'd disappeared completely or if there was another *me* lying in my driveway with a chewed-up neck? A sort of shell or shadow to occupy my space until I'd done whatever it was I was supposed to do here. And if so, would anyone notice the difference? I knew Gabriel would be able to tell because I could no longer feel the bond between us. Presumably neither could he. It didn't feel like it had been cut, nothing so permanent. It just felt like a few strands had started to unravel. They were going to need to be woven back together if I wanted to repair the connection between us, but maybe after this I wouldn't need to.

I questioned Sebastian about the possibility of a shadow self occupying my place in the real world.

"What is real, Rowan?"

Oh great! Now he decided to go all cryptic and ambiguous on me. Well, I don't do cryptic. Or ambiguous. Or even obscure.

"Is there still a version of me in my world, the one we just left behind? The one where Gabriel still is?" I couldn't be more straightforward than that.

"Yes, there is," he confirmed, telling me that as long as I continued to breathe here, I would breathe there. The trick was to not stop doing it. That was good to know because I didn't want Gabriel grieving for me prematurely. Not when I was actually feeling pretty good right now. Sebastian seemed amused by my reaction to this. I had no idea why, because it seemed perfectly logical to me. "Still don't believe it?" Sebastian asked, completely misreading the expression on my face. Before I could respond, he pinched me on the arm—hard.

"Ow!"

"Not dead—get it?"

"Okay, okay, I get it. I'm not dead!" My arm smarted, and I rubbed it. Having an extra joint in his fingers meant he could really put some oomph behind that pinch. I decided not to give him a reason to do it again.

"What happened, Rowan?"

I gave him a quick recap on everything he'd missed—which

meant everything that had happened from the moment I'd stepped outside my front door in response to Laycee's text message.

"It was a ruse?"

"Yeah, it was a ruse," I agreed.

"So you offered yourself in place of your friend."

I couldn't tell if he was more puzzled or disappointed by the notion. Either way, he didn't get it. "Of course," I told him. "She would have done the same for me."

"Would she? I wonder . . ."

His voice trailed off, and I decided to let it go. I had a feeling I could talk myself blue in the face and Sebastian still wouldn't understand why I thought it necessary to save Laycee. I sighed. Sebastian really didn't understand human relationships.

"I had no choice," I explained. "Katja used Laycee as bait, and I couldn't let my best friend in the whole world be terrorized by her . . . or worse. And besides"—I gave him one of my best smiles—"she intended Oscar to feed from me."

"Then why didn't he?"

"Things got out of hand." That was putting it mildly. "I honestly didn't think Katja was going to, you know . . ." With the first two fingers of my hand next to my open mouth, I parodied fangs. My ridiculously bad imitation made him grin in spite of himself.

"Surely you must have known what she intended?"

Yeah, well, there's knowing and *knowing*. I decided to bring us back to the reason we were there. "So, you found a loophole?"

"Actually . . . no, I don't think I have."

I stared at him. "But you told me you had. That's the only reason I agreed to come with you!"

"Rowan, let me—"

"Isn't there some sort of rule about angels not being allowed to lie?"

"You were dying, Rowan! If that happened, then Gabriel's soul would have remained trapped in your body and died with it. His refusal means it cannot be released in your world." His anger made me take a step back. "I didn't have enough time to search for a loophole; you didn't give me enough time. It's not like I can just look it up on the Internet."

I hadn't realized that Sebastian even knew what the Internet was.

He was pissed and with good cause, and I really couldn't blame him. After all, I *was* dying. "I told you you'd make a good escort."

My joke broke the tension, making him laugh. I put my hand on his arm and apologized. "So, is there anything we can do?"

"I think there may be a way, but this is all unproven. Nothing like this has ever happened before."

Now his face was filled with worry, only I wasn't sure which one of us he was more worried about. Me, Gabriel, or himself. I told him I'd take an unproven *maybe* over a definitive *no* any day of the week.

"What are you suggesting, Sebastian?"

"You must take the reason for Gabriel's decision out of his hands."

I must . . . do what? I stared at him, trying to grasp what it was he was saying by reading between the lines. I was pretty sure I had it, but I wanted to be certain. "Are you saying I . . . ?"

"Gabriel wouldn't take back his soul because it would mean also taking your life, but if that was no longer an issue . . ."

"Then he could return to being an angel."

"Precisely."

"So I guess going the whole bell, book, and candle route isn't going to work?"

He smiled at me, a sad, sorrowful look. "There's no time, Rowan. This is the only option left to you."

"I didn't think that was going to work anyway," I told him.

I blew out a breath. If I've learned one thing since accepting the possibility of running into supernatural creatures during a late-night visit to the supermarket, it's never to assume you know what they're talking about. Have them spell it out if necessary, every damn word. I got the part about me and my life, but what about Gabriel's soul? This was going to be a one-shot deal with no going back to try something else. If I was successful, I would remain a permanent resident of the Dark Realm. If I failed, I would remain a permanent resident of the Dark Realm. In either scenario, I was going to get a change of address.

"You said Gabriel's soul would die with my body in my world because he's refused it." The angel nodded, "So what happens to it when I die here?"

"Here you are in a different realm. If you die here, only your soul is forfeit. No matter what Gabriel may be now, his soul is that of a celestial being, and it cannot remain in the Dark Realm. Once released from your safekeeping, it will be returned to the Light to wait until it is reclaimed again."

"You're sure about that? Going back to the Light and everything?"

"Of this I am completely certain." His eyes glowed with an intensity I found a little frightening. They seemed unnaturally bright, but perhaps that was due to the lack of natural light.

"I'm dying back there, aren't I?"

He nodded, and I saw his eyes had become pools of fire. "You don't have much time left."

There was nothing else to say. Nothing for me to do except hope and pray that Gabriel would understand why I was doing this. That my sacrifice was all I could give him. That I loved him too much not to do this. And that, if there was a way, we would be together again. I guess I must have looked pretty awful, because Sebastian opened his wings and invited me to step inside his embrace. It was warm among the feathers, and as I laid my head against his chest, I inhaled the fragrance of sandalwood and myrrh. A sense of calm washed over me, making me feel safe.

"This will work, won't it, Sebastian? I mean, it's got to."

"No one can know for sure, Rowan. A Fallen has never refused to take back what was surrendered, so it is impossible to know what repercussions there may be. But"—putting a finger beneath my chin, he raised my head so I was now looking at him—"if there is any chance of success, then it has to be in your willingness to sacrifice everything for him."

I would take it because a tiny, microscopic chance was better than none at all. Rustling his feathers, Sebastian opened his wings, and I stepped out of the warm circle he had created, rubbing my arms at the sudden chill. He gave me what I'm sure he thought was a very reassuring smile. It was on the tip of my tongue to tell him that only his dentist would want to see that many teeth all at once, when it struck me that there were suddenly too many teeth in that smile. Way too many.

An angel can never give his soul to the Dark Realm, nor can he enter such a place while still in possession of it.

We were at the Void, a place that was not only within the boundaries of the Dark Realm; it was pretty much the heart of the place. And yet Sebastian was here with me. He was an angel, so how could that be? Narrowing my eyes, I took a few steps back, looking hard at him as I did so. Was it my imagination, or did he look different somehow? His wings, his hair, his skin? Everything about him seemed just a little darker than it had before. And it was a darkness that had nothing to do with the poor light. It was a darkness that came from within.

"Rowan?" The sound of my name was accompanied by a rustle of feathers, and as he spread them wide, I noticed very few that were now colored red or gold. Most of his feathers had turned completely black. "Rowan?" He said my name again, only this time it was coated with suspicion.

"How is it you can be here, Sebastian?" I challenged. "Angels cannot enter the Dark Realm in possession of their souls. You said so yourself!" I was feeling panicky, and the muscles in my throat were threatening to seize up.

He stared at me, his face a mix of curiosity and pride. Curiosity about what I would do next, and pride that I had been able to see him for what he truly was.

"My soul is . . . adrift," he said in a voice that told me any further explanations would not be forthcoming.

"Oh, Sebastian—no!" Conflicting emotions rolled through me, suddenly making me wonder if I could believe anything he'd told me in this place. Except this was Sebastian—and I liked him! "Perhaps I can help—"

"No!" he barked harshly. "Along with your fixation about dying, Rowan, I'm starting to think you have something of a hero complex. Gabriel, Laycee, a little old lady crossing the street. You can't save everyone, and you have to realize that not everyone wants to be saved." Staring at me, Sebastian softened the harshness of his tone with a smile. "Some decisions must be allowed to reach their own conclusions, Rowan. This is one time when you must accept that your concern would do more harm than good."

I flinched at the rebuke. He made it sound like I was the town busybody, poking my nose into things I shouldn't be and stirring up trouble. He must have sensed I was about to step back because his hand shot out and he caught hold of my arm. Those long fingers, which hadn't bothered me before, now seemed menacing as they overlapped my wrist. He flexed his fingers, and all I could think of were the small bones in Laycee's wrist grinding together as they were broken. She had to be on her way to the hospital by now, if not already there. I prayed Gabriel was with her. She would need someone to make sense of all she'd been through. It ought to be me, and I was suddenly furious that Sebastian had taken me away.

"What's happening to you, Sebastian? You're changing."

"It's being here. I cannot be this close to the Void without feeling its effects."

Sebastian was struggling with something; I had no idea what, but I didn't think it would be a good idea for me to hang around while he dealt with it.

"How do I do it, Sebastian?"

He stared at me, and I could tell he wasn't sure exactly what I was asking him. And then his eyes cleared and he understood. Lifting his head, he gestured to the abyss behind me. I turned. Of course. I had to give myself to the Void.

"There is another option," he said in a whisper.

I swung around to face him. "What other option?"

"You could always offer yourself to the Wraith in exchange for Gabriel."

I snorted in disbelief. "Sebastian! Gabriel is an angel who is now an Original Vampire. He has offered to remain in the Dark Realm! What could I possibly have that would make the Wraith choose me over him?"

"You're a Promise with an angel's soul still in your safekeeping."

"But you said a celestial soul can't remain in the Dark—it will return to the Light of its own accord."

"Once it is released. But if that did not happen, if it were to remain with the Promise . . ."

Oh shit. Sebastian was suggesting that I could secure Gabriel's release from the Dark Realm if I offered myself in his place, but only with his soul still in my possession. Where was the sense in that? The whole point was making sure Gabriel could get his soul back. Apparently being this close to the Void was affecting Sebastian's critical thinking. Why else would he think that I would consider offering myself under such a condition? If I was going to remain in the Dark Realm, then I was prepared to be like everyone else there—soulless.

Suddenly I didn't know what to believe. Was Sebastian lying to me now, or had he been lying to me previously, or had he just been lying all along? Averting my eyes from his too-sharp gaze, I did a hasty mental rewind of everything he had told me about being a Promise. My purpose was to safeguard Gabriel's soul, even if that meant giving it up. I wasn't going to allow myself to become some sort of sick trophy the Wraith could gloat over whenever the mood took him. I grabbed Sebastian by the arm.

"If Gabriel's soul is released it *will* return to the Light—that was the truth, wasn't it?"

"I . . . I . . ."

Sebastian looked as if he was in pain, and his wings began to rustle alarmingly. He clutched at his head as his eyes began rolling wildly.

"Sebastian!" I yanked on his arm, pulling him back. Grabbing hold of his face, I made him look at me. "It *will* return to the Light?"

"I . . . yes," he hissed at me. "It will return."

Good, that was all I needed. I let go of him and turned away. I was out of time and out of options, although there really hadn't been any other choice. As I turned to face the Void, I felt long fingers snapping around my wrist.

"No, Rowan, don't! I can't let you do this."

"Why not? You said it was the only way."

"I was wrong!"

He was lying. There was a wild look in his eyes, and I wondered how I could have ever mistaken them for something as beautiful as a sunrise or sunset. They were the fire pits of hell. I felt his fingers tighten on my arm and realized he was going to try and stop me from throwing myself into the Void, which meant he had been telling the truth about this. Giving the Void my life would offer Gabriel a chance at redemption. Choosing to take it was entirely up to him, but regardless, he was worth the sacrifice.

"Sebastian, please let go of my wrist. You're hurting me." You would have thought I'd asked him to pluck out his wings feather by feather from the look on his face. "Sebastian . . . *please!*" I gave him a pretty convincing wince. "I sure as hell can't outrun you so long as you have those." I gestured to his wings with my free hand. It took another ten seconds of internal deliberation before I felt his fingers loosen, and I made a big show of rubbing my wrist.

"I'm sorry, Rowan, I never meant to hurt you."

I stared at him, and saw that he was sorry, and for a moment he looked just like the Sebastian who had gotten me a blanket and tucked it around me. And then I saw something else in his face. A resolve that said, for reasons I knew nothing about, he was going to prevent me from doing what I needed to do.

I don't know if it was intuition, my non-poker face revealing my hand, or just a change in my body language, but Sebastian became suddenly wary. For all I knew, he was able to sense the determination that now rose up inside me. I was still running my thought process through to its conclusion when I felt his hand on my shoulder. I let myself be turned around so I was now facing him. His eyes were glowing like small twin suns.

Ah, Sebastian! What happened to you?

Timing was going to be crucial, but I'd recently taken a vampire by surprise, so I figured my chances were just as good with an angel. It was possible for a girl to get lucky twice in the same night, wasn't it? I made a show of looking Sebastian over, hoping it would confuse him enough to drop his guard. I let my eyes linger on his taut abdomen, and then do a lazy drift down his waist and hips. Thank God his jeans were tight! I was only going to get one shot at this, and if I missed, there would be no second chance. Ever.

This was the moment I wished I was one of those girls who could make their eyes swim with tears on command because I really needed a little extra something right now, but you have to work with what you've got. Gabriel always told me that pulling my teeth over my lower lip was a big turn-on. I prayed he was right.

"Sebastian?" I took a step back, looking up at him and wearing what I hoped was an expression of anxiety, remorse, and confused sexual longing. He dropped his hand.

I dragged my teeth across my lip. He licked his. His face became flushed, a sheen of moisture appeared on his upper lip, and he had what I was hoping for. An erection.

"Sebastian?" I said his name again, making my voice low and husky.

"Yes?" he said, swallowing once . . . twice.

"Fuck you!"

I raised my foot and kicked him squarely in the groin. His eyes widened, and his mouth become a silent O of shock as he fell to his knees, hands clutching at himself.

I took off.

CHAPTER 25

I was never one for sports at school. I hated gym. Couldn't climb a rope if my life depended on it, and fell off the balance beam enough times to know I might have difficulty passing a sobriety check sober. I also developed an acute aversion to anything that had to be played with a ball—volleyball, basketball, softball, or soccer. Not sure about tennis (no one at my school actually knew how to play), and of course football was a no-no. Back then the only padding a girl wanted was in her bra.

Oddly enough, I did like track. I wasn't very good at it, but there was something about running in an oval and keeping in your assigned lane that appealed to my sense of order. My high school coach would have burst his spleen in joy and disbelief at the acceleration I achieved sprinting away from the angel.

It was forty, maybe fifty feet to the edge of the abyss. It could easily have been a mile, it seemed so far away, but once I committed, there was no point worrying about distance. I was either going to make it or I wasn't. And not making it wasn't an option. I don't know if Sebastian thought screaming my name at the top of his lungs would make me stop, but it didn't. Guess that was another disappointment I'd dealt him. Keeping my arms tucked close to my sides, with my focus firmly fixed, I forced my legs to pump as hard as they could, propelling me forward. I heard a *whoosh* of air behind me. Shit! Sebastian had recovered from his kick in the balls a lot faster than the last guy I'd done that to. As this last thought fizzled in my head I saw the Void, and it seemed a part of it rose up to meet me in welcome. I didn't know if Sebastian could follow me down, but I was going to bet he couldn't. The Void was for those who had a soul to add to its numbers. I was betting that having a soul that was adrift didn't count.

Seeing the edge, I called on the last of my reserves and exploded like a human cannonball, throwing myself out into the space above the murky flow beneath me. My hair streamed out like a banner, and I felt something catch the trailing curls. It was Sebastian's long fingers. I tried to pull away, but the angel tightened his grip, and I felt my hair being twisted in his grasp. I gulped back a sob. It was exactly what I had done to Katja in order to save Laycee. Sebastian was going to pull me out of the Void and back onto solid ground, where I doubt my blow to his pride would go unpunished.

And then everything just stopped as a mighty roar rose up from beneath me, filling every inch of the cavernous space. Like a jealous lover, the Void didn't believe in sharing. Recognizing I had already offered myself, it was not going to let Sebastian take me away. I watched in awe as a sonic wave pushed the angel back across the cavern floor. He got to his feet in an angry rustle of feathers, a bewildered look on his face. Poor Sebastian! He really had no idea why I was doing this.

I closed my eyes and lay suspended in midair, waiting for whatever was going to happen to happen. Was I supposed to say something? Make a formal declaration of my intention to give my life, my soul, to the Void? It crossed my mind that perhaps the Wraith had put some sort of whammy on me, one that meant the Void wouldn't take me, after all. Would it be better or worse to spend eternity dangling a thousand feet or so in the air?

"There you go again, Rowan," I murmured to myself, "rushing headlong into something without knowing the consequences."

And then gravity kicked in. My arms began pinwheeling, and my legs kicked wildly as I went into free fall. I could feel my heart jackhammering behind my ribs, and the sudden change in pressure made my ears pop. The air rushing past me was hot, almost unbearably so, and I could feel the inside of my nose dry out as my lips began to crack. I closed my eyes, fearing they might boil up and pop out of my head like some grotesque cartoon caricature.

I don't know how I was still able to breathe, or what I was dragging into my lungs, because air, or anything like it, did not exist down here. All I could feel was the most terrifying rushing sensation. My stomach had lodged itself somewhere behind my left knee, and I was actually too scared to be scared. I should have been thinking about Gabriel, about how much I loved him and what my sacrifice would mean for him, but all I could think about was Alice falling down the rabbit hole and wondering if it had been this bad. And as I continued my downward spiral, the oddest thought occurred to me.

Will I die when I hit the bottom?

I could see the brilliant light even though my eyelids were closed. I wanted to turn away, but I wasn't sure if my head was still attached to my body because I couldn't feel anything from the neck down. If I was now in the same predicament as poor Oscar, then getting my retinas fried by a dazzling white light was kind of a moot point. As a disembodied head, what difference would it make?

I told myself that my head had to be attached to the rest of me because my brain was still working. The apparent numbness did not necessarily mean I was missing anything vital, like arms or legs. I performed a mental checklist of my extremities. Picturing my fingers in my mind, I moved them one at a time, grateful when I felt them respond. My physical inventory revealed nothing broken or missing, and I appeared to be lying, if my sense of touch wasn't impaired, on velvet cushions.

Gingerly I opened my eyes. The last time I had been in the presence of a brilliant light, the result had changed the course of my life. I wasn't going to rule out the possibility of a similar outcome this time. I blinked—and did it again a few more times just to make certain what I was seeing wasn't a mirage. And then I pinched myself—a lot harder than Sebastian had. Nope, nothing changed. Everything was still there. I was lying on a half-dozen multicolored velvet cushions in a garden.

I love the orderly disorderliness of an English country garden, and that was exactly what I was slap bang in the middle of. The grass, an amazing shade of lush, velvety green, was just begging to be walked on with the bare soles of my feet. Flowerbeds overflowed with a riotous array of color as plants jostled leaf and stem with their neighbors for growing room. The heavy scent of roses drifted on the air, mingling with honeysuckle, lilac, and lavender. And those were just the fragrances I recognized right away. There were other heady perfumes that, given time, I was certain I could name. I cast my eyes over the almost orgiastic display of color. My brain was able to name pansies, carnations, and marigolds as well as peonies, delphiniums, and foxgloves. Unfortunately, there were more blooms that I couldn't put a name to, flowers I'd never seen in any gardening magazine. But I had no trouble recognizing the roses. What self-respecting garden would be complete without them? Only this one seemed to have every variety and color imaginable. The sheer spectacle threatened to send me into sensory overload. I told myself that if I was to die right now, at this very instant, I would be content. If the last sight my eyes beheld couldn't be Gabriel's face, then this would be my second choice.

But . . . what if you actually are dead?

Thankfully that perceptive insight was put on hold as a voice coming from above my head said, "How nice to see you, Rowan. I wasn't sure if you were going to make it."

Shielding my eyes with my hand, I stared up. He had his back to the light, so his face was in shadow, hiding his features, but he held out a hand. It seemed a strong, capable hand, and as his fingers curled around mine, I noticed the nails were beautifully manicured. You can tell a lot about a man from his hands. As I got to my feet, he reached down and brushed a leaf from the skirt of my dress.

I don't usually wear dresses, and this girly number was definitely not something that would ever find a home in my closet. It had puff sleeves, a sweetheart neckline, and a bodice decorated with pearl buttons. The full skirt draped over what felt like three miles of tulle. I looked down at the froth of material billowing around my calves, wondering what had happened to my own clothes. And then I recalled Gabriel's emergence from the Void and figured it was probably best that I was wearing something else. Whoever my thoughtful provider was, he had not included underwear to go with my new outfit. Shoes either, which meant I got to walk barefoot across the grass, so it wasn't a complete loss.

"You should wear dresses more often," my host said, leading me over to the shade of an elm tree, where a table and some chairs were grouped beneath the boughs. "You look positively enchanting."

No one, not even Gabriel, had ever used the word *enchanting* to describe anything about me. I found it old-fashioned and courtly, and perfectly appropriate for the setting. I remembered to straighten out the back of my skirt before I sat down in the chair that he pulled out for me. I became mesmerized by the table. It was set exactly the way I imagined it would be for afternoon tea provided by the kitchen of an English country manor house. All the china was the same floral pattern, with just the right number of knives and forks with which to spread jams and savories and eat pastries.

The sandwiches, and there were several plates of them, were properly de-crusted and cut into triangles, and they sat next to smaller plates of tarts filled with preserves and alongside cakes dusted with powdered sugar and bowls of crystallized fruit. There were even scones and—my goodness!—clotted cream. I had no idea if I liked scones or clotted cream, which, now that I thought about it, sounded kind of gross, but I knew you couldn't have one and not the other. They went together, kind of like pancakes and syrup or steak and fries.

"One lump or two?" my companion asked, holding a cup and saucer in one hand and some sugar tongs in the other.

I had always thought sugar tongs were nothing more than a fancy prop. But grasped inside the metal teeth was a single cube of dazzling white. The bowl of the fine china cup was translucent enough for me to see exactly how much of the dark liquid it held. I don't drink hot tea, so I had no idea how many lumps was proper, but as I always drink iced tea sweetened, I figured I'd take hot the same way.

"Three?" I said hesitantly.

I received a smile in response and heard a pleasant plinking as the sugar cubes hit the side of the bone china cup. If I was being horribly greedy, then my host was far too charming to say so, and in my defense, the sugar cubes were awfully small.

"Sandwich?"

A plate of the little white triangles was held out to me. My stomach was still trying to settle itself, and I couldn't guarantee I was going to be able to keep the tea down, much less a sandwich. The prospect of upchucking all over my new dress seemed too risky a chance to take, so I politely declined. The plate was returned to its designated spot on the crowded table, and I busied myself with my teaspoon in my cup. Even stirring was an art—too vigorous and I was in danger of sloshing the contents over the rim and into the saucer.

Surreptitiously I looked at my host. Dark-haired and dark-eyed, he was undeniably handsome, with an aura of urbane sophistication about him. His pinstripe suit was, no doubt, custom tailored and was beautifully accented by a crisp white shirt, blood-red tie, and matching silk in his breast pocket. He looked like some wealthy Wall Street executive or the CEO of a Fortune 500 company. He even wore a tiepin and cufflinks, and the stones decorating both matched the larger one in the ring on his pinkie. I thought they looked like rubies.

"Where am I?" I asked.

He looked at me as he stirred his own tea. I didn't notice how many sugar cubes he had put in. And when he smiled, his eyes glittered like pieces of jet. "Do you like it? I created it especially for you."

I had no idea why he would say such a thing. Perhaps he told everyone he brought here the same thing. Especially the women. But if he wanted to impress me, then he'd done a good job, and I wasn't about to be a rude guest. His reasons were his own, and knowing them would not change my appreciation of the beauty that surrounded me. Someone had gone to a lot of effort.

"It's lovely," I told him. "Everything I could have wanted and more."

A bee, its legs already heavy and yellow with pollen, found its way to the vase of fresh flowers on the table. It settled on a rose, content to meander through the crimson petals, seeking to add to its load. Any more pollen and getting airborne was going to be a serious challenge.

Following my host's example, I raised the delicate china cup to my mouth and took a sip of tea. Gaaack! It was awful! I almost spat it back into the cup. People actually drank this stuff? Maybe the Founding Fathers had been on the right track dumping it in Boston Harbor. Masking my distaste as best as I could, I put my cup back on the table. My host raised an eyebrow of concern.

"My apologies, Rowan, would this be more to your liking?" He waved a hand and my cup and saucer was instantly replaced by a tall glass filled with amber-colored liquid. A slice of lemon decorated the rim and condensation beaded the outside. "I forgot your preference when it comes to drinking tea."

How would he know what I preferred?

Taking a sip, I had to admit it was, hands down, the best glass of sweet iced tea I'd ever tasted. I removed the slice of lemon from the rim, twisting it over the open glass and dropping it into the liquid. And I found myself looking across the table at my host. Despite the splendor of the scenery all around us, he commanded my attention.

"Didn't your mother ever tell you it's rude to stare?"

My mother hadn't stuck around long enough to tell me much of anything, but I couldn't expect him to know that. "Actually no, it was my father who told me," I said, "and I'm sorry if I'm staring, it's just that you bear a very strong resemblance to someone."

"A former beau perhaps?"

I shook my head. No, that definitely wasn't it. If I'd ever been asked out by someone who looked like him, I would have run a mile in the other direction. In spite of his charm and magnetism, both of which he had by the bucket-load, there was also an inherently dangerous quality about him. One that was very different from anything I had experienced. Sometimes Gabriel felt dangerous, and when I sensed whatever prompted that feeling rising in him, the danger made me feel reckless and wanton. I was able to give free rein to such feelings because I also knew that with Gabriel I was perfectly safe. He was never going to let anything truly bad happen to me. And although I had no doubt this handsome stranger could make me feel just as reckless, just as wanton, for him the thrill was all in the chase. It would be over the moment he caught me. In more ways than one.

I narrowed my eyes and tried picturing him in a different setting, to see if I could bring to mind whoever it was he reminded me of, and then it came to me. I blurted out the name of Hollywood's current bad boy, who had a blockbuster movie opening Christmas Day.

His dark eyes flashed in amusement. "Perhaps it would be a truer statement to say he looks like *me,* rather than the other way around."

Now didn't that put all those tabloid stories in a completely different light?

"Well, I doubt that he ever hosted a tea party or looked as well dressed as you," I said. "Your suit is beautiful."

"Thank you. It's Armani."

My knowledge of men's fashions had been expanding since I'd begun dating a vampire, and even though the only suit I'd seen Gabriel wear was his birthday one, I was confident he had to have at least one Armani in his closet. He wasn't the kind of vampire who couldn't dress up when the occasion called for it.

I took another sip of my iced tea. "Can you tell me where I am, exactly?"

"Purgatory."

I almost choked on an ice cube. Waving off his concern at my sudden coughing spasm, I reached for a linen napkin, holding it to my mouth while I brought my spluttering under control.

"Why so surprised, Rowan?"

"Well, let's just say it's not exactly how I imagined it to be."

Putting his cup and saucer on the table, he crossed his legs and smiled at me. "You think it should be all fiery pits and suffering? Demons running amok with pitchforks? Horrific screams of the potentially damned being tortured?"

"Yeah, something like that." I took a more cautious sip from my glass.

"Permit me to share a secret. To some people this *is* purgatory."

It was hard to imagine anyone not finding something to delight the eye or soothe the senses in this garden, but I do know there are people who have what I consider an unnatural dislike of the outdoors. Especially all the things that make it the outdoors. But if this was Purgatory, did that mean that this time I really was dead?

"Sebastian warned me about that," he said with a knowing smile, "your obsession about being dead. Only he couldn't tell if you were terrified by the prospect or eager to embrace it." He waved an expansive hand. "But do not concern yourself. For you this is simply a garden. Even I can create something that is beautiful for no reason other than it pleases me to do so. And doing this for you gave me a great deal of pleasure."

I looked away, feeling strangely embarrassed by his words. It was as if he wanted to show a part of himself to me that no one else had ever seen. And I had no idea why. When I was certain my coloring had returned to normal, I looked back. My companion was filling a plate with sandwiches, adding a few of the jam-filled tarts and a cream-filled puff pastry for dessert. I watched as he expertly snapped open a linen napkin, draped it across his leg, and balanced his plate on his crossed knee.

"Um, speaking of Sebastian, how is he?" I wasn't such a bitch that I didn't feel bad about what I'd done.

"As well as any male can be who's just experienced the excruciating pain of being kicked in the balls. He'll recover."

"Oh . . . well, I am sorry about that."

"What? That he'll recover?"

"No, of course not! I want him to recover. I meant I'm sorry about having to kick him in the first place."

"I'm sure he deserved it," he said, surprising me. "But you should know that not everything Sebastian told you was a lie, Rowan, and he isn't completely bad, at least not yet. He's just confused. Once he makes up his mind and declares himself, he'll feel much better and"—he paused long enough to give me a searching look—"be less prone to making errors in judgment."

I couldn't speak for past history, but it wasn't that difficult to work out what he considered Sebastian's most recent error in judgment to be. Me.

"What does he need to decide about?" I asked curiously.

"Whether to walk a path in this realm or . . . the other. Trust me, he'll find it less exhausting when he no longer has to divide his allegiance."

Was that why he tried to stop me from throwing myself into the Void? Personally, I would have thought any error in judgment on the angel's part had been brought about by his close proximity to the Void, not because of anything I might have done. However, I hoped his struggle—and he had definitely been fighting with something—came to an end before any irreversible damage was done. Now I suddenly felt bad about my attack on him, although I couldn't say for sure whether he thought trying to stop my course of action was a duty to the Dark or the Light.

"Are we still in the Void?"

My host laughed. It was a very comfortable, masculine sound. "No, if we were, this would not be half as pleasant. I'm sorry to say a question regarding your suitability has been raised."

I gave my own laugh. Part indignation, part nerves. "What's wrong? Isn't my soul bad enough?"

I hated this feeling of always being one step behind everyone else. The bee busying himself with the contents of the vase on the table probably knew more about what was going on than I did. I watched as another triangle of bread disappeared into my host's mouth. I couldn't be sure, but I thought whatever was between the two pieces of bread was . . . moving.

"Everyone's soul is dark enough for the Void," he said in answer to my flip remark. "Unless, of course, you are a newborn or Mother Theresa." He selected another triangle and held it up in his fingers. I told myself not to look at the sandwich. "The problem isn't with your soul, Rowan, it's with your motive."

"Wanting to save Gabriel isn't good enough?"

"Wanting to save any vampire is too good, but this particular one?" He held up a forefinger and waved it back and forth in a negative motion. "And I should tell you, before you ask, your efforts were wasted. You still have full possession of both his soul and your own."

"And I'm alive?" He hadn't actually told me that.

"Well, you're breathing, aren't you?"

I felt the hot prick of tears sting my eyes, which made me angry. I had tried my best and failed. My best, and only, attempt had all been for nothing. Now this handsome, suave man was going to do what Sebastian hadn't been able to—hand me over to the Wraith so he could bring me out on Sundays and holidays, parade me around, and no doubt use me to coerce Gabriel into being his lapdog. It was going to be a special kind of hell for both of us.

CHAPTER 26

"So when is he coming for me?" I asked, furiously blinking away my tears.

My host looked surprised. "Who?"

"The Wraith. You're going to hand me over to him, aren't you?" I spread a hand across the table. "Isn't that what this is all about? The condemned woman's last meal?"

This time when he laughed, he threw back his head. "You are delightful, Rowan! I'd almost forgotten how much so." *Yeah? Well, big whoop.* "I have no intention of handing you over to anyone, and besides," he said, gesturing with his sandwich, "the person you knew as the Wraith is no longer in charge of this dominion."

Somehow I didn't think it was because he'd been given a promotion. "What happened to him? Did he do something wrong?"

"Very much so," he said, looking pleased with himself. "He took it upon himself to go beyond the scope of his abilities and perform a task he was not suited for."

"What did he do?"

The look he gave me said he was surprised that I did not know. "Why, he is the one who orchestrated your loss of memory, Rowan. Causing a Promise to forget their true purpose is forbidden. By both sides."

His expression might, or might not, have been an apology.

"I would have thought my memory loss would have been an advantage."

"Ah, now that's the same mistake my predecessor made." Sighing, he brushed some imaginary crumbs off his lap. "If it were permissible, then such an affliction would prove to be most advantageous; however, sometimes we find ourselves constrained by rules that are not of our making."

"And making me lose my memory is against those rules?"

"Indeed it is."

"So are you in charge now?"

He tipped his head in assent. "This meager fragment of the Dark Realm is indeed under my authority."

In my mind, I saw the hooded robe gliding across the clearing once more. I wanted to ask what had happened to him, but I also feared I wouldn't like the answer.

"And are you also called the Wraith?" I asked, instead.

"No, I go by a very different name."

It was on the tip of my tongue to ask, but something made me hold back. I had the feeling his name was something I would be better off not knowing.

"Most wise," he murmured from across the table.

"Was making me lose my memory really that big a deal?" It didn't seem to me that I'd been hurt by it, and Gabriel appeared to be dealing with it just fine.

"When the terms for binding each Fallen to its Promise were set, it was decreed that they would be sacrosanct. Nothing would be allowed to compromise the purpose of a Promise."

"When did all this happen?"

"Sixteen ninety-two."

My jaw dropped open in surprise. I'd been a walking amnesiac for more than three hundred years? Talk about a jolt to the system. I frowned as I ran the date in my head, knowing there was something significant about it, but I couldn't recall what. It didn't help my concentration to feel his cool stare regarding me as he poured more tea. So what had happened two hundred years after Columbus landed in the New World? Damned if I knew.

Seeing my obvious struggle, he said, "Would it help knowing you were in Salem, Massachusetts, at the time?"

"Salem, Mass—the witch trials?" I asked, aghast.

"Yes. I suspect your consorting with the vampire was as close as Cotton Mather ever got to seeing a truly supernatural being."

"But why make me forget?"

My answer was a shrug of his shoulders. He knew, but for whatever reason he wasn't going to tell me, and I took the hard glitter of his eyes as a warning. I felt a sudden chill, as if the sun had suddenly disappeared behind a cloud. I wanted to believe this wasn't happening, but I knew all too well it was real. I wanted to scream and shout and pull my hair out at my stupidity, but in all fairness it had never occurred to me that throwing myself into the Void might fail. Everything had happened so fast, I hadn't had time to consider unforeseen consequences. And now I was dressed in some getup that my grandmother might have worn, having tea with . . . just who exactly? Who was this person sitting opposite me with his impeccable suit and impeccable manners? Well, he wasn't a man, that much I knew, and I'd suspected from the beginning he wasn't the Wraith. So did that mean he was a demon?

I felt as if the answer was staring me in the face; I just couldn't see it. If I trusted my instincts, I might be able to feel the truth of him, but I couldn't latch onto anything solid enough to pin down. There was a familiarity about the way he said my name and in the way he looked at me. It was a familiarity that felt right and oh so wrong at the same time. And somehow it was linked to the way he refused to call Gabriel by name, although I couldn't explain why I was so certain of that.

I forced my gaze to drift over the garden so I could catch my breath and try to decide what I should do next. The shadows had not moved, and the sun was still shining. The flowers were in full bloom, all dancing for attention with the scent of a hundred different varieties blending into one glorious fragrance. I picked up my glass of iced tea and drained it, watching with childlike glee as it was magically refilled the moment I put it down.

"So what happens now?" I asked, keeping my voice as calm as I could.

"Now we get to the crux of the matter. A dangerous precedent has been set: the vampire's desire to protect your life at the expense of his own soul, and your willingness to surrender that same life in order to give him back his soul." He clicked his tongue behind his teeth and shook his head. "It has caused quite a commotion, to say nothing about a massive headache, *on both sides*. Such altruism is completely unacceptable."

Yeah, I just bet it was. I could only imagine the shockwave our love had sent through the Dark Realm.

"I have had to take steps to ensure such unprecedented behavior never occurs again," he said with a weary sigh.

It wasn't in my best interest to know what kind of steps, so I didn't bother asking, but I felt he had some say in what would become of me now that I was here. In the Dark Realm.

"What are you going to do with me?"

Putting his elbows on the arms of his chair, he steepled his fingers and rested his chin on them. He stared at me for the longest time before finally asking, "Would you really sacrifice all you are for him?" My throat tightened, preventing me from speaking, so all I could do was give a single nod of my head. His expression changed to one of bewilderment. "But . . . *why?*"

"Because I love him," I managed to say as my throat magically released itself.

He waved a hand, and everything on the table vanished, including my glass of iced tea. "Love," he sneered, "is the biggest lie of all."

"That's only because you've never known it," I blurted out.

He stood up so suddenly his chair tipped over, and it took only three angry strides for him to reach my side. Grasping my wrist, he pulled me to my feet.

"Are you so sure this love you feel for the vampire can endure? That it will withstand temptation, greed, and lust, and all the other petty vices your kind are so easily swayed by?"

"Yes," I declared firmly. "If you had ever experienced love, true love, then you would know it can survive all those things and so much more."

Letting go of my wrist, he took a step back and looked at me, his eyes hooded. "Care to make a bet on it?"

"I—what?"

His question took me by surprise, and I stumbled, catching the edge of the table to steady myself. He repeated himself. I looked out at the garden, seeing the beauty, the grace, the perfection of each leaf and petal. And knew none of it was real.

"Well?"

"You're not going to let me leave this place unless I make that bet, are you?"

He shrugged. "The choice is yours, Rowan."

Yeah . . . right. He might not be the Wraith, but they were cut from the same cloth. Tricksters, deceivers, they lived only to play the game.

"Very well then," I said, hoping I sounded more confident than I felt. "What do you propose?" I had a feeling you only ever got one shot when you made a wager with someone like him, and I needed to make sure I didn't hang myself prematurely.

Gleefully, he rubbed his hands together. "Let us put this *affection* you and the vampire feel for each other to the test. Prove to me it is no passing whim, that it can withstand the ultimate trial and endure."

"What do you consider to be the ultimate trial?"

He seemed surprised that I would ask. "Why, time of course."

"And when I win?"

He chuckled, amused by my confidence. "I will release the vampire from his pledge to the Dark Realm."

I let out a slow breath and waited for the other shoe to drop. "And if I should lose?" I wasn't going to, but I needed to know what I was risking.

"The same thing I ask from all who wager with me."

"You want my soul?"

"Exactly," he said, grinning at me. His teeth looked very white, and very sharp.

Now that I knew the stakes, I needed to concentrate on the terms. "How much time do you intend to give me to prove my claim?"

"I like you, Rowan, I really do. Throwing yourself into the Void for the vampire! What will you do next?" Apparently he was quite tickled by my endeavor because he spent quite a while shaking his head as he continued to chuckle. When he was done, he asked, "Do you think I am generous by nature?"

"I think it depends on your mood," I told him honestly.

"Then be thankful I am in a very good mood." He grinned slyly at me, and I was immediately put on my guard. He was either incredibly confident of the outcome of our wager, or there was something he was counting on my not knowing. Either way I was probably screwed. "I will allow you to set whatever span of time you deem sufficient, but," he continued, "it must be fixed now. No later extension or deviation will be permitted."

"I can choose any period?"

This seemed too easy. What if I said I wanted a million years? He was expecting me to, I could see it in his face. There was something I definitely wasn't getting—and then it hit me! Sebastian and his fluidity of time remarks. He was going to let me set the time, certain I wouldn't think to define how it was to be measured. I could ask for a million years, but at some point, somewhere, that would be the equivalent of a single day as I knew it. I took a deep breath.

"I want the same amount of time that Gabriel was crucified, and"—I hurried on before he could cut me off—"I want the time to be converted into years as I know them and as they are currently measured in my present existence."

I had absolutely no idea how long Gabriel had been on that damn tree, or how much longer he would have hung there if I hadn't answered his call. Sebastian hadn't known either, but from the amount of blood that had soaked into the ground, I was certain it had been a while. "Agreed?"

"Agreed," he said, looking decidedly less chipper than a few moments before.

"How will you expect me to prove that our love has lasted?" Somehow I didn't think he was just going to take my word for it, or Gabriel's.

"An accounting will be kept."

"What sort of accounting, and by whom? You?"

I almost laughed out loud at the horrified look on his face. Such a task was obviously beneath him. "It will be as it always has been.

Every disagreement you have will be categorized and logged, along with every moment of pleasure. The tally will be kept in a secure place." Arching a brow, he gave me a long look before saying, "Agreed?"

My antagonist was secretly an accountant at heart. Who knew? The fact he had mentioned *disagreement* before *pleasure* was not lost on me, but I couldn't spot any glaring flaw in the proposal, so I nodded. "Agreed."

"Then we have a deal," he declared triumphantly.

I felt the ground shift beneath my feet, and the cold chill that had caressed me earlier returned with a renewed intensity. "Not quite," I said, holding up a hand. "There's the small matter of my memory."

"What about your memory? Has it not been restored?"

"This time."

The look on his face was a mix of hesitant curiosity. "What do you mean . . . *this time?*"

"I am still a Promise, right? Still safeguarding Gabriel's soul?"

"I have no interest in the vampire's soul!" he snapped.

As good as it was to know that, his declaration made me lose my train of thought for a moment. "Regardless, I'm still a Promise?" I repeated. He responded in the affirmative, and my throat was suddenly very dry. I could really use that glass of iced tea right now. "Can you ensure my memory will not be screwed up every time I'm reborn?"

"What are you saying?"

"I've been reborn a lot of times since the witch trials, and I never remembered who or what I was during any of those previous lifetimes. What if it happens again? It seems to me that it might look as though my purpose as a Promise was being compromised, and the rules were being broken . . . again."

The silence lasted quite a while, or it could have been ten seconds. My perspective was definitely becoming warped.

"Your argument is not without merit," he conceded finally. "I shall, how you say, level the playing field." I couldn't quite comprehend the look he gave me, but I'm pretty sure he didn't think I was going to get the better of him in any way. And he might have been right. After all, he'd played this game many times, whereas I didn't even know if there were any rules.

"As a Promise, you cannot be made a vampire. You cannot share the gifts bestowed or enjoy any of the advantages. Those are always given with a blood price. But because of my predecessor's eagerness to circumvent the rules regarding your status, I will extend you this courtesy. You will age as does the vampire you are bound to. Your body will not fall prey to disease or infirmity, and you cannot perish at another's hand. You will continue exactly as you are this moment, until you come to stand before me again."

"Are you serious?" I blurted out.

"You doubt my words?"

"No, absolutely not." It was more than I could have hoped for.

"*Now* do we have a deal?"

I nodded and held out my hand to him. "Sure, wanna shake?"

His eyes turned to pieces of black glass inside his head as he took my hand and pulled me to him. His other arm circled my waist like a band of steel.

"I don't shake hands," he said in a voice that made me think he'd stripped me naked and was licking me all over.

"And you're sure I get to keep Gabriel's soul?"

"Keep it, lose it, sell it to the highest bidder! I have already told you it is of no interest to me."

He pulled me closer, allowing me to feel how truly dangerous he was. A tangible presence wrapped itself around me like a shroud, and it was impossible not to feel the hard length of him pressed against me. Raising my hand to his mouth, he brushed his lips across my fingers. A shiver of unexpected desire ran through me. The arch of his brow told me he felt it too, and suddenly I knew if I ever got into bed with him, I would never get out again. At least not alive. He stroked the curve of my cheek, letting the tips of his fingers travel along my jaw and down my neck. I shivered as I felt them float across the edge of the sweetheart neckline, dancing across my cleavage.

And then he kissed me.

I didn't have to pretend to kiss him back because the moment his lips touched mine I wanted to. His tongue exploded in my mouth with an all-consuming passion, and I did nothing to stop him from taking everything and anything that he wanted. I was so overcome by my own need, consumed by a voracious, destructive hunger created from the darkest places in my soul, that I almost didn't recognize what was happening when he reached for a piece of me. With a coldness that was brutally ruthless, he shattered me open, stealing down inside and grasping a fragment of my soul. And I did nothing to stop him. Letting it slip through my fingers, I allowed this sliver of my essence to be ensnared by him.

Trickster, deceiver, and . . . seducer.

Satisfied, he withdrew from my mouth, his tongue making a final hungry sweep over my lips. "Now I understand why the vampire lusts for you so," he told me as his eyes took on a feral gleam.

Breathless and dizzy, I stared at him as the word *stupid* ran through my head, over and over. I watched as he pulled back his lips from his sharp white teeth and slowly unfurled his long tongue for me to see. There, embedded in the center, was the scrap of myself that he had stolen.

Leaning forward, his lips brushed my ear. "I will expect the rest in due course."

I pulled myself out of his embrace. I might not have gotten into bed with him, but I'd helped him pull back the covers. And worse, I had betrayed Gabriel with that kiss. In a daze, I looked around. What once had been a beautiful garden was now a parched and barren landscape. The magnificent elm tree had become nothing more than a twisted, gnarled husk, and the rank smell of decay filled my nostrils, making me nauseous.

I searched for any sign that life still existed in this place. But I found nothing. Everything was gone. *He* was gone, taking with him the token he had tricked me into surrendering.

Tricked you, Rowan, really?

The sound of demonic laughter pounded inside my head, making it throb painfully as the ground beneath me opened.

And I was falling . . . falling . . .

CHAPTER 27

Gabriel was all over me. Hands and lips everywhere, touching, feeling, reassuring himself that I had suffered no injury, come to no harm. Pulling me into his arms, he clasped me to him, his breath harsh and ragged in my ear. His arms were like bands of steel wrapped around me, his hold so tight I thought he might crack a rib. Having just recently been on the receiving end of that experience, I was in no hurry to repeat it, no matter how tempting it might be to test the truth of the demon's promise to me.

"Gabriel, . . . please . . . can't breathe!"

He shoved me away with enough force that I stumbled and fell backward.

"Don't you ever do that to me again!" he snarled, his face a mask of fury as he bent over me. "You don't go anywhere with that bastard, you hear me? *Anywhere!*"

I stared at him as he turned away and stomped off a few paces, keeping his back to me. It seemed that even the tattoos down his spine were rippling with undisguised anger.

What the hell? I could understand his rage, empathize with it even, because I know how fear can make even the most mild-mannered of us lash out. But this display of fury was way out of line and hurtful.

"Who are you talking about?" I asked, getting to my feet and brushing dirt off the ridiculous dress I was still wearing. Guess a wardrobe change hadn't been included in this trip.

Gabriel's eyes darkened, turning the color of an ocean during a winter storm. "Don't play me for a fool, Rowan—you know perfectly well who I mean!"

Dear God in heaven! Now it was my turn to let rip a little temper.

"Stop being such an asshole, and give me a break, will you? My head's pounding, I feel like shit, and I've just been—"

"SEBASTIAN!!!" he roared. "YOU ARE NOT TO GO ANY-WHERE WITH HIM EVER AGAIN—I WON'T ALLOW IT!"

His voice reverberated, almost knocking me down to the ground again. I stared at him, seeing nothing but murderous intent in his eyes. He was being unreasonable and completely unfair. Something I wasn't about to let go unchallenged.

"Excuse me? *You won't allow it?* Where the hell do you get off ordering me around like that?"

"You don't understand." He was still furious, but managed to bring his voice down a notch or two. "Sebastian is—"

"The only fucking person who's actually sat down and told me anything!" I yelled. "What are you so pissed about, Gabriel? That he told me all the things you wouldn't? Like what being a Promise actually means, and that I have your soul for safekeeping?" I barked out a laugh. "Or are you worried that I'm going to find out that you've refused to take it back from me?"

I watched as he folded his arms across his chest, and realized this was the first time he'd ever done that and not made my stomach flutter.

"Yeah, I'm pissed about all those things because they weren't his to tell," he said, narrowing his eyes. "But more than that, I'm pissed because he put you in danger by taking you to the Void."

The breath caught in my throat. "How do you know that's where he took me?"

He blew out an impatient breath. "Because he told me!"

"He told you he'd taken me to the Void?" I was stunned. Apparently the angel was not only confused about which side he wanted to play for, he was also suicidal. "Why would he do that?"

"Because I wouldn't give him any ice until he told me what he'd done with you! Personally," Gabriel continued, "I think he's been long overdue for a kick in the balls, and I'm damn proud of you for doing it, but you have no idea what these past few hours have been like for me. I've been in hell, Rowan."

Actually I'm pretty sure that's where I'd been.

"So is that how long I've been gone? A few hours?" Funny, it felt like a week at least.

He nodded. "And you should know no one believed whatever was left behind was actually you. Laycee refuses to leave your house until she can confirm with her own eyes that you're back with us." The ghost of a smile tugged at the corners of his mouth. "She threatened to deck Aleksei with a cast-iron skillet if he tried to make her leave."

"Oh Jesus! He's not going to hurt her, is he?"

He shook his head. "No. She is very protective of you, which is something he both understands and respects."

"Katja used her to get me out of the house."

"I know, she told me. Don't worry, Laycee will not be harmed because of what happened or because of anything she heard or saw. I give you my word."

Relieved, I exhaled the breath I hadn't realized I was holding, and the tension between us vanished as quickly as it had erupted.

"I thought I had lost you, Rowan . . . this time forever."

His anger crumbled as worry, fear, and grief took its place. I went and stood before him, smoothing a hand across his face as I pushed back his hair. Turning his head, he caught my thumb between his lips and pulled it into his mouth. I felt a sharp prick as his fang punctured the pad, giving him a taste of my blood. It was the reassurance he needed.

"I'm so sorry," I whispered, "I didn't know Sebastian was going to take me away. Everything kind of went crazy all at once. You must know that if I hadn't been so out of it, I would never have left you like that." He took in a deep breath and released my thumb. "I will never leave you like that again. I swear it." I needed his understanding more than his forgiveness. He gave me both.

Slowly I looked around, trying to get my bearings. We weren't in my yard, which was where I had expected to find myself, but like the Void, this was a place we were both familiar with. It was the clearing. Staring past Gabriel's shoulder, I recognized the terrible crucifixion tree, its thorny branches a testament to Gabriel's torture. Thankfully the blood that had bathed the ground had long since been absorbed by the earth. All that was left was a dark streak near the base of the trunk.

"In time, that too will fade," Gabriel said, solemnly. "It has been long enough, and every punishment must eventually end."

Beyond the perimeter of the clearing the same trees stood as silent sentinels, their twisted limbs and treacherous roots ready to catch the unwary traveler. Not that anyone came to this place without being summoned. Everything beyond the first ring was cloaked in darkness, but I could still feel the cold slicing open my chest as I struggled to breathe, and knew it had not diminished. It merely waited for me to step beyond the protection of the clearing.

"Are we going to be all right?" Gabriel asked, coming to stand behind me and put his arms around my waist.

"Not yet," I answered honestly, "but we will be." I leaned back against him and let the warmth of his body sink into me. His hair fell over my shoulder, and I inhaled the scent of his skin, soaking it up like a sponge. "Why are we here?" I murmured, turning my head so I could look up at him. "Why this place?"

His eyes were now the deepest shade of blue I had ever seen them, and concern furrowed his brow. "You seek answers, Rowan. What better place to find them than here?"

He was right. Here only the absolute truth could be spoken. Sebastian may have told Gabriel he'd taken me to the Void, but I was pretty sure the angel had no idea what had happened to me after that. It was going to fall to me to divulge the deal I'd made with the demon.

"Why did you give up the chance to take back your soul, Gabriel? Why pledge yourself to the Dark Realm?" I slipped out of his embrace and faced him. Taking his hands, I was grateful to feel his long fingers wrap around mine. "It wasn't just about me, was it? Tell me you had other reasons."

He sighed, and the warmth of his breath grazed my temple, lifting my hair.

"I had almost given up hope of finding you. Losing your memory also meant the bond between us was weakened somehow. I could no longer feel you, could not find my way back to you. The desolation was overwhelming. It almost destroyed me."

I gasped. It had never occurred to me that my blissful ignorance of Gabriel's existence would have been absolute torture for him, a torture he had endured for more than three hundred years.

"How *did* you find me?"

"It was pure chance. My sentinel, Tomas, saw you in the bookstore."

I was going to have to make sure I gave the elusive Tomas a big kiss when I finally met him. "I'm so sorry that it took so long."

"Ah, love, it wasn't your fault. You had no way to prevent what was done to you, any more than you could stop the sun from rising each morning."

Although it was true, it didn't make me feel any better. "So you made a decision to not let anything separate us again."

He nodded slowly. "I had just got you back, and, even though you didn't recall anything about our past, you seemed so happy to be with me. It was a side of you I had never seen before. I could feel your joy every time I took you in my arms, the rapture when you gave yourself to me—"

"My temper when I slapped you?"

He flushed with embarrassment, but not enough to prevent his dimple from winking at me. "Even that was wonderful to me—and I deserved it, too," he added hastily.

"But Gabriel . . . your chance at redemption. You've given up the possibility of returning to the Light, where you belong."

"Is that what you think?" I nodded, my throat suddenly too thick to let me speak. "No, no, love. You've got it all wrong." He took me in his arms and brushed the hair from my face with his palm. "Don't you understand, Rowan, *you are my redemption*. To have you love me as I am now is all I ever asked for." His brows pulled together. "You do still love me, don't you?"

"Yes, of course," I told him huskily, "but why didn't you tell me any of this?"

"I couldn't. I had no idea when your memory would come back or how much you would regain."

"But you knew it *would* come back?"

"Once a physical joining had been initiated, it was only a matter of time."

His sudden unease pricked my attention, and I looked at him. *A physical joining?* "Are you saying if you hadn't slept with me, I still wouldn't know, even now?"

He let go of me and took a step back, struggling with the consequences of his desire. The power to keep me safely ignorant had been in his hands, or in this case his pants, all the time. He just hadn't been able to smother his lust.

"That night on the porch," he said, dropping his voice to a low whisper, "I knew a strictly platonic relationship was going to be out of the question. I couldn't be with you, and not be *in* you. It would be like asking a starving man to have a seat at the banquet table, but tell him not to eat anything. Impossible."

He was right, and I couldn't let him shoulder all the blame. I'd been more than ready to jump his bones that same night. Who knows how long I would have been able to keep my hands off him? It was nice to know I hadn't been the only one struggling with irresistible desire.

"But if you knew sex would be the catalyst . . ."

"I hoped that by the time your memories returned, especially what it meant to be my Promise, you would have already accepted and understood my decision."

"You didn't know Sebastian would pay me a visit, huh?" I wasn't surprised to find I had conflicting feelings about the angel.

"Absolutely not!" Gabriel exclaimed, running his fingers through his hair. "My concern was with Katja. It never occurred to me that Sebastian would take it upon himself to interfere."

"Is that how you see it? Telling me the truth was interfering?"

"The truth is something I would never deny you, but I would have preferred someone other than Sebastian give it to you. His constant struggle with the choice he has yet to make can have dangerous consequences. Separating the truth as it actually is from what he wishes it to be is a challenge for him."

It was the most diplomatic way of calling someone a liar I had heard in a long time. And it gave me an idea who might have sent the charismatic angel to my back porch.

"Poor Sebastian," I murmured. "He's a bad angel who really wants to be good."

"You have always had a unique way of looking at things, Rowan." Gabriel drew in a breath and let it out slowly. I felt the muscles in my thighs stir at the sight of his chest rising and falling. "But it seems," he continued slowly, "that others are determined to reveal the knowledge that I alone am responsible for."

"I don't see anyone else here," I said, waving a hand around me. "Now might be a good time to tell me whatever it is I need to know."

He folded his arms, and my twitching thighs did their best not to collapse under the strain. It was good to know my earlier nonresponse had been nothing more than a reaction to the stress of the situation.

"If I had been able to block out my physical desire for you, thereby denying any possibility of your memory being restored, you would never know what being my Promise meant . . . and would have no idea that my soul was already forfeit."

"Already?" I asked, puzzled. "I thought you only did this a few months ago."

"In actuality, yes, but here"—he put his hand over his heart—"I made the decision a long time ago."

"I don't understand," I told him, more confused than ever.

"You are correct in thinking I did not renounce my soul for you alone. Although you bring a light into this solitary existence that makes every passing minute more precious than the last, you are not the reason I was created."

Whatever comment I was about to make died on my lips when movement between the trees of the outer ring caught my eye. The words I had been about to say were immediately forgotten as something slinked sinuously between the forest sentinels. Orange eyes glowed back at me, and I felt a strength of purpose coupled with a power that was far older, far deeper, and more fiercely compelling than anything I could conjure up in my wildest dreams. And I saw, moving in and out of the shadows with a lithesome grace that took my breath away, the leopard that had guided me here.

"They came to me in this place, long before the Wraith ever set foot here, and asked me to be their champion. I promised myself to

them, Rowan, agreeing to help ensure their continued existence, to make certain the balance between their kind and mankind did not swing too precariously in one direction. If I were to refuse them . . ."
He didn't say anything else; he didn't need to.

I had been so wrapped up in my own wants and needs, I'd forgotten about the petitioners who had asked to be given the glorious predator that was a vampire. I had no idea what sacrifices they had been forced to make in fighting for their survival. How could I know what it had cost them to turn to the Dark Realm, seeking an answer to their prayers. What it might mean, even now, if they were abandoned. Shame flooded through me at my selfishness.

Placing my hand on Gabriel's arm, I stared up into his eyes. A ring of gold now circled each pupil, signifying his own hunger.

"I would never ask you to forsake them," I told him, feeling the swell of emotion rising in me. "Never!" A chorus of snarls greeted my words, a chorus that, to my ear, rang with the sound of approval.

Taking me in his arms, Gabriel leaned down to kiss me, but I could still feel the lingering trace of another kiss recently bestowed on my lips. As much as I wanted Gabriel's sweet breath in my mouth, it was time for my confession. The kiss might not have been my idea, but I had done nothing to stop it.

CHAPTER 28

"You're not the only one with truths to share," I told him as I gently extricated myself from his embrace and put a small distance between us. If I was going to do this, then I needed some space.

"Rowan, love, what is it?"

"Don't!" I said, holding up a hand as he took a step toward me. "I need you to stay right there." This was going to be hard enough without the distraction of his touch. "Please, Gabriel, let me tell this my way."

"Very well." He shrugged in bewilderment, but remained where he was.

In a halting voice, I gave him a full accounting of Sebastian's visit to my back porch. What he had told me was my true purpose as a Promise, the restoration of my last elusive memory of that time, and the angel's slant on why Gabriel was refusing to take back his soul.

"He wasn't entirely wrong," Gabriel admitted. "He just didn't have all the facts."

"Would it have made any difference?" I asked. "You said yourself he tells the truth as he thinks it should be."

"Perhaps . . . perhaps not."

I then went on to tell him about Laycee's unexpected arrival—"And you're sure she's all right?"—and seeing the terrible condition of the starving Oscar, and realizing Katja was to blame, and my brilliant plan to get Laycee inside the house, and then everything pretty much going to hell.

"Did you take Laycee to the hospital to get her wrist set?" I asked when I was finished.

"Aleksei is taking care of that," Gabriel assured me. "He will stay with her until daylight if we do not return before then."

"But isn't he already at the hospital with Anasztaizia?" Although he had mentioned earlier that the Russian vampire was at my house, it hadn't really registered. I was filled with guilt at not asking about the beautiful Magyar sooner, and confused to hear Aleksei was with my best friend.

Gabriel frowned. "Why would Anasztaizia be at the hospital?"

I told him what Katja had said about the accident in the restaurant kitchen.

"Ah, now I understand. It was a lie, Rowan. Anasztaizia is perfectly well."

"And you're sure it's okay having Aleksei stay with Laycee?"

"I'll admit she seemed a little hesitant when I first told her who he was," Gabriel said, his frown deepening as he recalled the moment, "but then she seemed quite taken when she found out he and Anasztaizia are engaged."

"You told her that?"

"Was that wrong of me?" I shook my head, able to picture the relief on Laycee's face knowing Anasztaizia was spoken for. "When I left them," Gabriel continued, "Laycee was trying to persuade Aleksei to get his tips frosted." His forehead smoothed out as he grinned at me. "I probably don't want to know what that means, do I?"

"No," I agreed, smiling with him and thinking the next time I saw the big guy he'd be sporting a new 'do. I didn't realize Gabriel had broken his word to stay where he was until I felt him take my hand.

"What did Katja do to you once Laycee was safe?"

I hesitated, unsure of how to tell him another vampire had wanted to put me out of the picture, permanently. I didn't think it was possible to describe the depth of the animosity the Goth Queen had felt for me.

"I need to know, Rowan, but if it makes the retelling any easier, her maker, Ryiel, has also requested a detailed account."

That did make it easier. I had no personal connection to Ryiel, so

I was able to picture Katja in my mind and pretend I was speaking to him and not Gabriel. In a matter of moments, I had described her plan to have Oscar feed from me, knowing that in his condition he would kill me. The retelling was very cathartic.

"You have no idea how close I was to peeing-my-pants happy when you and Ryiel showed up," I told him.

"We should have got there sooner."

"Gabriel, don't!" I couldn't let him carry the blame for Katja's attack on me. "If Ryiel couldn't stop her from coming after me, then who could? You do realize she's a total whack job, don't you?" I paused and waited until he looked at me. "I'm just grateful you showed up when you did."

He turned my hand over and bent down to press his lips against the inside of my wrist. The gesture was wonderfully intimate, but as I looked down at his head, I thought of a different vampire.

"Did Oscar really have to be killed?" I asked, still shuddering over the almost casual way Ryiel had decapitated the vampire from the prairie state.

"It was for the best, love," Gabriel said, straightening up. "He was too far gone to be brought back. Even draining you would not have been enough, and being denied blood for so long meant he was in constant agony."

"Would Katja have known that?"

"Any vampire would have known."

Which made her action all the more heinous.

"So what did Ryiel do with her?" It was disappointing to hear the other Original Vampire had not been in favor of removing the exotic beauty's head. That was a treat reserved for starving vampires. Instead, he had decided a more hands-on approach was required for his wayward scion, an approach that brooked no interference from the outside world. "What did he do? Send her to some super strict religious order?"

"I think she would almost prefer that. Ryiel," Gabriel went on to explain, "lives in an abandoned monastery in the foothills of the Himalayas. That's why my return was longer than expected—"

"Stop it!" I could already see dealing with his guilt was going to be an uphill battle.

"Anyway, he lives in seclusion, cut off from the outside world."

"What does he do with his time?"

"He adds to his knowledge. He has the best archives of both human and vampire texts in existence. Have you ever heard of the Library of Alexandria?"

My brain took a trip down memory lane to high school. "Didn't it contain all the knowledge of the known world at the time? And wasn't there a fire or something that burned all the scrolls?"

"Fire yes, burned scrolls, not so many."

I stared at him with my mouth open. "Are you saying Ryiel has them?" I could only imagine what historians would give to be able to look at them.

"As I said, he adds to his knowledge."

"So what does he expect Katja to do there? Sort and catalog?" I know I wouldn't trust her around something as precious as ancient texts.

"He will expect her to reflect on her actions while she makes herself useful. Ryiel is a great believer in purging the mind with physical activity. I understand there are a great many rooms that need cleaning."

"What's to stop her from just leaving?" I couldn't imagine the psychotic vampire with a broom in her hands. Not with those nails.

"She cannot. Ryiel is her maker. It is impossible for her to leave without his permission, and after what he saw her do to you, I doubt he will ever grant it."

I still felt worse for Oscar. "Can he be buried, or does his body have to be burned?"

"He was a vampire, Rowan. It must be burned, but we could bury his ashes if you wish. Do you have somewhere particular in mind?"

"I think he would like it if we took him home and buried him beneath a Kansas wheat field. He was very kind to me . . . that first time we met."

I hadn't realized I was crying until Gabriel reached out and wiped a tear from my cheek. I could see the muscle in his jaw popping, and I realized he was doing his best to keep the possessive side of his nature under control. Not knowing where I'd been or what had happened to me hadn't been easy for him. And it was about to get considerably harder when I made my confession.

Keeping his voice low and as calm as possible, he asked, "What happened after Sebastian took you away?"

"He didn't tell you?"

He shook his head. "All he said was you had lost your temper and kicked him."

"And you didn't ask why?" Especially considering where I'd kicked him.

"Why would I? You would have had good reason." Gabriel's complete acceptance of my action was strangely gratifying, and I wondered if Sebastian realized what a lucky escape he'd had. Perhaps he did, which would explain his reluctance to share details. "So what did happen, Rowan?"

It took a few hesitant starts before I was able to get my narrative flowing, but once I did, I couldn't stop, and I told him everything. Including the *good reason* Sebastian's testicles got rearranged with my foot. However, he stiffened noticeably when I described the English garden and taking tea with my demon host. Not wanting him to think I was hiding anything, I left nothing out of my description. I even included the tiepin and cufflinks.

"You found him handsome then?" Gabriel asked, his fingers tightening around mine. I noticed he made a point of looking down at the ground.

"Yes, I did." Even though I knew it hurt him to hear me say it, I wasn't about to lie. Not here. The muscle in Gabriel's jaw popped furiously as he dealt with my admission, and when he had moved past it, I told him about the wager I had made.

Raising his head, he stared at me. "But . . . why would you do such a thing?"

His face had the same look the demon had worn when he had asked me why I was prepared to sacrifice myself for Gabriel. It was eerily uncanny.

"Gabriel, I had no choice—he wasn't going to let me leave unless I agreed to *something*," I said in my own defense.

"No, I don't suppose he would have." His manner turned grave. "You had best tell me all of it."

Now it was my turn to stare at the ground. Taking a deep breath, I recounted the terms, but when I came to the hardest part, how the deal had been sealed, my voice shook. Gabriel's lack of response seemed to confirm that my behavior was tantamount to adultery.

He placed a hand beneath my chin and raised my head until I had no choice but to look at him. "You did not betray me, Rowan."

"Then why does it feel like I did?" I retorted miserably.

"It was just a kiss. One you didn't ask for and one you certainly didn't initiate."

"But I didn't try to stop it either!" I confessed, jerking my chin from his grasp. "The truth is—I didn't want to stop him!"

"I know."

I flounced away in a swirl of torn tulle and began my own stomp around the clearing. It was difficult trying to figure out whether my anger was due to my own behavior or Gabriel's understanding support. Part of me wished he would get in my face and yell about how disloyal I'd been, and the other part wanted nothing more than to feel his arms around me and have him tell me everything was going to be okay. What was done was done, but it was fixable. *We* were fixable. It was only a kiss, and it was not going to come between us.

Except it wasn't *only* a kiss.

It was a kiss that I had wanted to last forever the minute the demon's lips touched mine. Sharing the passion and desire, I had allowed myself to become so wrapped up in those feelings, I never realized he was stealing a piece of me . . . until it was too late. And now guilt was tearing me apart. Guilt at not fighting hard enough to keep that piece from being stolen, and I had betrayed Gabriel. As well as myself.

"He took a piece of me!" I sobbed, falling to my knees. "He took a piece of me . . . and I didn't stop him!"

"Then we'll take it back!" Gabriel declared, pulling me into his arms.

I opened my mouth to ask how, but Gabriel pressed his lips against my forehead, my temple, my tear-soaked lashes, and dirt-streaked cheeks. He kissed my nose and my jaw, and seared a trail of fiery kisses down my throat. And then he took possession of my mouth, invading me with his tongue and cleansing away every remnant of that other kiss. He invited me into the velvet warmth of his own mouth, and hungry for him, I followed, sliding my tongue be-tween his fangs.

"Do you want to keep this dress?"

"I . . . what?"

"This dress." Taking a piece of the dirty torn fabric, Gabriel held it up in his fingers. "Do you want to keep it?"

I shook my head and watched as he slipped his hands inside the bodice and tore it down the front. He pulled open the two halves, and I heard the breath catch in his throat as he stared at me. Gabriel had seen me naked plenty of times, so I knew my body held no secrets for him, but the way he looked at me now, it was as if he was seeing me for the first time. My heat rose beneath the intensity of his gaze, and, inexplicably, I felt shy and awkward. I lifted a hand to cover myself.

"Don't," he rasped, stopping my effort easily and taking me down to the ground.

He dropped his head to my breast, running his tongue across my nipple before pulling the stiff peak gently into his mouth and scrap-ing it between his teeth. I moaned and arched my back, wanting more. His hand cupped my other breast, rolling and pinching that nipple between his finger and thumb until it was swollen and aching. He licked a path down to my stomach and then used his fangs to scrape over the sensitive place just below my hipbones. I shuddered and trembled as a different heat roared through me. My entire exis-tence was concentrated on his touch, and when he pushed apart my legs and used his tongue to stroke the center of me, I exploded.

Gabriel continued to worship me with his mouth, his silken hair sliding over my skin. Trailing a path along the inside of each thigh, he kissed and nipped his way to my core, where he suckled and licked, his tongue dipping inside my body while bringing me to the edge of ecstasy before pulling back. The third time he did this, I reached for a handful of his hair and snarled at him. Eyes glowing, he kissed me with a mouth that was glossy and slick and used his fingers to take me over the edge.

I was still rolling through my orgasm when I felt him inside me, each thrust of his hips more powerful than the last, and I wondered if I might come apart. But my body knew better than my mind, so hungry for my lover it wasn't about to let him go. Stretching and wrapping myself around him, I pulled his cock deep inside me, creating a delicious friction each time he withdrew, coating him with my own silky essence as he returned. My hips began to move of their own accord, and I took him even deeper inside me, until, when he couldn't hold back any longer, he bathed both of us in white-hot fire. And as I reveled in the glow of his climax, I opened my eyes and saw that above me, every thorny branch of the crucifixion tree had burst into flower.

CHAPTER 29

I don't know how we got back to my house. There are some things it's better not to ask. I was just thankful that whatever power had returned me home had also managed to re-dress me in my pajamas, even if they did smell faintly sulfuric. Laycee came bursting through the front door and threw her arms around me. Too emotional to speak, we cried as we held on to each other.

"Laycee, I—"

"No," she said, putting her hand against my mouth. "Later. We can talk later. I'm just glad you're back."

She took hold of my hands and squeezed both of them with hers. With both of hers.

"Your wrist—it's really fixed?" I gasped in amazement. I had been expecting to see a cast or lots of bandages, but it was as if the bones had never been broken.

"Oh yeah, it's fixed." She looked over her shoulder as Aleksei came down the porch steps. "He took care of it for me."

I was stunned. "You can do that?"

"Yeah, I can do that," Aleksei replied, looking slightly abashed. "Is good to see you have come back to us, Rowan."

Leaning forward, Laycee put her lips to my ear. "You have some unusual new friends. This one I like, the other two not so much." I stared at her and simply nodded, not knowing what to say. "I'm going to go home now," she told me as she kissed my cheek. "We'll have that talk later."

I watched as she followed Aleksei to the big black car now parked in my driveway. He opened the passenger door for her and then got in on the other side. The BMW was gone, along with Ryiel's car, and I was thankful to see there was no sign of Oscar's body.

"Aleksei's taking her home?" I asked Gabriel as we both watched the sedan drive away.

He murmured something under his breath. Probably a comment about my stating the obvious, but I was too exhausted to ask him to repeat it.

"Come, let's get you to bed," he said, picking me up in his arms and carrying me into the house. The last thing I remember was the sound of the front door being kicked shut . . .

This time when I opened my eyes, I knew exactly where I was, and I came awake in the very best of all possible ways. Rolling on top of me, Gabriel pushed himself deep inside. A fine sheen of sweat made his skin slick, making me dig my nails into his arms to hold on. I watched the pulse throbbing at the base of his throat increase with each thrust of his hips. He looked down at me, and I was bathed in a sea of blue and gold so bright it was almost blinding, and then his lips pulled back and his fangs dropped. He was close to coming.

"Do it!" I urged as I danced on the edge of my own explosive climax.

Dropping my hand from his arm, I pushed aside my hair, giving him free access to my neck. The walls of my bedroom shook at the sound of his possessive sexual snarl, and every muscle in my body clenched, throwing me headfirst into a storm of sensual release that came from both his cock buried deep inside me and his fangs at my throat.

I ran my hands gently down his back and sides, feeling him tremble above me as his own orgasm exploded through him. Slowly he retracted his fangs, sealed my neck, and then rolled off me and onto his back. We lay side by side, both gasping for air.

"That," I managed to say when my breathing had resumed a more manageable flow rate, "was very intense." And then my stomach growled.

Taking charge, Gabriel got out of bed, giving me a spectacular view of his ass as he went to find breakfast. Returning with toast, scrambled eggs, bacon, and coffee, he insisted I not get up. I wasn't about to argue, even if it did mean crumbs in my belly button.

"How long was I out for?" I asked, cradling a mug of coffee in my hands.

"Almost forty-eight hours," he told me.

"You didn't stay here, did you? I mean you can't, not in the day-time."

"I did think about taking you to my place, but Laycee wouldn't allow it," Gabriel said with a smile. "It's good that it's winter and the nights are longer. I didn't have to be gone from you for that long."

"Where is Laycee?"

"I called and told her you were awake. She will be here in a little while."

Taking the now-empty mug from my hands, he put it with the rest of our breakfast plates on the tray he'd left on the dresser, and then got back into bed with me. I lay in his arms, twirling a lock of hair around my finger, watching as the curl straightened and then bounced back . . . straightened and bounced back.

Gabriel put his hand over my mine. "What is it?"

"There are some details about the wager that I haven't told you."

"I know that you're not going to age any more, that he fully expects you to default, and it was never my soul he wanted, but yours."

I twisted around to look at him. "How could you know any of that?"

"I felt the change in your body the moment I took you in my arms in the clearing. As for the rest"—he shrugged—"I know him, Rowan."

"You know him?"

Taking my hand, Gabriel put it to his mouth and brushed his lips across my knuckles. I put my head on his chest and inhaled deeply, letting the scent of his skin soothe me like a balm. For a long time he didn't say anything, his only response the lazy sweep his hand made up and down my back.

And then he sighed, kissed the top of my head, and said, "Did you know that angels are created in pairs?" I stared up at him, wondering if this was his not so subtle way of avoiding my question about knowing the demon. "I thought, perhaps, Sebastian might have mentioned it," he added.

I shook my head. "No, Sebastian never mentioned anything about it. So why is that?"

"They didn't used to be." His hand paused in the downward motion. "The first angels were each created from a single orb of Light, but in doing so an unexpected imperfection was revealed."

"What kind of imperfection?"

"One that made an angel believe he could be thought equal to the Creator. As a result he was cast down."

Cast down?

"Oh my God, you mean like when Satan was cast out of Heaven . . . ?"

Gabriel nodded slowly. "Satan, Lucifer, the Devil. He answers to many names, though I doubt he would recognize his own if it was spoken aloud. Still, it is enough that you are aware of his existence, and because of his action it was realized that an orb of Light was too powerful for any solitary creation. The potential would be better served if divided between two celestial beings."

"You mean like angel twins?"

A small frown puckered his brow. "Not really. There are no common traits to be shared, although an awareness of the other always exists, even if opposite sides are chosen." The gesture I made with my hand said further clarification would be much appreciated. "From the moment angels are brought into awareness," Gabriel continued, "they are given the choice to walk in the Light or the Dark Realm. Some choose right away, some take longer—"

"And some have a hard time making up their minds," I said, thinking of Sebastian.

"It is not an easy decision, Rowan, and once made, it can never be reversed."

This time when he did not speak, I understood the reason why. His silence told me exactly who the demon was, and why he had wanted me. "He was created with you, wasn't he?" I said softly. "You shared the same orb of Light, only he has always belonged to the Dark Realm."

"Yes . . . he was drawn to the Dark from the very first."

Now I knew why the demon had seemed familiar to me, and why I had allowed him to kiss me as I did. And there was something else too. A catch in Gabriel's voice told me who it was that had supplied the means for his capture so long ago—a capture that had culminated with a terrible disfigurement and abandonment on the thorny limbs of the crucifixion tree.

"No wonder he wouldn't use your name," I murmured.

"No, I don't suppose he would," Gabriel said, leaning down and kissing me lightly on the mouth. "There is, however, one thing about the wager you have not told me."

"What?"

"How much time did you get him to agree to?"

Unable to believe that I had overlooked such an important detail, I told Gabriel what I had asked for, as well as how it was to be converted, calculated, and measured. He stared back at me, his expression completely unreadable.

"What is it?" I asked, pulling back from him. "Aw shit, I screwed up, didn't I?"

I threw back the covers and had one foot on the floor when Gabriel's strong arms pulled me back on the bed and rolled me beneath him. He kissed me long and hard, leaving me almost breathless when he was done.

"No," he said, grinning down at me. "You didn't screw up."

It was on the tip of my tongue to ask him how long he had been crucified, but I stopped myself. I was afraid it wouldn't be enough. Instead I was suddenly overwhelmed by the realization that if the lesser beasts had not petitioned the Dark Realm, then Gabriel would be suffering still. There was an outside chance the demon might not know how long Gabriel had suffered, but I didn't believe that. I couldn't shake the nagging feeling that I was missing something, thinking that perhaps he had been a little too quick to agree to my terms regarding the amount of time needed.

"What is it, love?" Gabriel cupped my chin in his hand as I shared my concerns. "You may never have dealt with someone like him before, Rowan, but remember, he has never dealt with anyone like you."

I surrendered myself to another long, hard kiss.

"His arrogance may prove to be his downfall. It would not be the first time," he added darkly.

"I guess I'm just worried that there's something I'm not seeing," I confessed.

Taking me in his arms, Gabriel smoothed the hair from my face. "You are returned to me, and that is all that matters." His lips brushed mine in a gentle, featherlike kiss. "In the meantime, you have given Ryiel enough time to begin his search."

"Ryiel? What's he got to do with this?" I asked, startled.

"I told you he has all those ancient texts. He is certain one of them dealt with the nullification of demonic wagers."

"Will it also make the demon return what he stole from me?"

"I don't know," Gabriel answered honestly, "but he wanted a part of you."

He didn't say anything else, he didn't have to. Though he tried to hide it, I could read the worry in his eyes.

"And you think Ryiel has the answer somewhere in all his books?" Gabriel nodded. "But how does he even know about it?" I asked.

"I told him. He feels responsible, love, and he wants to help." Gabriel stroked his fingers lightly up the inside of my thigh, making me quiver. "Let him do this, Rowan. There really isn't a better vampire to help us."

"Can I ask you something about Ryiel?" I stayed his fingers with my hand.

"Of course." Curiosity made him frown slightly.

"Ryiel is a Fallen . . . hasn't he found his Promise yet?"

Picking up my hand, Gabriel threaded our fingers together. "Ryiel found his Promise many centuries ago, but he chooses not to make the necessary connection in order to free his soul."

Now it was my turn to frown. "Why not?"

Gabriel shrugged. "His reasons are his to keep, and right now I couldn't be more grateful for his desire to remain a vampire. He always was the most knowledgeable of us."

It was the first time I had ever heard him refer to the other Fallen, and while I wanted to bombard him with questions about them, I knew this was not the time.

Tucking me back against his side, Gabriel turned thoughtful. "Are you sure you're okay with not aging?"

As it seemed there was nothing I could do about it, I didn't see the point in the question, but I answered it as honestly as I could. "I think it's going to take a little while to sink in, but yeah, I'm okay with it. Why do you ask?"

"It can be a difficult adjustment to make."

"Well, let's just take it one day at a time, okay?"

He kept silent as I snuggled back against him, beginning to comprehend some of the radical changes my life was about to undergo, changes that were more complicated than simply replacing my diurnal lifestyle for a nocturnal one. Of course, I would still be able to go out during the daytime, but it made more sense to me to keep my waking hours the same as Gabriel's.

"I'm not going to be able to live here for much longer, am I?" There was an unexpected lump in my throat at the thought of leaving the house my great-great-granddaddy had built.

Gabriel dropped a kiss on my shoulder. "You don't have to leave right away, but eventually people will start to notice that you're not getting any older. That neither of us is."

"And I should leave before they start asking questions, right?"

"It would be easier all around," Gabriel told me in a low voice. "As much for them as for you."

Of course, this was something he and every other vampire in existence dealt with all the time. The need to always be on the move, careful not to arouse suspicion. Reinventing themselves and never getting too close to anyone. I was so grateful I wasn't going to have to deal with this alone.

"I'll have to come up with a plausible excuse to explain why I'm leaving." It wasn't going to be easy. I'd lived in this town all my life, but people had left before me, and others would in the future.

"Why not tell them the truth?" Gabriel murmured above me. Twisting myself out of his arms, I sat up and looked at him, convinced he'd turned delusional. "Well, as much of it as you can," he amended.

"What do you mean?"

He stroked the pad of his thumb over my lower lip. "If you're going to be spending the rest of your life with me, wouldn't it be natural for you to move away and come live with me?"

I don't know why I assumed that we would continue to live separately, but the idea that Gabriel might want me to move in with him had never crossed my mind. It shouldn't have been that much of a surprise, given his possessive nature. I suppose a part of me had figured we'd cross this bridge eventually, but not quite this soon.

"You really want me to do that?"

"Of course, and if you don't like my apartment, we can always get something else. Anywhere you want." He grinned. "Although I have a feeling once you see the size of my bathroom, you're not going to want to leave!" I slapped him playfully on the arm. "Of course," he continued, "if you prefer, you can always say your new living arrangements are because of something a little more permanent."

"You're worried about how Laycee is going to react, aren't you?"

"She is a woman of remarkable fortitude who should never be underestimated," he said seriously. She was also the only person who now knew all our secrets. "Don't you think she might feel better if she knew how committed I am to you?"

I caught my breath. "You mean . . . like saying we're engaged or something?"

"Yeah, that's exactly what I mean. Only I don't think there should be any *something* about it."

Leaning over the side of the bed, he grabbed his jeans from the floor and pulled something out of the pocket. With fangs fully extended, he placed a small velvet box in my hand. Opening the lid, I was dazzled by the brilliant bolt of red fire that winked up at me, and I forgot how to breathe.

"Rowan Marie Harper, will you marry me?"

Taking the box from my hand, Gabriel slipped out the ring and slid it on the third finger of my left hand, already knowing what my answer was going to be.

"Are you sure?" I asked, completely blown away by both the ring and his proposal. "I mean, *do* vampires get married?"

"Funnily enough, when they find someone they love, they do. I hope you don't mind if we exchange our vows at night. I'm told it's very much in vogue right now."

I was so overwhelmed I couldn't speak. Overwhelmed and on the verge of tears. Throwing my arms around his neck, I kissed him, delighted when he surrendered to me.

"If I had any idea this was how you would thank me," he said when I finally let go of his mouth, "I would've gotten you something bright and shiny a long time ago."

"It's not the ring," I said, feeling another swell of emotion. "It's the fact that you gave it to me." Then, like any girl with a new bauble, I extended my arm and watched the gem sparkle.

"You can tell Laycee it's a red diamond," Gabriel said, kissing my shoulder. "I thought it would be perfect for you." He cupped my chin as my lower lip began to wobble. "Awww, sweetheart—don't cry."

I couldn't help it. The dam burst, and I began sobbing like a baby. Secure in his embrace, I let myself go into emotional free fall. When I finally managed to regain some semblance of control, I reached over him and pulled open the nightstand drawer.

"Has Christmas already been and gone?" I had no idea what day it was, much less the date.

"Not yet. Why do you ask?"

"Well, I was going to give you this for Christmas, but if it's not the twenty-fifth somewhere in the world, it's close enough to be okay." I placed my own small velvet box on his chest.

He opened it . . . and said nothing.

"Ohhhh . . ." Disappointment formed a hard knot in the middle of my chest. "You don't like it, do you?" It was a stupid thing to ask.

Gabriel looked up at me, his eyes totally changed. Brilliant gold pupils centered in a sea of hot electric blue. "It means more than you can possibly imagine," he said huskily. "Put it on me."

My fingers shook as I took the slender band out the box and hesitated over his hand. Impatiently he stabbed his ring finger forward and I slid the band on. Twin bands of platinum cradled a circle of deep mahogany between them, the colors and substance complementing each other perfectly. And, like mine, it was a perfect fit.

"Are you sure you like it?" I asked worriedly. It seemed so plain when compared to the dazzling hunk of carbon he had given me.

"I couldn't have asked for anything better," he said, rolling me over so I was beneath him once more.

I could tell as he slanted his mouth over mine that his way of thanking me was going to involve an awful lot more than a kiss, and I felt my body ignite for him, the heat inside me matching the gem on my finger. Unfortunately, the sound of a car pulling up outside the house told me Laycee had arrived.

"Gabriel—we don't have time!"

Taking my hand, he put it on his shaft, moving it up and down.

"Sweetheart," he said nuzzling my neck, "there will always be enough time."

CHAPTER 30

Six months later . . .

I found Laycee sitting on the porch swing, sipping a glass of iced tea. "Don't get up," I told her, "I can help myself."

I hadn't been sure that Laycee would want to move into my house, considering what she had been through in the front yard. Bad memories might linger, but with Jake about to get custody of his kids, it seemed like a no-brainer. "It's okay if you don't want to," I'd told her as she helped me reduce the contents of the living room to a number of large brown shipping cartons. "I can always put it on the market."

"Don't you dare!" she'd admonished. "I refuse to raise my kids anywhere else." She promptly burst into tears, which was how I found out what Jake had given her for Christmas—actually more like Thanksgiving, if her due date was correct. "Damn hormones!" she wailed, wiping her eyes.

Now, as I put the pitcher of iced tea back in the sparkling new fridge, I smiled to see it had a water and ice dispenser in the door. Still, I couldn't help feeling a wave of nostalgia for my ancient Frigidaire with the iffy motor. Laycee had felt awkward, bad even, about wanting to completely remodel the kitchen. She hemmed and hawed and danced around the subject so much, I eventually had to take matters into my own hands. The look on her face was priceless when she walked in and saw all the old appliances missing.

"Unless you want me to buy the first ones I see," I told her, gesturing to the big, empty spaces between the counters, "you better go choose what you want and get them delivered." After that, installing a new air-conditioning system and water heater was a piece of cake.

Carrying my glass of tea outside, I joined her on the swing seat. That, she had assured me, was not going to be replaced. The air was warm, but the humidity was still bearable and would be for another month or so. My dad's hydrangeas were blooming, and the light scent of jasmine filled the air.

"So, what do you think?" Laycee stretched out her legs so I could admire her new shoes.

"Ah, I see you got them." I made complimentary oohing noises over the Louboutins she was wearing, a birthday gift from Gabriel and me, but the high heels made me anxious. "Do you really think it's a good idea to wear them in your condition?" I had nightmares about her balancing the extra weight on such a thin heel.

"Don't worry; I won't actually walk in them until after the baby gets here." She gave me a look that was only slightly greedy. "Was Eye Candy serious when he said I could choose a pair every year if I wanted?"

"Yes, provided it won't be a problem with your guy." I added.

"Oh, don't worry, my guy is very comfortable with having friends who are stinking rich," she said with a laugh.

Apparently, Jake had been impressed to learn that Gabriel owned an apartment in the very classy Colonnade Towers. Laycee forgot to mention that it wasn't just any apartment, but the penthouse suite, and also that Gabriel actually owned all the apartments in the building. As well as pretty much most of the real estate you could see from the penthouse terrace. And he'd been right about his bathroom—it was huge.

I grinned at her. "Speaking of the big lug, where is he?"

"He's taken the kids for ice cream."

I sipped my tea. "Ah, how's that going?"

"The kids are just wonderful," she answered. "They're really happy to be back with their friends, and honestly, I'm not asking for much more than that. I'm taking each day as it comes."

I watched as she slipped off her new shoes and placed them neatly beneath the swing. "You sure there's only one in there?" I asked, watching in amazement as she managed to tuck her feet beneath her and sit down.

"Yep, that's what the doc says. Guess it's gonna be a big one." She took a sip of her tea and became pensive. "We never did have had that long conversation, did we?"

"No," I answered with a slow shake of my head. "We never did."

"Do you think we could do it now?"

"Are you sure you want to, Layce?"

"Yeah, I think it's as good a time as any—ooooh!" She grabbed my hand and held it against her swollen abdomen. "Baby Jake's kicking." The feel of movement beneath my palm took my breath away and stole a piece of my heart. "I'm not asking for any explanations," Laycee said, continuing to hold my hand in place, "but I need to talk to someone."

"Do you want to see someone professional?" I didn't know how I would get Gabriel to agree to this, but if Laycee felt it was necessary, then somehow I would.

"Puhleeeze!" She rolled her eyes. "I'm okay talking to you right here, right now, but really, Ro? If I tell anyone else, they're going to send me for a sleepover in the nearest psych ward." She paused and a frown creased her brow.

"Everything okay?" Not knowing much about the nuances of pregnancy, I became worried every time her brow wrinkled.

"Yeah." She moved my hand off her belly. "Baby Jake's gone back to sleep."

Linking her fingers through mine, she took a breath. "This is the only time I'm going to say this, understand?" I nodded. "I know what I saw, Rowan, and vampire chick was exactly that."

"Exactly what?"

"A vampire."

"Ah."

"Yeah, you bet your ass, Rowan Marie Harper."

She let go of my hand and picked up her glass again. I noticed it shook. Not enough to spill, but enough that I noticed. That night had been a truly horrifying experience, and it wasn't something either of us could pretend hadn't happened.

"Is there anything I can say to help you with this, Laycee?"

She shook her head and put down her glass. "No. I don't know what you went through when you were gone, but I know that it was something you can never explain." She turned to me, her eyes unnaturally bright. "And I also know you didn't come back the same."

The lump that suddenly filled my throat was the size of a bowling ball, and I could hardly get my words out. "What do you mean . . . not the same?"

"I saw what she did to you, Rowan." For the second time in my life I didn't know what to say to my best friend. I had never wanted Laycee to get up close and personal with a vampire, and certainly not one like Katja. "By the way, what happened to her?"

I had to clear my throat before saying, "Ryiel took her away."

"Ryiel? Big guy, dark hair?"

I raised my brows, surprised she remembered.

"You're not likely to forget someone who looks like that," she said in response to my questioning look. "And the view from your bedroom window is real good."

She hadn't been kidding when she said she'd seen everything. "And you still want to live in this house?" I asked with a wry smile.

"Nothing happened *inside* the house, and Jake's promised to landscape the hell out of the front yard for me, beginning with having a proper driveway put in." She nudged me with her elbow. "So, what did Ryiel do with psycho vampirella?"

I hoped it was just the light playing tricks, but it seemed to me that Laycee's eyes glazed over a bit at the mention of the Original Vampire's name. I put it down to her current unpredictable hormonal state.

"He took her to an abandoned monastery in the Himalayas."

"You're kidding, right?"

"No." I shook my head and took a sip of tea. "Apparently Ryiel doesn't have much use for the *modern world*." I made quotation marks in the air. "He lives pretty much secluded from society, with no TV or Internet or anything."

"Uh-huh. And what d'you suppose they'll do with no TV and all?"

"Gabriel tells me he's very scholarly and spends most of his time examining ancient texts." She didn't need to know that he was searching for a way to nullify my wager with a demon.

"Yeah, well, I think the Kama Sutra could be classified as an ancient text," Laycee pointed out drily.

For a few moments neither of us spoke, our attention captivated by a hummingbird at the feeder. Its head bobbed up and down as it helped itself to the bright red mixture Laycee replenished with an almost religious fervor.

"You know that even though she did what she did to me, I'm not like her. Katja, I mean." I said in a low voice.

"Yeah, I know, but wherever you went, it changed you, Ro. I don't know if you had an out-of-body experience or something, but I do know you came back different. You *are* different." She reached for my hand and squeezed it gently. "Eye Candy isn't the only one who notices things about you, and you're more like him now . . . and less like me."

I could feel the tears welling up in my eyes, and I fought to regain my composure before speaking. "So . . . what are you saying?"

She took a deep breath. "I will always be your friend, Rowan, and in my heart I will always love you, but," she paused, "this is a small town and people talk. And if they don't talk about you, then they surely will about that man of yours." I wanted to tell her that I'd make sure Gabriel behaved, but she shushed me with a wave of her hand. "I may not know Eye Candy as well as you—actually," she gave a throaty laugh that was reminiscent of the old Laycee, "I *know* I don't know him as well as you—but I trust what I see. He's not like other men. No matter how you dress him up, or down. He doesn't fit here, and neither do you. Not anymore."

As usual, Laycee had got to the heart of the matter—telling me everything I already knew but hadn't quite faced up to yet. I was different, and it wasn't just because I now lived in a swanky apartment on the ritzy side of town. I wondered what Laycee would think if I told her that Gabriel and I slept in a bedroom that had protective runes covering the walls, while a five-hundred-year-old sentinel stood watch outside?

"People will notice, Rowan," Laycee repeated. "Not at first, of course. They'll think you've got the best plastic surgeon in the world, but eventually they'll see you're not the same. And they will talk."

"What do you want me to do?"

"You have to move on with your life, Rowan. Move on and leave us behind. Me and Jake and the kids. I can't deal with having vampires in my life. Knowing about Gabriel is hard enough, but I can't see him or you or the big Russian guy anymore. Please don't ask me to."

This was one of the adjustments Gabriel had warned me about. Not so much my difficulty dealing with the people in my life, but their difficulty in dealing with me. Laycee was right, of course. Katja had proved that being around me could also be dangerous, and now I had baggage of a different kind: a powerful demon with an unhealthy interest in me, and let's not forget a confused angel who had already shown he could be treacherous. As much as it hurt—and it felt like my heart was being shredded—it would be better if I was out of her life. Laycee had no place in her life for anything supernatural, and I was going to respect her wishes.

"Would it be okay if I sent you a postcard every now and then?"

"You better! How else am I going to see all the great places you're going to visit?" She shifted on the swing seat, repositioning herself so she was now facing me. "Remember what I told you out at Rosie's the night you first saw Eye Candy?"

"You told me lots of things," I said, blinking furiously and sniffing. "What part did you have in mind?"

"I told you to grab your happiness when it presents itself—no matter how it comes packaged." She gave me a smile that lit up her face. "I'm glad to see you took my advice, even if the packaging isn't quite what I expected."

"Yeah, well that and not eating yellow snow were the best tips you've ever given me."

We hugged each other, recognizing that our friendship had detoured down a different path. We would always be friends, but each of us sensed something had been lost. We would not grow old together, or share stories about our children or grandchildren, or complain about the crotchety old geezers our husbands had turned into.

"I will love you till the day I die," I whispered in her ear.

"Yeah? You better mean that, because I got a feeling that's not going to happen for a very long time." Tears of her own now spilled down Laycee's cheeks. "Damn hormones," she muttered, fishing a tissue out from her sleeve.

I was helping her to her feet when the sound of knocking made both of us turn our heads. Laycee took my hand as we went to the front door together. It was still light, but nighttime was just around the corner. The sky had become a canvas of deep purple and indigo, and the horizon was bathed in red and gold.

"Hey, Gabriel, how are you?" It always threw me when I heard Laycee use his name.

"Couldn't be better," he replied, giving her a smile that was nothing short of beautiful. "How's the baby?"

She rested her hand on the crest of her stomach. "Couldn't be better. Rowan got to feel him kick earlier."

I saw him reach for my hand and then snap his arm back. Noticing the gesture, Laycee gave him a concerned look and asked, "What's wrong?"

"I, uh, I can't come in," Gabriel said, looking slightly embarrassed.

"What's wrong, are you sick or something?"

He shook his head and looked at me, his hair dazzling in the dying embers of the day. "I can't come in," he repeated with a grin. It took me a moment to realize just what he was saying. Oh my god—*he couldn't come in!*

I turned to Laycee. "You finally got the deed to the house registered, didn't you?"

She flushed, and combined with the glow of being pregnant, it made her look radiantly beautiful. "Yeah, I'm sorry it's taken us so long, but filing the paperwork makes it all so *final*. Jake and I wanted to give you some time . . . you know, in case you changed your mind."

"I'm not going to change my mind," I said firmly. "I really want you and Jake to live here, and be happy, and raise at least another three or four kids in this house, okay?"

She began tearing up again, but managed to give me a puzzled look before wiping her eyes. "How'd you know? About the deed being filed? Jake only took the paperwork in this morning."

"I can't cross the threshold," Gabriel said in a low voice. "I'm a vampire, Laycee. I need to be invited in . . . by the *owner*."

"Oh."

I watched as a half dozen different expressions crossed my friend's face—all of them variations on possibilities of things that might be. Or not. She wavered for a moment, and then I saw her make up her mind, and knew what she was going to say before the words left her mouth.

"Do you want to invite me in, Laycee?" Gabriel asked, keeping his voice low.

She shook her head. "No, Gabriel. I don't think I do."

This time the smile he gave her was positively angelic. "Then you don't have to," he told her.

He turned to go, but Laycee stepped onto the porch and stopped him with her hand on his arm. "Promise me you'll take care of my girl," she said, looking up at him. Taking both her hands in his, Gabriel leaned down and put his mouth next to her ear and whispered. Her eyes glittered brightly as he let her go, and we both watched him walk down the driveway to go lean against his latest toy—a Lamborghini he'd christened Lola.

"Are you okay?" I asked, seeing Laycee swipe at her cheek.

"You know what he told me?" She reached for my hand, and I shook my head. "He told me he'd give his life for you."

"He doesn't have to," I told her as my heart whispered good-bye. "He's already given me his soul."

Have you read the first book in Carla Susan Smith's vampire series?

A Vampire's Promise

TRUST YOUR INSTINCTS

Rowan Harper is nothing but a smart-mouthed bookstore clerk with a crappy love life on the night she walks into Rosie's Bar. Most of the drama in her life is borrowed from her best friend's adventures. But when she meets Gabriel—tall and movie star gorgeous— everything changes. Never mind that she turns down the drink he offers, or that he brims with secrets she can't begin to guess at. He ignites a desire in her she never suspected—and shows a fascination with her she can't explain.

He has no family, no job, no bank account; he knows where she lives and her favorite flower. An aura of mystery cloaks him, even as Rowan grasps for facts, even as she fears an answer that could destroy her happiness. Gabriel can guide her through a wonderland of new sensations. But only if Rowan trusts him enough to follow . . .

Winner of the OKRWA "Finally a Bride" contest.

Carla Susan Smith owes her love of literature to her mother, who, after catching her pre-teen daughter reading by flashlight beneath the bed covers, calmly replaced the romance book she had "borrowed" with one that was far less risqué, and much more appropriate. Carla was encouraged to include different genres in her reading tastes, and romance—paranormal romance, in particular—has always been her first love.

Born and raised in England, she now makes her home in South Carolina, where she lives with her wonderfully supportive husband, awesome son, and a canine critique group (if tails aren't wagging, then the story isn't working). When not writing, she can usually be found in the kitchen trying out any recipe that calls for rhubarb, working on her latest tapestry project, or playing catch-up with her reading list. Visit her at www.CarlaSmithauthor.com.